WITH *Love* IN *Sight*

THE TWICE SHY SERIES

CHRISTINA BRITTON

DIVERSIONBOOKS

Diversion Books
A Division of Diversion Publishing Corp.
443 Park Avenue South, Suite 1008
New York, New York 10016
www.DiversionBooks.com

For more information, email info@diversionbooks.com

First Diversion Books edition March 2018.
Paperback ISBN: 978-1-63576-196-2
eBook ISBN: 978-1-63576-195-5

LSIDB/1801

This book is dedicated with oceans of love to my children, the most amazing son and daughter I could have been blessed with. There are no greater treasures in my life than you.

And to Eric, who has been my champion since day one, for never giving up on me and always, without fail, believing in me. Even though I refused to put a sword with a secret compartment in the hilt in this book. I love you, hunny.

Chapter 1

"My dear, who is that lovely blonde thing being partnered by Mr. Davies?"

"Miss Mariah Duncan. She is quite the popular young lady this Season."

Miss Imogen Duncan just barely heard the words over the din of the orchestra and the hundred or so voices that rose up like the squawking of so many peahens in the glittering ballroom. But at the sound of her sister Mariah's name, she started.

She peered around the column she'd been practically propping up the past hour and spied a group of older women conversing on the other side, their jewel-colored turbaned heads bent together. Squinting, she tried to make out their features before giving an irritated huff. She could see their blurry outlines, but all details were completely lost.

She clenched her gloved hands, helplessness coursing through her. How she wished for her spectacles. But no, they were safe on her dressing table back at home where her mother decreed they should stay when she forayed into public. Of course, that was not the most convenient place for them as far as Imogen was concerned. She would much rather have them perched on her nose. But she had learned to pick her battles long ago, and this was one she could not hope to win.

The women, having fallen silent for a moment, struck up their conversation again, drawing Imogen's attention back to them.

"She certainly is the best of this year's batch of hopefuls. The men are drawn to her like flies to honey," said the third lady.

"With those looks, do you blame them?" chimed in the first, her voice dripping boredom. "If I had a figure like that I'm certain the young bucks would be at my heels as well."

Irritation reared its head, wiping out Imogen's initial benign feelings for the women. It was not the first time she had overheard remarks of this nature, and it would certainly not be the last. Was that all that people in this blasted city cared about, whether a woman was beautiful?

She scanned the crowd that twirled about on the floor, trying to make out her sister. Even with Imogen's impaired vision, Mariah stood out right away, with her pale, almost white hair piled high on her head and the beacon of her white dress with the faintest hint of pink at the hem and bodice. She held herself with a poise, moved with a lithe grace that was unmatched by any of the other ladies present. Imogen did not need her spectacles to know that her sister outshone the rest.

But why could no one concentrate on the sweetness of her spirit? Looks were all well and good, but more importantly, Mariah had an uncommon kindness to her. If only people could see beyond her face.

"Who do you suppose will be the one to catch her?" asked the second, breaking Imogen from her reverie.

"She is prettier than her sister Frances, who married the Earl of Sumner several years ago. I don't see why the chit couldn't land herself a marquess before the year is out."

"Her father would be a fool to accept less," said the first. "With her face, she could get a duke if she wanted."

Imogen frowned. The women's comments were making her skin crawl, as if she'd just been immersed in a tub of dirty water. She began to back away, determined to rejoin her mother so she no longer had to hear the mercenary comments being directed at her sister. But the next words stopped her cold.

"Wasn't there another sister?"

Every muscle in Imogen's body froze. Her feet felt nailed to the floor. To her dismay, she found herself holding her breath and leaning closer.

"Yes," the third woman answered after a thoughtful pause, "I believe there was. Plain thing, awkward to the point of being painful to watch. I wonder whatever became of her?"

Imogen did not want to hear this. So why couldn't she move? What kept her rooted to the spot as those horrible women talked about her?

"Ah yes, I remember her now. Plump little mouse of a thing. Always squinting. She came out the same year as Lady Sumner. She was completely eclipsed, of course, and no one ever thought of her after that. Not that they ever did before, poor girl. I believe she had one more Season after her sister married, but her mother's effort was wasted, to say the least."

"I hear she's back in town for Miss Mariah's debut."

One woman clucked her tongue in sympathy. "It can only be worse for her this time around. There's no chance of her making a match now. Not at her age."

"Well, at least Lord and Lady Tarryton can be assured they will have one daughter at home to see them through old age."

Their titters reached her, finally propelling her from her hiding place. Tears burned her eyes as she sidled behind the women and through the thickly milling crowd, making certain to stay well out of their view. She could not bear to see the pity in their eyes if they caught sight of her. She should have moved away at the first mention of her sister. It served her right for listening in on gossip that was not meant for her ears.

What was incorrect about anything those women said about her, after all? She *was* awkward, and plain, and a spinster quite firmly on the shelf with no hopes for marriage. And she knew, even without hearing the words aloud at home, that her parents held the belief that she would be with them for the remainder of their lives. So why did it hurt so very much to hear three ill-mannered tabbies talking of her that way?

Imogen worked her way through the ballroom, knocked this

way and that by the mass of bodies, tears blurring her already useless vision. She blinked them fiercely back. Now was not the time, not here in front of all these people, most of whom probably thought the same of her as those women did, if they thought of her at all. But it seemed her heart would not listen, for it repeated in an endless litany what she fought so hard to forget: that she would remain unloved by any man, with no future, no hope for a life of her own.

She bit her lip as a sob threatened. Spying the open terrace doors to her right, she swiftly changed course and headed for them. No one, not even her mother, would begrudge her a few minutes alone.

The coolness of the evening air settled about her, and it was only as the faint breeze turned her cheeks icy that she realized her tears had not been held in check and had in fact left wet trails down her face. She swiftly clamped a hand over her mouth as another sob welled up in her chest. No, the terrace was no good. She needed to get further away. She grabbed her skirts in both hands and flew down the stone steps into the garden, needing the cover of darkness so she could give vent to what was quickly breaking through the surface.

She sped along the well-tended paths, deeper into the dimness of the foliage. The lanterns that had been strung about grew sparse the deeper she went, but it was still not private enough. And as her eyes darted about uselessly, skimming the darkening vegetation for a hiding place, she called herself ten times a fool. She was six and twenty, for goodness' sake. She'd had eight years to come to terms with her unmarried state. She had realized upon her first entrance into Society that she would not take, that she would be the focus of no man's affections. It was no surprise to her.

It was not as if her life were horrible, however. Her dear sister Frances, of the much-lauded brilliant marriage, was the unhappiest woman Imogen knew. Seeing how miserable she was made Imogen realize the heartbreaking truth that no marriage at all was better than being mired in a heartless union.

And Imogen truly was blessed in so many ways. She had the love of her family and security. There were many women in the world in much worse situations than she. But to hear herself spoken of as if she were not a person in her own right was almost too much to bear.

She so very rarely allowed her control to slip. Her future was not something she permitted to invade her thoughts, though it was always in the back of her conscious mind, like an evil specter waiting to haunt her. So when it did break through her defenses as it did now, it was with a cruelty that stunned her.

She began to stumble about, having difficulty staying on the path now that moonlight was the only thing guiding her. Several branches caught on her dress and slapped her arms. In vain she once again wished furiously for her spectacles.

That wish was compounded upon only seconds later when she ran smack into a very large, very warm, very male person standing in the shadows. Two strong hands clamped firmly on her upper arms. Before she could call out for help, the man's mouth found hers in the darkness.

She stood stupidly for a long moment in shock, aware of the hard, lean body pressed to her own, the faint scents of sandalwood and soap, the lips firm as they plundered hers. She had never had a man so much as embrace her other than her father and brothers, much less had one kiss her. And such a kiss! She felt as if he were stealing the very breath from her.

Something that had been dormant in her up until then flared to life. Her limbs began to tremble, her fingers itching to grip onto him. But when the man gave a groan, his tongue pushing into the recesses of her mouth and the taste of brandy overwhelming her, she was finally jolted back to herself. She lodged her hands between their bodies and, planting her feet firmly on the ground, shoved with all her might.

• • •

Caleb Masters, Marquess of Willbridge, was having a fine time. He was pleasantly inebriated, had won a hefty sum in the card room, and was waiting in a cool garden for a very willing widow with a taste for sexual adventure. He didn't have long to wait. Suddenly she was there, throwing herself against him. Ah, so Violet was even more eager than usual. He grinned, gripping her arms, and thanked his lucky stars for lonely, mature women just before he claimed her mouth with his own.

Unexpected sensations bombarded his fuzzy brain. What wonderful changes were these? Typically, Violet tasted of sherry and smelled of some cloying scent she'd had made up for her on Bond Street. But now she tasted pleasantly of lemonade, her lips soft and slack, her breasts full and pressing into his chest. Her scent was heady, a simple, clean smell with a faint hint of something citrusy that was altogether mouthwatering.

There was something new and exciting about her tonight. He longed to run his hands down her body, to explore the delectable roundness of her. But even one such as she required a bit of wooing before doing the deed. More than willing to take his time tonight, he deepened the kiss...

And was shocked when he was pushed violently away. He stumbled back, catching himself on the hedge just before he toppled over.

He straightened, frowning as he brushed leaves from his jacket. "What's gotten into you, Violet? You've never been missish about my advances before."

A soft, outraged gasp followed his surly comment. Instantly a strange feeling of unease uncurled in his belly. He turned to the woman, looking at her fully for the first time in the dim moonlight.

Instead of the inky, artfully arranged curls he had expected, he could just make out light-colored hair, pulled back severely from a full, heart-shaped face. And where a shockingly low-cut silk gown should have been was a modest, plain affair lacking even a single flounce or ruffle.

The incensed voice that came from her was the final blow.

Whereas Violet had a throaty voice that you could feel clear to your toes, this girl had a trembling, light tone that barely carried on the faint breeze.

"How dare you assail me in such a fashion, sir."

Suddenly disgustingly sober, he felt the full weight of his mistake. Even one as debauched as he would never molest an innocent woman. Collecting himself, hoping to smooth over his gaffe, he flashed his most charming smile, the one that had gotten him out of countless scrapes, and bowed deeply.

"My abject apologies, miss. I was waiting for another, you see, and I fear I mistook you for her."

There was no reaction from the diminutive woman. She stood silently, her arms hugging her middle. It was only after a long moment of waiting for a response that he noticed she was trembling. Moonlight glinted on the unmistakable wetness of a tear on her cheek.

His *ton* persona disappeared in an instant. Oh hell, what had he done? He rushed to her, extracting a handkerchief from his waistcoat pocket, and closing her fingers around it when she made no move to grab it herself.

"I'm so sorry. Please don't cry." Now that he was closer to her he could see the utter misery etched on her face.

She sniffed, pressing the handkerchief to her eyes. "No, it's not you. It is I who must apologize. I was looking for a place to hide and should not have come upon you so unexpectedly."

Despite her words, the guilt he felt from pawing an innocent woman was enough to make him want to swear off drinking for the next decade or better. But knowing a tennis match of apologies would do no one any good, he looked about for a place where she could rest and collect herself. Spying a stone bench not far from where they stood, he took hold of her elbow and guided her to it. She sat gratefully, attempting a small smile up at him in the gloom.

He sat beside her. "Hiding? Whatever were you hiding from?"

"Just unpleasant people, is all."

"Has anyone harmed you?"

"No, nothing like that. I only overhead some distressing comments about myself. It is my own fault, I suppose, for I should not have stayed to listen." Her lips twisted in the semblance of a smile, but it didn't reach her eyes. They were a light color, but in the pale moonlight he couldn't see their hue.

"It is most certainly not your fault," he said. He felt a strange protective surge for this lady. The sensation gave him pause. He might have some morals when it came whom to seduce, but he was certainly no Galahad. He had never been overly concerned with the innocent female population, had never cared for their dramas or troubles or desires. But it was as if everything suddenly shifted in the space of a heartbeat. Who was this quiet, tragic woman? She was quite a bit older than the debutantes he was forever skirting. And yet it was obvious from her dress and lack of jewelry that she was unmarried.

He placed a hand over his heart and bowed in his seat. "Forgive me, but as there is no one about, perhaps you will allow me to introduce myself. I am Caleb Masters, Lord Willbridge."

Dawning recognition lit her eyes. "Ah yes, I have heard of you." She looked back in the direction of the ballroom, a faint frown marring her smooth face. "Perhaps it's not wise for me to be alone with you."

"You may be assured, you are quite safe with me. My reputation, though deserved in many areas, has been grossly twisted in others."

For the first time a hint of humor lit her face. "So you are not a consummate rake and womanizer?"

He smiled slyly. "Oh yes, that's true."

She laughed then, and the sound was like bells.

"But you have not told me your identity," he persisted.

She sobered. Clearing her throat, she replied in a very small voice, "I think perhaps that would be ill-advised."

"Ah, I see. You are trying to be mysterious. Well, you are succeeding admirably."

"No, you mistake me," she said in some alarm. "Such subterfuge is quite beyond me, I assure you."

"I was teasing," he said.

Even in the dim light he could see the dark flush that stained her cheeks. "Of course you were," she murmured. "But you see, even if we were to meet publicly I could never acknowledge you, having never been formally introduced. So it is best if we leave things as they are."

He looked down at her bent head. He knew he could tease her identity from her, and quite easily too. But he also knew if he did he would cause her even more distress. He watched her hands clench in her lap. No, that he could never do. He was guilty of enough in his life without adding that to his list of sins.

"As you wish," he said in a light voice.

She nodded, the movement jerky. "I think I had best go back inside."

As she rose, he stood along with her and held out his arm. She looked at it uncomprehendingly for a moment.

"I will not allow you to traverse the wilds of the Morledge gardens without a chaperone," he said. "There is no telling what kind of beast may be lurking about."

A ghost of a smile passed over her face. But as she took his arm and they turned for the lights of the ballroom, he thought soberly that for one as sweet and innocent as her, she could encounter no worse beast than him.

Chapter 2

Imogen was achingly aware of the muscled arm under her hand. She should have run from him the moment he had released her from that unexpected kiss. Any proper miss would have. But she had stayed. And then he had shown himself to be quite kind, and she found she didn't want to leave him.

He was not at all how she had assumed one of London's most notorious womanizers would be. There was a gentleness, an unfeigned consideration in him that belied every claim she had ever heard. And oh yes, she had heard the stories. How he gambled and drank till dawn, seduced innocent and experienced women alike, and gloried in every dangerous pastime a man of his ilk could get up to. It was amazing what people would say in front of one when one was considered nigh invisible.

And he had kissed her. *Her*, plain and awkward Miss Imogen Duncan. Granted, he had not intended to, had believed her to be someone else. But even so.

They reached the shadows that hugged the side of the town-house just before the bright light pouring off the terrace, and she stopped. He halted beside her.

"I suppose I must leave you here." His voice was low and shivered through her.

She nodded. "It really wouldn't do—"

He held up a hand. "Say no more. I would not have your reputation harmed, as it certainly would be were I to walk you back into the ballroom from the seclusion of the gardens." He bowed gallantly over her hand. "Thank you for your company this evening, my mysterious lady. I pray we meet again."

Imogen blushed and curtsied. "Lord Willbridge."

With utmost will she pulled her hand from his warm grasp. The loss of his touch was almost heartbreaking in its intensity. Before she could reconsider she spun about and raced up the stairs to the terrace, the back of her neck tingling with awareness of his presence behind her. She made it to the safety of the ballroom, blending into the milling crowd with little trouble before swiftly locating a small alcove to take shelter in. Once carefully ensconced, partially hidden behind a heavy velvet curtain, she dared to peek out.

Her vantage gave her an unfettered view of the terrace doors. In spite of her appalling vision, she knew the second Lord Willbridge strode back into the ballroom. Heat shot down her spine. He was so incredibly tall, so commanding and magnetic. She wished she could look on him clearly so she could soak in the masculine beauty of his features in the bright candlelight.

As if in answer to her desire, he turned and headed her way. She gasped softly, ducking deeper into the shadows. There was no way he could have seen where she was hiding…could he?

To her horror—and secret delight—he stopped directly in front of her alcove. Had she reached out from her hiding place she could have touched him. He was so close to her that she could see every glorious detail of him without the need of her spectacles.

In the pale blue cast of moonlight, he had been handsome. But in the blaze of the hundreds of candles that lit the Duchess of Morledge's ballroom, he was breathtaking. His copper hair shone, tousled in the way so many of the young men attempted to mimic but failed at miserably. His sapphire blue evening coat and striped waistcoat were cut to perfection, accentuating his broad shoulders and narrow waist. His legs were long and muscled under the tight, dove-colored breeches, and he held himself with a delicious arrogance that only those completely sure of themselves could hope to attain.

His pale eyes swept the crowd with intensity. A look of frustration passed over his face, and Imogen knew, with her rapidly beating heart, that he was looking for her. She breathed a small sigh of relief when he passed without incident, ignoring the strange twinge of regret in her chest. Thank goodness he had not seen her, she told herself forcefully.

After some time she decided to take the chance and peer out again. He was a short distance away, too far to see anything clearly but close enough to know it was he. Nor was he alone. His long body was curved in an intimate way over a woman Imogen could not identify. She squinted. By the way the woman was tossing her jet-black curls, rapid words issuing in a low tone from her ruby lips, she seemed angry with him. Lord Willbridge leaned in and whispered something in the woman's ear. His companion tittered and plied her fan over her daringly exposed bosom.

Imogen ducked back into her alcove. So he had not been looking for her. *Foolish girl*, she berated herself. He had been in the gardens with the purpose of meeting another, after all. She remembered his kiss with sudden vividness, his mouth hot on hers. But it should not have been her—it should have been this other one he kissed, the one with the black curls and porcelain skin and clinging crimson silk gown. As she felt her heart twist, she resolved to remember that.

• • •

"I wonder," Caleb mused the following afternoon as he rode his horse through Hyde Park, "if I were to describe a woman to you, would you be able to tell me her identity?"

Sir Tristan Crosby glanced at him with the bleary, red-eyed look of one who had overindulged the night before. But he smiled all the same as he kept his horse in pace with Caleb's. "Never tell me someone has caught your eye."

"No, not my eye," he replied thoughtfully. The woman last night had been no beauty, and from the looks of her she was quite firmly on the shelf. But she had been pretty in a wonderfully wholesome way. Her clothes, though plain and modest, had obviously been well made, and her manners had been impeccable. Perhaps she was a sister of someone of note, he thought, or even a paid companion of one of the wealthier members of the *ton*.

But she had been sweet, and real. He'd lain awake this morning contemplating the quiet sadness that had been present in her eyes, wondering who she was. Despite knowing that he would not be good for someone like her, that he would be the last person someone of her obvious innocence should associate with, he wanted to find her, to ascertain she was well.

"I saw her in some distress," he finally answered, because something needed to be said.

Tristan quirked one golden eyebrow. "Distress? By your own hand?"

Caleb scoffed. "Come now, you know me better than that. She was an innocent, and you know I don't make advances toward the likes of them." But then his gut twisted and he squirmed in his saddle. He remembered the kiss, her outraged reaction. No, he was not entirely without blame in her tumultuous evening. Damn it, was he destined to sully every good thing he touched?

He mentally shook himself. But no, it had been an accident. *As had the other*, his mind whispered. A brief flash of his young brother's still, lifeless face jolted him and he brutally brushed it aside.

His friend's curious voice broke through his darkening thoughts. "Well, out with it, man, and I'll do my best. Unlike you, I'm not above eyeing the occasional virgin."

Caleb ignored the residue of memory. He had managed to keep it from overwhelming him for the better part of a decade. He could certainly push it aside now.

He turned his mind to the recollection of the woman from the night before. "She was slight, but with a rounded figure. Light hair severely styled. Pale eyes. Plain, but pretty. Her gown was very modest, no decoration of any kind."

"You have succeeded in describing nearly every wallflower and spinster in town."

Caleb blew out a frustrated breath. "Yes, that's what I was afraid of." He'd known it was a fruitless attempt, but he'd had to try regardless. Her quiet sweetness and innocence had given him a peace he had not felt in too long.

Tristan appraised him. "I must say, she doesn't seem your type at all."

"I told you, she did not interest me, not in the fashion you're implying. I was concerned, is all."

Tristan held up one hand. "Have it your way, man. Didn't know you were so damned gallant. I'll have to remember that in future."

Caleb grinned, though it felt strained. They both knew that "gallant" was the last word anyone would apply to him. "See that you do."

A short time later they turned out of the park. As they were parting, Tristan turned to him. "Why don't you join Morley and me later? We'll be making a visit to the Incomparable Miss Mariah Duncan. Perhaps it will get your mind off of your mysterious lady."

Caleb laughed. "Not sure I'll be welcome in such a lady's drawing room."

Tristan rolled his eyes. "Come now. You may be a degenerate, but you're a blasted marquess, with enough money to buy her father over tenfold. There's much that can be overlooked with those attributes."

Caleb considered for a moment, recalling the flaxen-haired beauty he had seen briefly the night before. She was a stunning creature to be sure, though not at all his type. Still, it might be fun. Yet another distraction in a long, weary line of them.

"Well then," he said, "with that argument, how can I say no? I shall be there."

• • •

So captivated was Imogen by her book and the world of Lilliputians within, she didn't immediately hear the soft rapping on her bedroom door. It wasn't until the person let herself in and called her name that she realized she had a guest at all.

"Imogen. Reading again, are we?"

"Frances." Imogen rose with a broad smile, placing the book aside and hurrying to her sister. She bussed her on the cheek and drew her to the small sitting area in the corner of her bedroom.

Just a year younger than Imogen, Frances had been her closest friend and confidante in their youth. Now, however, her sister was the Countess of Sumner and at her husband's country seat in Northamptonshire for most of the year, so Imogen rarely saw her. That Frances was in London at all, much less during Mariah's come out, was a wonderful bit of chance.

"I cannot stay long. I'm afraid I come with unpleasant news."

Imogen took in the new lines of strain bracketing Frances's mouth and frowned. "I admit I found it strange you were not at the Morledge ball last night. Is something wrong?"

Frances sighed. "Only that James has urgent business at one of his minor estates, in Rutland. We have to leave immediately."

"Oh no, Frances." Imogen wanted to weep at the unfairness. To lose her sister's companionship was just too much to bear amidst the turmoil this horrible Season was putting her through.

"Can't you tell him you'll stay and follow him later?" she tried. "Surely he doesn't need your presence."

"No, I could never do that," Frances answered. "A woman's place is with her husband. He has decreed I join him, and so I must."

Imogen shivered at the bitterness that colored her sister's words.

Frances drew herself up. "But I did come for a reason. I wanted to talk to Mariah directly, but she is already busy in the drawing room with Mother, preparing for the day's callers, and I could not drag her away." Her troubled gaze lowered to her own tightly clasped hands. "I wish I had more time, that I could have given her my advice in person." She looked once more on Imogen with a desperate fierceness. "But I do believe you may be the better one to talk to, as I well recall the stubbornness and blindness of youth."

Alarmed, Imogen leaned forward and covered her sister's hands with her own. "What is it?"

"You have to watch out for Mariah. She is so sweet, so innocent. I used to be like that. It seems a dream, but I remember." Her voice had grown wistful, but she shook herself and continued, gripping Imogen's hand tightly. "Make certain that whomever she chooses loves her. Not just a regard, but a true love. If he does not care for her in return, do everything in your power to dissuade Mariah from accepting him. Do you understand what I'm saying?"

Imogen did. Her heart ached for Frances. Her sister had loved her husband at one time. But Imogen knew equally well that her husband had not returned those feelings. Oh, he had made a good show at first. But it had quickly become apparent that his display had been more for Frances's dowry than anything else.

The flush of impotent fury heated her face, but Imogen forced down her emotions. It would certainly not do Frances any good if she were to rail at her about the earl. But Imogen knew if she could go back in time and stop her sister from entering such a union, she would, with no hesitation. Barring that, the least she could do was to promise this and to protect Mariah from the same fate.

"Of course I'll watch out for her, Frances. I'll warn her. Mariah will not be unhappy in her future marriage. I promise."

Frances seemed to deflate in relief. Tears shone in her eyes, but she quickly blinked them back. "Thank you. I knew I could count on you. I thank God every day that you were never trapped in such a situation. After Mariah there is only Evaline to worry about, though she may prove difficult in this regard. The three boys we need not concern ourselves with, but our youngest sister is so headstrong, I fear it will take both of us combined to make certain she does not make a bad match of it. Though she has a few years before her come out, and so we still have time to counter Mother's influence and see her happy."

Taking a deep breath, Frances stood. "And now I really must

be going. James will be wondering where I've gotten off to." The words were said briskly, though flattened at her husband's name.

Imogen forced a smile and, after embracing her sister, saw her out the door.

She leaned back against it for some time after Frances had gone. Lord Sumner had made her sister into the shell of a person she was today. She had a vivid image of Frances as she used to be, so open and full of hope and life. Now she was a pale copy of that bright girl.

Grief for the loss welled up, but Imogen tamped it down. Now was not the time. She was expected downstairs in the drawing room. A quick look in the mirror, a swift patting down of errant strands of hair, and she hurried from the room.

Before she even made it to the curving staircase that descended to the first floor, however, she could hear it: a deep rumble of male conversation, as if their house had been invaded by the low, unsettling sounds of thunder. She pressed her lips together. So it had begun already. Which meant she was late. Which in turn meant her mother would have her head.

Well, she admitted to herself as she started down the stairs, perhaps she had been forgetful due to Frances's troubling visit. But an even larger part of her simply had not wanted to be there, in a drawing room full of strange men. The very thought was almost enough to make her break out in a rash. It was always like this before she attended some social event. All those people she didn't know, conversing around her in ways she would never be able to. Their eyes flitting over her as if she were invisible, or worse, looking on her in pity. But the one thing that truly paralyzed her was the thought of someone actually talking to her. She never knew what to say, knew that her natural shyness could be seen as rude to most, but was unable to do a thing about it.

She paused on the bottom step. Strange, then, the ease she had found with Lord Willbridge. She could not remember ever being so swiftly comfortable with a stranger in her life. Not that anything could come of it. Yes, he had been wonderfully nice, much sweeter and more considerate than she could countenance. But he must be that way with everyone. He could not be so popular otherwise, especially as his reputation was so shockingly unfortunate. To him, she could not have been anything special, just another female to charm. One he would not give a second thought to once he was out of her presence.

But she would never forget that wonderful moment, how handsome he had been, how cherished she had felt in being listened to, even for so short a time.

Just then she became aware of a cloying scent, strong enough to tear her from her thoughts. She wrinkled her nose and looked up. The hallway was full to overflowing with hothouse blooms, their cards all on prominent display. Not a single surface was left unadorned, some bouquets even gracing the floor.

Her mouth literally fell open. She shut it with an audible click. Granted, there had been all manner of flowers pouring into their townhouse since Mariah's debut several weeks ago. But this went beyond what she had come to expect.

Stepping into the veritable sea of flora, Imogen moved toward the drawing room door. The muffled murmur of male voices and laughter grew louder, and she tensed, her steps faltering beside an enormous potted plant. It was then she remembered her spectacles.

Damn and blast, she had forgotten to leave them on her dressing table. If any visitors had seen her with her spectacles on, her mother would have had an apoplectic fit. But how Imogen hated having to remove them.

With a small sigh, however, she reached up and pulled her spectacles from her face. Immediately her vision blurred, the colors of the flowers mixing in a jumble, as if someone had poured liquid over a beautiful watercolor painting. The strain behind her eyes began almost immediately as they fought to focus. She squinted, trying to make out the obstacle course of small flower-covered tables, the drawing room at the far end of it.

Taking a deep breath and squaring her shoulders, she moved around the monstrosity of a plant and started forward. She had not taken two steps before she stumbled into a very large person. Her nose landed in his cravat, and immediately she was assailed by the familiar scent of sandalwood. She closed her eyes, somehow knowing who she would see when she looked up.

And then he spoke, pounding the final nail into her coffin of mortification.

"We really must stop running into each other in such a manner."

His voice, that same wonderfully rich baritone she recalled from the night before, sent shivers down her spine. Raising her eyes to his face, she attempted a smile of greeting but felt it wobble dangerously before it disappeared altogether.

"Lord Willbridge, what a surprise to see you here." But not truly, she reflected. Why wouldn't a man of his caliber be among the horde that was flocking to Mariah?

"And you as well. Are you here to visit with Miss Mariah Duncan then?"

She wanted to laugh. But she knew if she did she might cry. And if she cried there would be no stopping it.

"No, I live here," she mumbled. That seemed to shock him into speechlessness. As he gathered his wits, she became aware that they were not alone. They had an audience.

The butler she knew, of course. But the other two gentlemen she was having trouble placing, being as they were just large blurs. She squinted. Of course, she remembered them. The men had been here several times before.

She curtsied. "Sir Tristan, Lord Morley, it is a pleasure to see you again." She knew her throat had closed, that her voice had dropped to a whisper. She turned to the butler. "I can take the gentlemen in to see Miss Mariah, Gillian. Thank you."

As the butler moved off, the two men bowed to her.

"Ah, er, thank you. This is a fine welcome, indeed," the darker of the two responded in an overly cheerful way. Imogen knew that tone of voice well. It was the kind you heard when someone could not remember who you were and was trying to cover up their faux pas.

Lord Willbridge seemed to pick up on his friend's blunder as well. Standing as close to him as she was, Imogen could see the narrowing of his incredible pale gray eyes as he considered his friend. A mischievous glint sparked in their depths.

"As I have not had the honor, and you are known to the lady, perhaps you could introduce us, Morley," he drawled.

Even without her spectacles, Imogen could see the other man's eyes widen in dismay, his face going an interesting shade of pink. She felt a quick burst of pity; though she was tired of being forgotten, she certainly could not allow the poor man to suffer.

Pushing past the lump of anxiety in her throat at having the attentions of three very handsome strangers settle on her, she intervened. "My name tends to trip some people up, I'm afraid. It is a little unusual, you see." She turned to Lord Willbridge and extended her hand, trying to calm her trembling fingers with a deep breath. "I am Miss Imogen Duncan, my lord. Mariah's eldest sister."

Immediately he took hold of her hand and bent low. "Miss Duncan, it is a pleasure."

Did his lips just brush her fingers? Heavens, she rather thought they had. It was the merest touch, but it seared her straight through her thin gloves. Her mind was momentarily wiped clean, and she stood there for a moment unable to form a single coherent word.

"I thank you for showing us to the drawing room," Lord Willbridge said. "It is a treat indeed to be given escort by a daughter of the house."

It was just what she needed to thaw her from her frozen state. She smiled in relief and thanks up at him, saw the answering smile in his own eyes. Taking his proffered arm, she led the way, the two other men following behind.

A footman jumped to open the large double doors as they neared. Her useless eyes scanned the room, roaming over the sea of people until they came to rest upon a lone dark form in the far corner. Her mother.

The slight smile that had remained from Lord Willbridge's gallantry instantly fell. Teeth worrying her bottom lip, she curtsied to the three men, keeping her eyes averted.

"Gentlemen," she mumbled, and turned to leave them. But a staying hand on her arm stopped her.

"Thank you, Miss Duncan, for showing us the way. It truly has been a pleasure." Lord Willbridge's voice was so very quiet and kind. And those eyes of his, beautiful as no man's had a right to be, held her captive. With utmost will she nodded and, breaking free of his grip, retreated to the corner.

"What did Lord Willbridge say to you?" her mother demanded in a hiss as Imogen sat down close by.

"He was merely thanking me for showing him the way to the drawing room." Imogen retrieved her embroidery from the basket at her feet, hoping that would put an end to it. But, as ever where her mother was concerned, it was not.

"Why were you showing those men in here? Where was Gillian?"

"I ran into them in the hall. I sent Gillian back to his post at the door."

But instead of pacifying her mother, the explanation seemed to incense Lady Tarryton. "You should have been here long ago. I do hope you were not walking about with those horrid spectacles on." She gave a delicate shudder as she scanned the room. "I cannot think what people would say if you were ever seen in them. You will be labeled a bluestocking for certain. I do not want Mariah painted with the same brush as you. How will your sister fare in snaring a husband if that is the case?"

Very well, if her suitors are anything to go by, Imogen wanted to say. But she kept silent, turning back to the work in her hands, hoping her mother would do the same. This time luck was with her, and the tirade ended.

How often had she heard those same words, her mother's obsession with her daughters' reputations so extreme that she thought something as simple as a pair of spectacles would mean ruination for them all? Appearance was everything to Lady Tarryton; anything ugly or out of place was to be pruned from their illustrious family as brutally as a pair of shears lopping off a sick branch from a tree.

And Imogen was the most out-of-place branch there was.

It would do no good to think along this vein. Her mother loved her, in her own way. Imogen would just have to be content with that.

But now that Lady Tarryton's attention was elsewhere, Imogen could think about Lord Willbridge's presence. He had obviously come for Mariah; his surprise at seeing her here was proof enough.

It had been so very nice, though, to be acknowledged. As much as she hated conversing with strangers, she had found it wonderful to be seen not with pity, but as an equal. Without meaning to, her aching eyes swept about the room. Unerringly she found him, his copper hair a bright spot in a sea of pale blondes and dark browns. Was he looking her way? In the next moment he held his teacup up in her direction, a salute.

Her face going hot, she quickly looked down to her lap, her heart setting up a quick beat of anticipation. But for what? It was not as if he would ever court her. And friendship was certainly out. Men of Lord Willbridge's status in society did not seek out unmarried women for that sort of thing, even if they could.

No, nothing would come of this. It was just a small detour; soon she would be back on her straight, uninteresting path in life. She focused on her embroidery, jabbing the needle into the fabric with unnecessary force, ignoring the whisper of despair her heart gave.

Chapter 3

She was a spinster.

Caleb sat watching Imogen as she bent industriously over her embroidery, alone in her corner but for her mother. It had shocked him to see her in the hallway. What were the chances of him finding the one person he had been thinking about so diligently since last night? Then to find she was a daughter of the house, Viscount Tarryton's daughter, sister to the Incomparable Miss Mariah Duncan? He had been stunned that the Fates could be so kind to him, then delighted in finally having located her. So much so that he had not fully recognized her situation.

But then they had entered the drawing room and she had escaped him, scurrying to the corner to sit with her mother. And even from his position across the room he could see her mother snap at her, saw the stiff cast to Imogen's shoulders as she fumbled for her embroidery, and the calm that settled over her face as she attempted to work quietly, a calm that did not fool him one bit.

Now he could take the time to observe her situation. And he was dumbfounded by what he saw.

She held the most pitied position a woman of her station could hold. The unmarried maiden sister, watching her younger siblings courted and married off before her. Forever expected to waste her life in service to her aging parents. Always a burden on others, hoping for her family's charity to ensure her future comfort.

Why was she not married? In the full light of day he could see even more so the quiet prettiness he had noticed the night before, detracted from by her severe hairstyle and gown. The latter was itself an unattractive yellow that gave a sickly cast to her skin. But the bones in her face were fine and delicate, and there was a fullness to her figure that could be alluring were it shown to more advantage. He had felt the lushness of her curves himself the previous evening. He could attest to their existence, though he would not have been able to guess at them had he first seen her thus.

But the thing that stood out the most to him, now that he was close enough to see in good light, were her eyes. Though they were tight in the corners, as if strained, they had a thick, curling fringe of lashes, and their color was the clear turquoise of a calm sea. Her hair was a lovely light brown. He wondered fleetingly how she would look with a few curls to frame her face, to soften the austerity of the style.

But he realized to his shame that if she had not stumbled upon him alone last night, thereby giving him a glimpse of the person beneath, he would have passed her over just as the other gentlemen in the room were doing. The way she held herself, how she seemed to quietly blend into the furniture, made her nigh invisible, especially with her beautiful sister glittering from the center of the room like a star.

He pulled his eyes from Imogen forcibly as her mother leaned in to harangue her once more, his jaw clenching in frustration. Would that he could do something. But no, it was not his place.

A short time later, his companions rose to take their leave. He rose along with them and went to make his farewell of the lovely Miss Mariah, stood before Imogen and her mother to make his bows. But when they turned to the door he found he could not leave just yet. He had seen too much of Imogen's soul bared the evening before to pass her over so quickly now. Damn and blast, but he would not treat her as all the others did. She deserved far better than that.

• • •

"Miss Duncan."

Lord Willbridge's voice was soft and achingly lovely with that deep, rich tone. But Imogen had been so aware of him—and trying so very hard to pretend she wasn't affected by his presence in the slightest—that she yelped and jumped in her seat, her embroidery clattering to the floor.

He immediately bent to retrieve it for her. But he paused as he went to hand it over. The strangest look passed over his face then, as if he were in pain.

"That is, er, a very interesting design, Miss Duncan," he choked out.

Frowning, Imogen looked down at her embroidery as she accepted it from him. It was a sad mishmash of colors, which in no way followed the design she had carefully pounced out onto the delicate fabric.

Her hand flying to her mouth, she fought back a horrified gasp. Face flaming hot, she quickly shoved the offending piece behind a cushion.

"I am not typically so abysmal at such things," she managed.

"Of course," he murmured complacently. Immediately she read the implication in his voice, that he would allow her to say such things but knew better.

She narrowed her eyes as she looked up at him. "You do not believe me."

The amused twinkle in his own pewter eyes promptly made her see her error. He was teasing her. All the tension, mortification, and pique drained from her.

"I assure you," he said, "I have no doubt as to your prodigious skills."

Amusement tugged at the corners of her lips. And then a little devil perched on her shoulder, and she found herself saying to him what she never would to another human being: "As I have a great many, you may just be surprised."

He grinned. "You have surprised me already, Miss Duncan."

"Imogen!"

Lady Tarryton's voice tore through the moment. Imogen felt her joy pop like a bubble at the surface of a pond, until not even the ripples of happiness were left behind. She kept her eyes at the level of her mother's chin. She could not bear to see the fury that must be stamped across the woman's face.

"Yes, Mama?"

"You are keeping his lordship from joining his friends. Please don't embarrass us."

Lady Tarryton addressed Lord Willbridge then, and Imogen could see her entire demeanor change. "Please do forgive my daughter, my lord. I hope this does not prevent you from coming back to visit with us. I am certain Mariah would love to receive you again."

Her mother's voice fairly oozed flattery.

Imogen felt sick to her stomach. Of course her mother would want Lord Willbridge for her youngest. Why wouldn't she? The man was a marquess, and rich, and handsome. But more importantly, he was quite the kindest man Imogen had ever known.

"Thank you, my lady," he replied after a pause. Was that aggravation in his voice? His face was smooth, a polite smile on his lips. But there was some angry spark simmering in his eyes. He turned to her then, and his anger disappeared. Imogen melted under his regard.

"Miss Duncan, it was a pleasure meeting you. I look forward to seeing you again."

With a bow he stalked from the room.

• • •

Caleb settled back into the plush velvet seat of his friend's carriage and sighed. The sight of Imogen getting bullied by her mother had left a bad taste in his mouth. What was wrong with the woman? Couldn't she see what a gem her eldest was?

Tristan settled beside him. "That was her, wasn't it, Willbridge?" he asked. "The girl you mentioned earlier."

Malcolm Arborn, Viscount Morley entered the carriage then. He knocked on the trapdoor with his ebony walking stick and the carriage lurched forward, away from the Incomparable Miss Mariah's home. Away from Imogen.

"What are you blathering on about, Tristan?" Morley drawled as he adjusted his cuff.

"Willbridge here has taken a fancy to Miss Duncan," Tristan replied with a wide smile.

Morley shrugged. "Who hasn't? She's a beauty. Not many are immune to her."

"Not Miss Mariah Duncan, you dolt. Her sister, Miss…" He frowned. "What the devil is the chit's name?"

"Damned if I can remember."

Caleb looked from one to the other in exasperation. "Truly?" he exploded.

Both men looked at him in shock.

"It is Imogen. Miss Imogen Duncan. She gave her name to you right there in the hall. She saved your ass, Morley, from the embarrassment of not remembering it in the first place. It was a damned sight kinder than I would have done."

Morley looked on him as if he'd grown two heads. Tristan, however, smiled widely. "You truly do fancy her."

Caleb would not even bother acknowledging his friend's idiocy. He leveled a hard stare at each of them. "Just because she has not the outlandish beauty or sparkle of her sister does not make her a nonentity."

"What the devil has gotten into you, Willbridge?" Morley asked. "Why the sudden sermon? I have never once seen you ask a wallflower to dance. You seemed quite content to concentrate on the flashy, generous widows who clamber after you."

Caleb clenched his jaw and turned his attention to the window. Every word Morley spoke was true. He had never concerned himself with women like Imogen before. He had been more than happy to pretend they did not exist. They had never done anything for him, had never helped distract him from the unending guilt that had ridden him for the past decade. He had needed the constant stimulation of knowledgeable women to erase the painful recollection of his past sins.

So why did he suddenly feel mortally offended over the way one unpopular maiden sister was treated?

He knew the answer, of course. If she had not stumbled upon him last night and he had not been fairly smacked in the face with her distress, if he had not taken the time to soothe her, if she had not let him glimpse what lay beyond the façade, he would even now be sitting as these two, happily oblivious to such women.

When he contemplated the way he had tripped through life before, overlooking the Imogens of the world, he felt very small. Even worse, he wondered how many times he had passed by Imogen herself, his eyes sliding over her as if she were a part of the scenery.

"You are right, of course," he finally answered Morley. "I'm as guilty as the next in that I ignored women of her position before."

But not any longer, he vowed.

• • •

Yet another ball. Another chance to stand or sit about with nothing better to do. *I must be getting rather good at pretending to be a potted plant*, Imogen thought with a bit of wry amusement.

She stood beside a row of seated matrons, her mother among them. Already Mariah twirled about on the floor, all grace and sweetness. Her sister spotted her as she passed close by in the arms of her partner. She grinned and rolled her eyes. Imogen smiled back, watching as Mariah was swept away in a turn. Imogen loved all of her siblings equally, but since Frances's marriage she had become especially close to Mariah. Though the girl was younger than her by eight years, she always felt the need to be Imogen's champion and protector. It frustrated Mariah to no end that others could not seem to see her sister.

"I vow," she had proclaimed to Imogen just that afternoon as they had returned from a drive in the park, "I will accept no man unless he treats you with respect. I shall accept no offer of marriage unless the man shows you the common courtesy of acknowledging your presence."

Mariah was of course referring to her disgust of the last hour, in which a great number of gentlemen had ridden up to the Tarryton carriage to pay their respects. Mariah had made a point of forcing each of her admirers to greet Imogen. But as each of them had slid their eyes over her older sister briefly with the barest nod before returning their full attention to her, Mariah's ire had grown.

Imogen had placed her gloved hand over Mariah's and given it a squeeze. "It has always been thus, even when I was eighteen and fresh on the marriage mart. Don't worry yourself over it. I'm quite used to it by now."

"Used to it? You may be, but I will never get used to it. No, unless I can find a man who can be decent and kind to you, my dearest sister, I will not accept his hand."

Imogen had been touched. But secretly she thought that Mariah would be in for a long wait.

She was pulled from her musings as she was jostled from the side. She caught herself against the wall, but only just. The gentleman who had bumped into her gave her only the faintest glance and a mumbled excuse before he moved off to join his group. Imogen sighed. No, she was quite invisible.

She stilled. Just how invisible *was* she? She quickly made a face and then looked about furtively. While most people about her were blurry, those close to her showed not the slightest hint of having seen her.

Feeling her daring grow, she grabbed her skirts in both hands, her feet flashing as she performed a jaunty little dance step. Not even her mother acknowledged her, and the woman was seated beside her. She stifled a laugh behind her gloved hand. Truly? She was that invisible?

There must be a certain freedom in no one noticing you. Her sister was always watched, her every move commented on. If she was less than flawlessly groomed, her manners less than perfectly polite, it would be talked about by all and sundry. Such was not the case for herself, however.

And so, lifting her skirts, she performed a small but perfectly executed twirl.

A low chuckle behind her made her stumble and gasp. And then a warm hand was on her arm, helping to steady her, and she was looking up into Lord Willbridge's laughing gray eyes.

Chapter 4

Caleb had thought, after seeing Imogen rudely jostled and thrown off balance, that he would be playing the white knight in pushing through the throng and coming to her aid. He was proved wrong, however, as he came closer and caught sight of her performing a surreptitious little jig, followed by a smothered laugh. Relief and a spurt of humor ran through him. Behind her calm exterior there seemed to hide a bit of a minx.

Grinning, he came up to her just as she was completing a beautiful little twirl. The laugh that escaped him was completely involuntary, and he was sorry a moment later when she stumbled because of it.

He steadied her. "I don't know who your partner was, but I'm quite envious of him."

She blushed furiously and looked down at her toes. He hooked one finger under her chin and forced her gaze back up.

"No," he gently chided, "I'll not have you go back into hiding. I quite liked the lady I met so unexpectedly in Lord Tarryton's drawing room, and I would very much like to see her again. Is she still in there, do you suppose?"

To his delight Imogen burst out in a small, surprised laugh. "I'm afraid most people are not privy to that particular lady."

His smile grew. "Well, you may tell her I feel all the privilege of having glimpsed her then, even for so short a time."

"You should feel so," she quipped. Her eyes widened as if just realizing her own audacity.

He laughed quietly. "It was quite an unexpected thing, to

finally be gifted with your identity. I searched far and wide for it, you may be assured."

She cocked one eyebrow in disbelief. But there was also something else lurking in her turquoise eyes. Hope, perhaps?

"No, I truly did," he insisted. "Well, as far and wide as one morning would allow."

"You can be assured that if I had known running pell-mell through a dark garden was a way to secure a man's attentions, I would have done it years ago." Her expression was serious, but there was a teasing light in her eyes that lit up her entire face.

He liked her. He truly did. There was something wonderfully substantial about her, and she had a surprising sense of humor that completely caught him off guard. The dark cloud that seemed to constantly shadow him disappeared for a moment.

He held out his arm. "Walk with me?"

When she looked at him in doubt, he motioned with his eyes toward the matrons sitting close by. They were beginning to cast them covert glances, clearly curious as to his presence on this side of the ballroom, though to his relief her mother had yet to notice his arrival.

She flushed. "You know, I was perfectly invisible until you turned up, my lord," she chided playfully. She took his arm and he began to thread her through the crowd.

"You can be assured, you have my heartfelt apologies. The matrons and chaperones have eagle eyes, I fear. I know you will not hold it against me when I tell you that there are times I feel like a bit of prey they have in their sights."

She laughed lightly, keeping her gaze straight ahead, her eyes squinting as she scanned the crowd, a small smile on her surprisingly lush lips.

Lush? Surely that adjective had not just popped into his thoughts. He shook his head. "You are an enigma to me. I cannot make you out. Why do you hide behind such a façade?"

"An enigma," she murmured. "That is a new one. I fear what you see with me is what you get."

He frowned. "Oh, come now, Miss Duncan. You forget, I've glimpsed it. There is much more to you."

She shook her head, her lips compressing. "That's very kind of you, but not true in the least."

He stopped near the wall and turned her to face him. "Stop it."

"Stop what?"

"Disregarding my compliments." He was unable to hold back the tinge of frustration in his voice. Truly, why could she not see he was being honest with her? What force had her believing she wasn't worthy of a compliment? He thought back to his visit to her drawing room. Her mother was not a warm woman. From the look of her he doubted she had ever had a kind word for her eldest. Anyone would feel emotionally bruised after living with that.

He realized that she was staring up at him with a curious expression. He smiled, effectively banishing the strange mood that had momentarily overtaken them. "It isn't well done of you, you know. When a woman receives a compliment, she should simper behind her fan and bat her lashes."

"Oh dear," she said in mock concern. "And here I've forgotten my fan."

They had a wonderful moment of shared laughter. Truly, she had a lovely laugh. She didn't giggle behind closed lips but let out a chuckle of true mirth. He had a sudden and complete moment of peace as he hadn't had in years.

The music ended then. He cocked his head, listening, and then turned back to her. Holding out his hand, he gave her a crooked smile. She looked at him quizzically.

"I would be honored if you would gift me with the next dance, Miss Duncan."

She was already shaking her head before he finished. "Oh, no," she said. "No, you don't want to dance with me."

He kept his hand out. "I assure you I do."

She contemplated him for a long moment before she set her chin and reached out with trembling fingers to grip his own. He grinned down at her before leading her out onto the floor.

• • •

A cotillion was just starting, the sets forming as they took their places. Imogen's heart beat rapidly in her chest. What devil had compelled her to accept him? She wondered. The same devil, she suspected wryly, that had her bantering with him so boldly just minutes ago. She felt as if a stranger had invaded her tonight, one with a daring that Miss Imogen Duncan had never possessed.

Mariah was in the same square formation. When she spied Imogen her face lit up. Imogen grinned back, her every nerve ending alive. And then Mariah's gaze drifted to Lord Willbridge at her side. Her eyes widened, and she looked back to Imogen, her brows raised. After that there was no time for more as the musicians struck up their instruments.

How many times had she danced about the drawing room back at Hillview Manor with her sisters, laughing and carrying on even as they pretended they were at a grand London ball on the arm of a handsome stranger?

But now she was. And every time her hands met those of Lord Willbridge she felt a jolt go straight through her to her very toes.

"You surprise me yet again, Miss Duncan," he murmured in her ear as they passed. She looked at him quizzically. When they met again, he leaned in once more.

"You have not stepped on my toes once. Is there anything you cannot do?"

She gave a small sputter of laughter. "Please," she scoffed as they parted.

When they came back around again his lips were once more at her ear. "For shame, Miss Duncan. Remember, take a compliment honestly given."

"Even if said compliment is bordering on insult?"

He chuckled. "Not an insult," he said as they came around again. "You'd be surprised how many times my toes have been trampled."

She gave him a teasing glance. "Well, as you are leading, perhaps the fault is your own."

She blushed as his quiet laugh reached her. The excitement of the exchange had her bursting with energy. She never felt this comfortable with someone, always overthinking what she was saying. But he brought out a confidence in her that she had never before possessed.

She could certainly get used to this.

All too soon, the music ended. Lord Willbridge led her to the side of the room and bowed low over her hand. "Thank you, Miss Duncan. You dance beautifully." He grinned and melted back into the crowd. Imogen found she could not erase the smile from her face even if she had wanted to.

• • •

Later that night, just as she was settling under the covers, there was a knock at Imogen's bedroom door. Before she could answer it, Mariah flew in. She skipped over to the bed and jumped up, settling herself against Imogen's side.

"I thought you would be dead on your feet, Mariah," Imogen whispered, tucking the blanket about her sister. Mariah snuggled beneath the covers and laughed quietly.

"I vow I cannot rest. I have been replaying Lord Willbridge's actions in my head. I have never seen anything more dashing."

Imogen grinned. "He quite surprised me, I admit."

"He is a lovely dancer, Imogen. It was wonderful of him to single you out. I have heard he does not ever dance with unmarried young ladies. Though he is a rake, I found it gallant of him. Were you very shocked?"

"Yes," Imogen admitted, her mind full of those lovely gray eyes. "But for shame on you for calling him a rake. He has never acted anything but the perfect gentleman with me."

Well, she amended, her cheeks warming, perhaps not always so perfectly gentlemanlike. The kiss he had given her upon their first meeting certainly did not fit into that category.

Mariah's clear blue eyes were wide. "Were you very tongue-tied? I know how it is for you with people you have just met. I worried for you."

"Strangely enough, I was fine. He has a way about him. He put me at ease immediately."

"Do you think he means to court you?"

Imogen gave a shout of surprised laughter before clamping her hand over her mouth. Their gazes swung to the door for a long moment, but all was silent. They both exhaled in relief. If their mother had discovered Mariah out of her bed, she would have launched into one of her many recitations on needing sleep for beauty, and neither could bear that.

"Are you mad?" Imogen whispered.

"And why couldn't he be interested in you?" her sister came back hotly. "You are beautiful, and wonderful, and any man would be proud to have you for a wife."

Imogen looked at her askance before muttering, "I think you are the one who needs the spectacles."

Mariah swatted her on the arm. "Stop it. I hate it when you do that. You cannot take a compliment."

Imogen's mouth fell open.

"What?"

"Lord Willbridge said that very thing to me this evening."

Mariah sputtered on her laughter. "Did he now? My opinion of him has just grown tenfold."

"Well, I do not care that the two of you are in harmony with your thoughts. He has no designs on me, and that is final."

Mariah rolled her eyes. "Fine. You may be gloomy and fatalistic to your heart's content. I, however, have the right to think whatever romantic notions I may." Her expression turned dreamy. "He is so deliciously handsome."

Imogen didn't think such a statement required an answer. But she agreed wholeheartedly.

Mariah sighed happily and launched into a recounting of the evening, most especially Lord Willbridge's attributes. Imogen listened with half an ear as an unexpected thought occurred to her. Why, she wondered, had he paid her the compliment of a dance? He was handsome, and popular, and could have had his pick of the ladies present, despite his unfortunate reputation. Why had he chosen her?

And then a realization hit her, with all the force of a runaway horse. Perhaps it was not her company he was after.

Imogen recalled Mariah's rant in the carriage, when she vowed she would only choose a husband who paid her sister the courtesy of his attention. Lord Willbridge had been present in their drawing room yesterday afternoon, obviously there for her sister. Perhaps he had decided on Mariah for a bride and realized that the way to her heart was through Imogen. Why did she not see it before?

She felt mortified to her very soul. For a very short, very sweet moment, she had believed that perhaps he had searched her out for herself. Not in a romantic nature. No, he could never desire her for that. She ignored the way her chest squeezed at that thought. But maybe he had liked her, had seen something in her that no one else had, had perhaps wanted to be her friend. Was that so very bad to imagine?

She became aware of a deep quiet in her room. Mariah had finally nodded off, her head pillowed on her arm, her nearly white hair a thick plait draped over her shoulder. Imogen gently smoothed a stray wisp from her sister's cheek before snuffing the candle and snuggling down beside her.

Imogen vividly recalled the promise that Frances had extracted from her. If Lord Willbridge truly was trying to get to Mariah in this way, she couldn't fault him for going to extremes to try to capture her attention, for her sister was being courted aggressively on all fronts. But she would not allow any man who did not love Mariah to win her. A true innocent, the younger girl would not be able to guard her heart if a man such as he besieged it.

It was up to Imogen, then. Her lips twisted. Could fate be any more cruel, that she should have to protect her sister from the attentions of a man who was becoming all too dear to herself?

But she must be certain that Mariah was protected. And she would not allow herself to be used, no matter how he smiled at her and made her knees turn to jelly.

She resolutely closed her eyes.

Chapter 5

Caleb entered Lord Avery's musicale the next evening, scanning the crowd for a particular, unlikely face. It no longer had the power to surprise him, this desire to see Imogen. She was such a refreshing change from the dissolute crowd he typically hung around. There was an artlessness to her he was drawn to. And her quick wit, along with the unexpected joy she had displayed when he had danced with her, had been charming and completely without artifice.

His chest felt lighter than it had in longer than he cared to remember. He desired her companionship, looked forward to being not the consummate rake but a gentleman who could take pleasure in a woman's company simply for the sake of being with her.

As he moved through the brightly lit house, he still found no hint of her or her family. He fought down a wave of disappointment, pasting a smile on his face as he joined several of his friends in a light discussion, headed off the advances of a certain married woman, and worked his way toward the music room. Eventually he passed the threshold, taking in the quiet cream and sage opulence, the doors into the adjoining drawing room thrown wide to enlarge the space. Seats had been placed in rows down the length, and there she sat toward the front, two seats in from the aisle, quite alone and scanning her program. There was no sign of her mother or sister, though he had no doubt they were about somewhere and that Imogen was meant to hold their seats. He moved toward her.

When he was still a distance from her, she suddenly looked his way, her eyes tightening at the corners as she squinted. A peculiar kind of joy filled him, a feeling he had come to associate with her presence. He smiled. As he came closer to her, she returned it, but only just.

"Miss Duncan, you are looking well this evening." He motioned to the chair next to her. "May I?"

She nodded quickly and he sat, taking the aisle seat. Her hands clenched on the program, and he could easily imagine her knuckles turning white under the material of her gloves.

"I was hoping you would be here tonight," he said.

Her eyes flew to his. "You have been looking for me?"

"Of course."

"Why?"

The question took him aback. "Why?" he repeated.

"Yes. Why were you looking for me? I know I'm not the normal type of company you keep." She stuck her chin out. "Do you care for my sister, my lord?"

It had taken every bit of strength she possessed to force the words past her unwilling lips. Once they were out, she wanted to recall them. She lifted her chin a fraction more and waited, ignoring the faint trembling in her hands and the even more furious trembling in her stomach.

He sat back, the breath leaving him in a disbelieving huff. "I'm sorry, what was that?"

Did she truly have to repeat herself? "Do you care for my sister?"

His mouth hung open for a moment before he shut it with an audible snap. "What does your sister have to do with anything?"

She looked down at her lap. "Many men have pursued my sister. And yet she has shown none of them favoritism."

There was a charged pause before he blurted, "And? What has this to do with me?"

Was that annoyance in his voice? She swung her gaze up to his incredulous one. "It has everything to do with you."

"Explain," he demanded.

She began to feel incensed at his attitude. "It is no secret my sister and I are exceedingly close. It really was only a matter of time, I suppose, before someone realized her affection for me and decided to use it to gain access to her."

His face fell slack. "Is that what you think of me?" Disbelief and hurt colored his voice. "Do you actually believe me such a cad?"

Uncertainty snaked under her skin. "I don't know you well enough to disbelieve it."

He studied her a long moment. "You are right, of course," he finally said.

Imogen's stomach dropped. "I am?"

"Yes. You have no reason to believe my seeking you out is honest. We have known each other but a matter of days and have not had more than the slightest of conversations." His voice dropped then to a whisper, pain coating his words. "And if you knew the half of what I have done, you would run screaming from me this instant."

Imogen was shocked speechless. Before she had time to recover he continued in a firmer tone, "But know this: I am not after your sister for a relationship, be it honorable or not. I do not wish to disparage her, Miss Duncan," he said slowly, carefully, "but she is not at all my type."

Instantly her ire returned. "Not your type?" she asked in disbelief. "How can she not be? She is wonderfully sweet, and beautiful, and graceful. She would make you a fine marchioness if you had a mind to make her your wife."

He sputtered out a laugh. "You are her greatest champion, I see."

The ridiculousness of the situation hit her. Here she had been accusing him of using her to get to Mariah, and in the next breath she was berating him for not wanting her. But she could not back down now. She squared her shoulders. "I am."

"Well, you may champion her all you like, but it will not change my mind. I have no intention, nor have I ever had any intention, of making Miss Mariah my bride, as lovely a person as she may be. And," he added, enunciating each word with sharp precision, "I seek you out because I happen to like you."

Imogen slumped back into her seat, her teeth biting into her lower lip. "Oh," she breathed.

"Is it so very hard to believe that someone would wish to be your friend?"

"Well, it has not happened before now, so I am sure you can understand my surprise."

"More fools they, then." He grinned. "And all to my benefit, as I shall not have to share you." The smile fell from his face and he looked at her oddly for a moment. "Your sister is very lucky, you know, to have you as a champion. Not all siblings are so close."

She tilted her head and regarded him. "That comment seems to have a wealth of meaning behind it, my lord. Do you have siblings?"

He looked away, but not before she saw the flash of pain in his eyes. "Yes, there are four of us now. Though we are not close. Not any longer."

His wording jarred her. "Four of you *now*? Have you lost a sibling?"

"Yes," he mumbled. "A brother. But it was long ago."

Imogen wanted to reach out, to lay a comforting hand on his arm. But he seemed to shake off the sudden pall that surrounded him and turned to her with a smile. "Now then, what does Lord Avery have for us this evening, hmm?"

The abrupt change of subject left her reeling. He held out his hand. She looked at it blankly for a moment before she placed her program into it.

But if he could let the charged moment pass so easily, then she could as well. It was obvious he did not want to continue with it. She straightened and directed her gaze to the heavy vellum in his hand. "He is to have a soprano from Italy," she remarked as he glanced over the paper.

"Is he now?" Lord Willbridge murmured. "I wonder if this one is truly from Italy, or if she is from Italy by way of Gloucestershire like the last one." He leered sideways at her, and she smothered a surprised giggle.

"Surely not."

"Surely yes." He nodded knowingly. "Though don't let on. Lord Avery, I'm sure, had no knowledge of the deception, though how anyone could have been fooled by her atrocious accent I'll never know."

She laughed. "Well, to tell the truth, I could care less if she were from Italy or India or the East End. If she has a beautiful voice I will listen to it, and gladly."

"Do you sing?" he asked.

"Very rarely, and only when forced."

He grinned. "Then I shall have to force you."

Alarm filled her. "No, you would not dare." His answer was merely a lift of an eyebrow. She groaned. "No, promise me you will not. I would faint dead away were anyone to make me sing in public."

"Faint dead away? Come now. You are made of sterner stuff than that, Miss Duncan."

Just then the crowd began to pour into the room and take their seats. Imogen's mother and sister were on them in a moment.

"Lord Willbridge," Lady Tarryton gushed, simpering as she approached. "What a pleasure to see you, sir. We were so honored to have you in our drawing room the day before last. You remember my daughter, Miss Mariah Duncan, of course."

Lord Willbridge rose and bowed. "My lady, Miss Mariah. Forgive me; I seem to have taken your seat."

"Nonsense." She seated herself beside Imogen. "You are more than welcome to join us. Though perhaps you will see better over here, by my youngest. The view is quite unparalleled."

Imogen felt her face burn. Her mother could not be more obvious if she tried. She expected Lord Willbridge to follow the barely concealed command. Not many dared oppose her mother, and if they did, it was done once and never again.

But to her surprise he sat down firmly next to her once more.

"If the seat is so fine, then please take it for yourself. I would not have you give up such a prime spot for me."

Imogen's gaze flew to her mother. She had a macabre desire to see how the marquess's refusal would affect her.

Lady Tarryton's syrupy smile lost some of its sweetness. "Ah yes, thank you my lord. Most kind of you." She fell into a tense silence, and Imogen could almost hear the wheels turning in her mind. As she expected, it wasn't long before her mother recovered.

"Imogen," she said, a sudden gleam lighting her eyes, "why don't you come sit over here and give Mariah your seat, dear?"

As Imogen gave a small sigh and went to rise, Lord Willbridge reached out and laid his hand on her arm, forcing her back down. She landed in her seat with a grunt. Lady Tarryton gasped.

"Miss Duncan has offered to share her program with me, and I would be most obliged. I'm a complete dunce when it comes to music, you see, and she has promised to explain it to me as the night progresses," Lord Willbridge said.

Imogen's mother blinked owlishly at him.

"Ah, certainly. How…noble of my daughter." She gave him a perplexed smile before turning her attention to the front of the room. Mariah, on her mother's far side, smiled slyly at Imogen before turning forward as well.

Imogen was silent as the soprano took her place and began. And then, under cover of the singing, she leaned ever so slightly in Lord Willbridge's direction, bending her head toward the program to give the appearance of explaining the song. He took the hint, smart man, following suit.

"How in the world did you do that?" she whispered.

His eyes were wide with feigned innocence. "Do what?" he whispered back, before ruining the effect and grinning.

"Oh, you are good," she mumbled. "I wish I could manage her half as well as you."

"It is a simple matter of surprise," he replied. How he managed to insert such a scholarly tone into his whisper she would never know. "Keep her on her toes. And deflect, deflect, deflect."

She raised one eyebrow at him. "Is that your secret? I thought it was an excess of charm."

He winked, returning his attention to the performance. "Well, there is that."

Imogen simply shook her head in awe.

Suddenly sharp fingers gripped her right arm. Imogen just barely kept from gasping aloud. She turned quickly to face the furious countenance of her mother.

"What do you think you're doing?" Lady Tarryton demanded in a harsh whisper.

Imogen schooled her features back to her usual calm lack of emotion. "Nothing, Mama."

"You've been making a positive cake of yourself with Lord Willbridge. I don't know what you think you are doing, monopolizing his time like that. But I mean for him to marry Mariah."

As if that wasn't painfully obvious, Imogen thought, fighting to keep her visage serene. She stared at a spot just over her mother's shoulder, an ache starting up behind her eyes that had nothing to do with the dim light and her lack of spectacles.

"He is not interested in you in that way, you know," her mother added, seeming to become only more furious in the face of her daughter's calm silence. "You may as well get it through your head now, and save yourself heartache later."

As Lady Tarryton turned away from her, finally ending her tirade, Imogen slowly returned her gaze to the front of the room.

No, she thought, surprised at the painful throb her heart gave, he certainly was not. And never would be.

Chapter 6

A week later, Imogen and her family set out for the Knowles's yearly house party. Everyone in the carriage was bleary-eyed and yawning as they left London, the rising sun sending slanting shafts of newborn light in to touch on their weary faces. No one, however, was going to fight Lady Tarryton on the ridiculously early departure she insisted on. The past sennight she had done nothing but berate Imogen for the time Lord Willbridge spent with her and bemoan his lack of attention for Mariah. If getting a jump on all the other marriage-minded females was what it took to content her, then they would all gladly get up at the crack of dawn.

For Imogen, despite the constant haranguing she got at home, had never been happier. Every night Lord Willbridge unfailingly sought her company out. No matter where they were, whether it be a ball or a card party or even Almack's, he was there waiting for her, a smile on his face. They spent no more than the proper amount of time together, either in dancing or simply walking and conversing. But it was the loveliest time of her day, the part she looked forward to the most.

She could not understand the draw she had for a man of Lord Willbridge's looks and status. But then, why should she have to understand his attentions to find happiness in them? Perhaps he was as lonely as she was. She supposed that even a man such as he could get lonely at times, could be tired of the constant stimulation and excess and want just a simple friendship with nothing else expected of it.

And now she was off to a weeklong house party, and he would

be there. A small thrill worked up her spine. It unnerved her, for she feared it was not the typical excitement a person would feel for a friend. And it was growing more pronounced by the day. It could be a dangerous thing indeed, if she were not fully aware that he had no designs on her whatsoever.

She knew she must tell herself this daily, or she could easily lose her heart to the man. But, as always, it caused her a small twinge of pain beneath her breast. Which was silly, as she certainly had no intentions of falling in love with him.

An uneasiness crept within her. No, she thought, she most certainly was *not* falling for him. That would be foolishness indeed. She would not allow it. He was a friend and nothing more.

But deep inside her was the whisper of a thought: if her heart had a mind to, there was nothing her head could do to stop it.

To keep these thoughts at bay, she concentrated on what she had heard of the house that lay before them. The Tudor-era building had not been altered externally since it was first built. No hodge-podge of renovations from different times and eras: It would look much as it must have three hundred years ago. And the gardens were said to rival the house in beauty, stretching for acre upon acre.

Imogen gave a soft sigh. How she wished she would be able to see them properly. But her mother had already decreed her spectacles should disappear before their arrival and not come back until they were well on their way back to London. She adjusted them more comfortably against the bridge of her nose. Already she felt the familiar ache behind her eyes at the mere idea of being without them for such an extended period of time.

As if on cue, her mother's sharp voice filled the carriage. "Imogen, for goodness' sake, won't you put those spectacles away?"

Imogen started from her musings and automatically reached up to remove the wire frame before she stilled. What if she left them on? What if she finally stood up to her mother and insisted on being able to wear them in public? For a moment her fingers trembled, anxiety over disobeying her mother warring with her deep desire to finally see the beauty in the world around her.

After a moment, the latter won out. She forcefully lowered her hand to her lap. "I've heard such lovely things about Pulteney Manor that I would like to be able to see it as we come up the drive," she replied, her voice measured and calm.

Lady Tarryton blinked several times before compressing her lips to thin lines. "Very well. But be sure to put them away before the carriage stops. Really, Imogen, someone might see."

Imogen swung her gaze out the window, swallowing a strange impulse to laugh. Someone might see? How ironic.

She had a flash of Lord Willbridge's splendid managing of her mother at Lord Avery's musicale. What would happen if she attempted such a thing? Imogen had always followed her mother's edicts, as it made life easier for everyone involved. When her mother insisted that she refrain from wearing her spectacles in public, Imogen complied, though it gave her a dreadful headache. When her mother took charge of her fittings at the modiste's, picking out colors and styles she deemed appropriate for someone of Imogen's status in life, Imogen sat quietly by, knowing they would look appalling on her but believing it was not worth insisting on gowns more to her own taste. Because when Lady Tarryton was unhappy, the entire household felt it.

But now she saw that it did not necessarily make life better. Perhaps, just perhaps, the small things in life were important too, despite the temporary setbacks they caused. Mayhap it was time to do a little pushing back. Just because she was destined to live life at home, it did not need to be an unhappy life. After all, soon her siblings would grow up and marry, and she would be left alone with her parents. If she did not begin asserting herself before that happened, she would forever be miserable.

Fighting to wear her spectacles in public was ridiculous, in so many ways. But it was a start. And she knew her mother well; even something this small would be a battle in its own right. The Battle of the Spectacles. She laughed softly to herself. She supposed she could just wear them and be damned. But she loved her mother, and defying her went against every fiber of her being.

However, her drab world had recently been graced with a wonderful burst of color: she had the unprecedented novelty of a friend, one who sought her out and laughed with her and made her feel she was something more than a spinster with no future. Imogen noticed an increasing desire to view and enjoy the world about her, which was growing more difficult by the day without the use of her spectacles. She was tired of living a half life, of seeing everything in a constant blur.

At least this small skirmish had been won. Her eyes soaked in the surrounding area, noting the guardhouse at the beginning of the Knowles's property, the long, tree-lined drive, the bright flashes of color from the wildflowers that lay low to the ground. It seemed to go on forever, and Imogen craned her neck, hoping to get a glimpse of the famed grandeur of the house.

Suddenly the trees opened up, and the house loomed in the distance, all red brick with stone dressings, the many mullioned windows glittering. A large clock tower soared above the central doorway, the gold fittings gleaming in the sun. Several liveried servants stood at the ready on the sweeping stone staircase. Rolling lawns stretched out on either side of the circular drive. And in the center a magnificent marble fountain in the shape of a sea serpent spewed water high into the air.

"Oh," Imogen breathed. Mariah pressed close to her, the better to see the view as well.

"What a beautiful house," she said. "How I long to go exploring."

"Really," Lady Tarryton cut in, "one would think you both were raised in a barn. Hillview Manor is nothing to sneeze at."

"Of course not, Mama," Mariah soothed. "But there is always something wonderful and exciting about someplace new."

Imogen ignored the exchange, taking the time to absorb every bit of the scenery she could. Her eyes swept up over the three-story façade, studying the rows of windows. She wondered if Lord

Willbridge was here already, if one of the rooms that soared above them was his, if he was watching their approach even now. That same thrill shot through her again at the thought of him, and the unbidden images scrolled through her mind of them meeting in the mornings over breakfast, joining in on outings, relaxing for games in the drawing room after dinner.

Her mother's voice broke through her thoughts, sweeping out the pleasant pictures with a harsh dose of reality. "You have had your look. The carriage is about to stop—put away those spectacles now."

Imogen reached up, reluctantly pulling them off and sliding them into her reticule. She leaned back in her seat with a soft sigh. No, she would not be seeing those images come to fruition. It was lovely to dream of having a life where such things were possible, of course, but she had her place, and that place did not include joining in on games and outings and the like. But as the carriage rocked to a halt and the door was thrown open, she wished for the first time that her situation were quite different.

• • •

The day was a fine one, though Caleb wished they had set out a bit earlier. Very well, much earlier. But thankfully it was not overly warm, even though it was now past noon and they still had a fair way to go. He felt a swelling in his chest, a great burst of happiness that could not be contained, and began to whistle a jaunty little tune. He was glad they had decided to travel on horseback, that they had sent their valets on ahead with the luggage, that his cousin Frederick had had the good sense to throw a house party so close to the beginning of the Season. All in all, it was a promising start.

A growl cut through his song. "Will you stop that infernal racket, man? It's playing havoc with my head."

Caleb grinned over at Tristan before finishing his song in a particularly high pitch. Tristan winced. "What has got you so blasted happy?"

Caleb shrugged. "It's a fine day. Do I need another reason?"

Tristan shook his head and turned back to the road. "You're unnatural, you are."

Morley nudged his horse closer. "Tristan, you dunce, if you had not over-imbibed so dreadfully last night—and I daresay into the early morning as well—your head would be clear enough to know that his good mood has everything to do with a certain female's presence awaiting him at Knowles's home."

A belated look of understanding lit Tristan's face. "Ah, Miss Imogen Duncan will be there, will she?"

Caleb's smile vanished with the swiftness of the sun on a cloudy day. "How many times do I have to explain to you? I have no designs on Miss Duncan. I simply enjoy her company. She's refreshing."

"Hogwash," Morley scoffed.

"It's the truth," Caleb insisted through clenched teeth.

"You are deluded," Morley countered. "A man like you does not change overnight to such a degree."

"And how would you know, Morley?"

"Because I *am* a man like you, Willbridge," his friend drawled. "I have known you since Eton. And not once since we were at University have you deviated." He looked suddenly uncomfortable and exchanged a concerned look with Tristan before clearing his throat. "My apologies," he mumbled.

Caleb's jaw set. It took some effort to form words, for he knew just what was on their minds. They had been there the day Jonathan had died. They remembered the horror of it, and what it had cost him since.

"None needed," he replied in a patently false voice.

But despite the momentary dredging up of memories they'd all best forget, Morley launched on: "Now you are eschewing your friends and typical pursuits. You ignored a blatant invitation from Violet at the Morledge ball and have not visited her since. As a matter of fact, you have not been to visit with any of your other inamoratas, either. The signs are all there, man."

Caleb squirmed a bit in his saddle and tried for a tone of bored indifference when he said, "You are ridiculous. What signs?"

"Why, that you are more than halfway in love with Miss Duncan," Tristan said. Morley nodded in agreement.

"I am not in love with Miss Duncan," Caleb all but shouted. A bird launched itself from the bushes that lined the side of the road in a flutter of startled feathers.

"Methinks the man doth protest too much," Morley murmured.

Caleb huffed in exasperation. "Can I not have a platonic female friend?"

"No," both friends replied in unison.

Caleb shot them a glare.

Tristan held up one hand. "We just want you to exercise caution, is all."

"Caution," Caleb repeated dumbly.

"Yes," Morley said, "caution. We don't pretend to understand your interest in the girl. Perhaps she's just a novelty, something new to relieve your boredom. Now, don't go taking offense," he said as Caleb let loose a low curse. "Even if you just feel friendship for the girl, you know as well as I that gentlemen cannot form close friendships with unmarried females. You will get people talking, and then will ruin her reputation when you don't offer for her. At the very least she will be a laughingstock."

For a long moment Caleb didn't trust himself to speak. Finally, he said gruffly, "I will think on it, I promise you. Now, if you'll excuse me?"

Before he could say something he knew he would regret, he nudged his horse on faster, leaving the two men behind. Damn and blast their eyes, why did they insist on putting a lecherous spin on the one thing in his life that was pure and sweet?

But perhaps he no longer had the right to touch anything pure and sweet. The old pain shot through him, and with it came the unbidden image of laughing eyes closed much too early, blood on his hands that no amount of scrubbing could erase, grief etched on the faces of those he loved.

If he had not been so cruel, his brother would be alive. But with the loss of Jonathan, everything in his life had changed. And Caleb had not been the only one affected. His father had done his best to deny it when he had been alive. His mother even now attempted to tell him he was not at fault. But Caleb knew better. In his heart he carried that guilt constantly. So he lived the life he did to hold the pain at bay as best he could.

Until he met Imogen.

She alone gave him a calm peace from the turmoil in his soul. But had his need for that peace blinded him to how he could harm her reputation irreparably?

Was Imogen to be relegated to the list of lives he had ruined through his self-serving actions?

He could not think. His mind was full of faces, all of them scored with condemnation for his part in their misery. But now was not the time for this. Such thoughts would not help him figure out how best to deal with Imogen.

Caleb shook his head violently. Concentrating on the path before him, he kicked his mount to a gallop. And as his body and mind responded to the quickened pace, he watched as if from a distance as the memories of the past melted away.

Chapter 7

Later that evening, Caleb stood to the side of the group milling about the elegant gilt and burgundy drawing room before dinner. It seemed no one had refused the invitation to his cousin's house party; the room was full to bursting. And yet Caleb felt Imogen's absence keenly.

Just as he sensed the moment she entered; his chest expanded, his shoulders felt lighter. Indeed, the very air around him seemed less dense. Despite the urge he felt to cross the room to her, however, he forced himself to stay where he was. But he could not keep his eyes from her. She was as ever eclipsed by her sister, who shone as if she had been dipped in stardust. Even so, Imogen was all he could see.

He had taken time on the hard ride here to think deeply about his fascination with her. After his initial fury of emotion, Tristan's and Morley's comments had made him realize he needed to look with a critical eye at his feelings for Imogen. Why did she have this effect on him? What was it about her that drew him? But even after an hour of searching his mind, he was no closer to an answer. Now he studied her and forced the question on himself that had been at the periphery of all his musings that afternoon: did he desire her?

She was not his usual sort, of course. He always seemed to gravitate toward buxom, sultry women whose knowledge of the sensual arts sometimes eclipsed even his own. But Imogen was none of those things. She was small, though full-figured, and quiet. Everything about her spoke of calmness and virginity and innocence.

She looked at him then, squinting as always, and a small smile flitted across her face. But those eyes, he thought as he bowed to her, watching her take her place far across the room next to her harridan of a mother, he could drown in those eyes. Whole universes had been found in their depths. He never felt freer of the shackles of the past than he did when receiving a smile from those incredible turquoise eyes.

Did he desire her? He feared the answer was yes. For even as he considered it, he remembered with a suddenness that locked his muscles the kiss he had stolen from her that first night. Her body had been soft against his, and her lips, though slack with surprise, had been like the sweetest nectar. And he knew then that more than anything he would like to kiss her again.

He very nearly physically recoiled from the thought. It was *Imogen*, for goodness' sake. She was his friend, an innocent, and completely out of bounds.

Damn both Tristan and Morley to the very pits of hell. They had effectively ruined what to him had become one of his greatest pleasures. He could not now look at Imogen the same way again. How could he continue their relationship realizing as he did the way he felt for her?

And truly, how could he in good conscience continue it anyway? His friends were right, though he hated to admit it. If he continued to show her marked attention and it went no further, the entire *ton* would think he had played with her. She would be the victim of every joke for the remainder of the Season and beyond.

Just then Miss Mariah linked arms with Imogen and whispered in her ear. Imogen blushed crimson and murmured back, keeping her eyes averted. Miss Mariah glanced his way, giving him a small smile before turning back to her sister.

Caleb's heart sank. If those closest to them were beginning to believe there was something more than friendship, it was only a matter of time before the rest of Society did as well.

If he only had to worry about himself, he would damn them all and keep on his course. He had never been one to bow down to social dictates, and he did not intend to start now. But there was Imogen, who had enough sadness in her eyes and did not need it compounded upon by his selfishness. Despite the pain it brought him, he would have to break away from her.

Jaw set, he turned his back on her and walked purposely toward the nearest lonely widow, ignoring the pull he felt to turn about and go to Imogen's side.

• • •

As dinner that night wore on, Imogen found the food growing increasingly tasteless. Lord Willbridge had not looked her way once since the initial meeting of their gazes across the crowded drawing room. Instead, he had joined a stunning woman in a deep sapphire evening gown, her bosom fairly spilling from the fragile silk. After that he had made his way to another woman's side, this one in a lovely shade of emerald green that set off her auburn curls to perfection. And now there was the blonde he sat beside. Even with her blurred vision Imogen could see the melting smile Lord Willbridge gifted the woman, one that curled Imogen's toes from where she sat halfway down the length of the immense mahogany table. She endeavored to keep her eyes from him, but he drew her gaze time and again with his laughing gaiety and flirtatious manner.

Mariah, seated across from her, did not even attempt to mask her confusion. She ignored the gentlemen to either side of her, instead glaring with barely banked frustration at the marquess. Every so often she would shoot Imogen a disbelieving look before returning her attention to the head of the table.

By the time the women left the men to their port and returned to the drawing room, Mariah was a seething ball of rage. She wasted no time in pulling Imogen off to the side.

"What is wrong with Lord Willbridge?" she hissed.

Imogen looked about, making sure no one, especially her mother, was within earshot. "There is nothing wrong with him. Calm yourself."

"But he has been ignoring you all evening."

"I am not his only friend, you know. And if he lives in my pocket, people will begin to talk."

Mariah huffed. "Well," she hedged, "I suppose that's true."

"Of course it is," Imogen soothed. To her relief, the tense line of Mariah's shoulders relaxed a bit. But as they moved to join Lady Tarryton, Mariah took hold of her arm.

"But the women he has been flirting with! Imogen, it is not well done of him."

"Mariah," Imogen said with exasperation, "we knew his reputation long before this night. He is not a monk."

Mariah looked at her for a moment before sputtering in laughter. "No, he is not that."

As the women settled themselves, Lady Knowles stood up and garnered the attention of the room. "Ladies, I have to thank you all for joining us here at our home. I know it was rude to call you away from London for even so short a time as a week when the Season has just begun."

Murmurs travelled around the room. Not one of the ladies present would have declined this invitation, even had the party been extended to a full six weeks during the height of the Season. The Knowles's short but eventful house party, with the masquerade ball that finished it off, was a much sought-after invitation, looked forward to yearly from all echelons of society. Many a young woman had been known to fall into a dead faint at not having received an invitation.

Lady Knowles smiled benignly at the faces around her. "Tonight we shall be rolling back the rug for some impromptu dancing. Sir Frederick has a pianist from Vienna coming to regale us with songs. Tomorrow there will be a picnic at some medieval ruins that are not far from here. For those who don't wish for the walk, we shall have archery and such set up for your enjoyment here at the house."

Imogen listened with half an ear as the woman rattled on. A ruin! Now here was something she could get excited about. Forcibly pushing aside any unpleasant thoughts about Lord Willbridge's puzzling behavior, Imogen instead concentrated on the joys the following day would bring. And maybe, just maybe, her suspicion that he was purposely ignoring her would be proved wrong.

• • •

The drooping branches of the willow tree Imogen sat beneath acted as a kind of veil, partly shielding her from the partygoers who had risen from the blankets littering the lawn. The food had been enjoyed, and now they were tramping over the picturesque ruins of a medieval monastery, the moss-covered stone walls providing a lovely backdrop to the women's brightly colored dresses and bonnets.

But as usual, it was all a blur to Imogen. Before they had all left for the short walk to the ruins, footmen with hampers and blankets at the ready, Imogen had tried once again to fight the Battle of the Spectacles. She had covertly placed them on her nose, hoping if she was nonchalant, her mother, who was agog at her surroundings though she claimed herself unaffected, would simply not notice. But not a moment later her mother dropped back beside her, her voice a harsh hiss in her ear.

"Imogen, take those off at once." Her eyes, the same clear blue as Mariah's, were glacial.

"I would like to wear them, Mama," she said, clenching her hands in front of her.

"No, you will not. Why your father allowed you to get them is beyond me."

"Well, they do help me see," Imogen mumbled with some sarcasm. Her mother's eyes widened.

"Truly, I cannot imagine what has gotten into you, Imogen," she said. "I did not bring you up to be disobedient. Now do as I say and put those things away."

Imogen finally did, but with great reluctance. Once Lady

Tarryton saw the offending piece safely tucked away, she rejoined her friends.

And now Imogen was left with a muddied view of what had promised to be a lovely sight. Though, she thought wryly, perhaps she could see it as a romantic filter, with everything a dreamy mix of hues. She peered from her bower, squinting at the people as they paired off and explored. She finally spotted Mariah, picking her way over some fallen rubble, hanging onto the arm of Sir Frederick Knowles's eldest son, Mr. Ignatius Knowles.

Suddenly, from the corner of her eye, she spotted Lord Willbridge's copper hair, a beacon she had been painfully aware of throughout the day. He ducked under a stone arch and into a small but mostly intact portion of the building. From the looks of it he was quite alone, which surprised Imogen.

Her lips compressed. The man had been a veritable Lothario the night before. His strange coldness had not abated, but had in fact worsened as the night progressed. Once the men had returned from their port to the company of the ladies in the drawing room, he had not stopped flirting with all manner of polished, welcoming women. There was not a moment he did not have one within his scope. And when the dancing had started, so much more carefree than that of a London ballroom, he had swung about partner after partner. Imogen had watched from her corner beside her mother, berating herself for the twinge she felt every time he passed her by without a flicker of a glance.

His strange manner had been present throughout the morning as well. Just once he had looked her way. But his eyes had been unsmiling, his nod to her curt. And then he had turned, and she could almost feel her heart cracking.

With no warning, no build-up, he had begun to treat her as all the other men of the *ton* did. She could not believe that he was truly a bounder, that all this time he had been using her to alleviate boredom. He was not a cruel person. She felt it in her very bones. So why would he suddenly act in such a way?

A slow burn began in her belly. It was not an emotion she

felt often, but she knew immediately what it was: anger. She was good and angry at him. Friends did not treat each other in such a manner. Though she had few enough of that species in her past, she knew it as certain as she knew her name.

Without thinking, Imogen rose. She glanced about for only a moment, her eyes straining to ascertain her mother was happily gossiping with her back to her before she pushed past the screen of drooping branches and swiftly headed in the direction she had last seen Lord Willbridge.

Chapter 8

It had been necessary for Caleb's sanity that he make an escape from the crowd at the ruins. His stomach roiled at the memory of Imogen, looking like a pale specter, forgotten by everyone. Including himself, he thought with a pang of guilt. She had seemed so lost, sitting alone beneath the branches of the willow tree. He had longed to go to her, to bring a smile to those sad eyes.

But he must keep his distance. Perhaps, he thought as he made his way past a tumbled-down wall and through another of those great stone arches that littered the ruin, he should just return to London. He had seen the hurt in her eyes earlier when their gazes had accidentally clashed, had felt it clear to his toes. Yes, perhaps that would be best. For the both of them.

It seemed, however, no matter what he decided to do he was destined to hurt her. Either he remained friends with her and risked her reputation being unfairly damaged, or she would feel he'd betrayed their friendship by turning his back on her. He cursed, picking up a small rock and throwing it with force back through the arch he had just walked beneath.

"Ow!"

Caleb glanced up sharply at the feminine shriek that echoed through the small space. Just then Imogen came into view, one hand rubbing at a spot on her thigh. He could only stare open-mouthed as she stalked toward him.

"If I had known your feelings ran in that particular direction, I would not have followed you," she grumbled, a frown creasing the space between her brows. She stopped several feet from him, and he was surprised to see not the cowed, hurt look that had been present on her face that morning but a tight-lipped anger.

"My apologies," he stammered. He wasn't quite sure how to handle this new Imogen.

"Your apologies?" she said. Her voice was still soft, but now held a level of tightness that made him inwardly cringe. "Yes, I suppose I do deserve them, though perhaps for more than you meant."

He eyed her warily. He had never seen this side to her, had never even thought she was capable of it. She always seemed so calm, so in control. Who knew that sweet Miss Imogen Duncan was capable of such a degree of anger?

"Why have you been ignoring me, Lord Willbridge?"

The question itself did not cause him to rush to her and take up her hands. It was the small catch in her voice, the slight quiver to her lips that did it. She was angry, yes. But also hurt, and he could see from the tense line of her shoulders and the jut of her chin that it took every ounce of bravery she possessed to confront him. Yes, he should escape, should make the break he had determined to. But he could not. Not when she was before him like this.

"I'm sorry," he murmured, his thumb rubbing the backs of her knuckles. "I am trying to do what is best for you."

"I don't understand." She didn't draw her hand away, but he could feel it trembling in his grasp.

How could he possibly explain this to her? Finally realizing that only a direct answer would suffice, he blurted, "There has been interest in the state of our friendship. My friends have begun to question it. I knew it was only a matter of time before others in Society begin to as well."

"Ah, now I do comprehend," she replied, coldness seeping into her tone. "You have been made aware of the repercussions of a friendship between us. You worry about the talk it may cause and how you are presented to your peers, having befriended one such as me. You need explain it no further." She began to draw her hands from his, but his grip tightened.

"No," he replied harshly. "That's not it at all. And why do you continue to belittle yourself? You know I think of you as my very dear friend."

"Forgive me if I doubt your words, but you have proved that to be false the last two days, my lord."

Caleb felt the flush of anger dim his vision. "I did it for your own benefit, not my own."

She raised a mocking brow. "*My* benefit? That is an interesting excuse to give. For I can assure you, I have received no benefit from having been ignored by you."

"Listen to me, you daft woman," Caleb growled, losing patience. "I don't give a damn what others say about me. I have flitted on the edge of what was proper for longer than I care to admit, and never once have I worried about what was said about me. But I would not have you hurt by any gossip that may arise from us becoming close. For that's what will happen if people begin to question our friendship. I don't want others speculating on us." He sighed in frustration. "They'll think I'm toying with you. I'd not have you laughed at," he finished lamely.

A strange look passed over her face, gone so quickly that he could not grasp the meaning of it. "I assure you," she said, "I do not give a fig what they all say about me."

He felt anger—and a bit of relief, truth be told—at her stubbornness. "You should care. They can make your life a living hell. I'm trying to protect your reputation by staying away from you."

"Don't you think I should be the one to make that decision?" she said, her quiet voice full of a steel he had never heard before. "Your friendship, as unlikely as it is, has given me the greatest pleasure I have had besides my siblings' love these past eight years."

He felt something long dormant in his chest flare to life. "As has yours."

"I have enough outside forces dictating what I do, what I wear," she continued fiercely. Her hand came up to her temple but dropped quickly. "But," she declared, her eyes boring into his, "I will not allow anyone to dictate who I am friends with."

"But your reputation—"

"And what will they do to me?" she demanded. "Will they shun me? Ignore me? I am fully used to such things, I assure you. And if I'm sent back to the country in shame because of it, so be it. It is where I want to be, anyway."

She was not listening. He cast about desperately, but the only defense he could see to use was the one he did not want to reveal to her. He did not want her knowing about his part in Jonathan's death, to have her look on him differently because of it. The very idea sent him into a cold sweat. But he must do something. Surely he could warn her away without telling her directly.

The ruined walls of the monastery seemed to be passing judgment on him. He would never be free of that one horrible moment. It would haunt him forever.

"Imogen," he began gruffly, "you do not know what kind of person I truly am, what I have done. I am responsible for horrible things, things that you would hate me for should you ever find them out."

Her eyes softened. "They are all past sins, my lord. We all of us have done things we regret. The point is, you do regret them."

He ran a hand over his face, even as he felt that wonderful release from the past that she, and only she, seemed to bring. He was losing the will to fight, but he dug deep. He had to tell her.

In that moment, she began speaking. "You and I are friends, are we not?" At his nod, she continued, "I am six and twenty, my lord. And in that time I have not had one friend—until you. I am not going to give you up so easily, I'm afraid. Are you so willing to give up on me?"

The last of his will vanished in a moment. Damn his weakness, his selfishness. He squeezed her fingers and stepped closer. "No," he said forcefully.

She smiled for the first time that day. "Then there is no question of us ending this friendship, is there?"

Her countenance transformed. He wanted to kiss her, he realized. The urge to draw her close, to gather her in his arms and feel her mouth beneath his, almost overpowered him.

He felt himself bending toward her, felt his heart gallop like mad in his chest. Her eyes widened, her lips parting. His brain took over then, fairly screaming at him, stopping him cold: *You fool, this is Imogen, not a common trollop!* He shuddered and pulled back.

Taking a deep breath to steady himself, he forced a smile. "No, there is no question of it," he murmured. "But we must take care. Despite your disregard for your reputation, it is of importance to me."

"Very well," she agreed quietly, her eyes bright.

He tucked her arm through his and began to lead her back through the ruins. He was a selfish creature, he thought with disgust. The truth of the matter was, he needed her. She grounded him as nothing else had in ten long years. He was settled and calm with her, who he should have been instead of who he was. If she was strong enough to brave the old tabbies of the *ton* to keep their friendship, then so was he.

And to hell with the strange surges of desire he felt for her. He could control them if it meant keeping her in his life.

• • •

It was a heady thing to fight for something so very important to her. Imogen had assumed initially that the wonderful fire it had sparked within her would fade with the day. But no, all through that warm afternoon, while she and Lord Willbridge joined Mariah and Mr. Ignatius Knowles in exploring the elegant, ruined lines of the old monastery, she had felt it continue to burn bright.

Later that evening, as Imogen was preparing for dinner, that daring spilled over into the Battle of the Spectacles.

Imogen sat at the dressing table in her room, smoothing the last bit of stubborn hair into place. She glanced over to the small clock on the mantle and realized it was time to fetch Mariah. Giving herself one last critical look in the mirror, she went to remove her spectacles. But at the last minute her hand stilled. Clenching her fingers tight, she rose and strode purposely to the door.

Mariah was just exiting her room as Imogen stepped out into the hall. Her steps faltered when she spotted her sister in her spectacles and she gave her a long appraising look.

"Well, it's about time." She smiled brightly and grasped Imogen's hand firmly in her own. Emboldened by the small act of support, Imogen squared her shoulders and directed their steps toward their parents' room. She hesitated but a moment before knocking.

"Enter," came her mother's strident voice.

Both their parents were within and looked up when she opened the door.

"Girls," their father greeted them absently, "you both look splendid." He returned to the book in his hand before the words were out of his mouth.

Their mother was less welcoming. "Why are you not heading down to the drawing room? And Imogen, remove those horrid things at once."

Mariah squeezed her hand reassuringly. Imogen's heart pounded like mad in her chest, her tongue dry as dirt. But she knew that if she didn't beard the lion now she would never be able to.

"No, Mama," she said quietly. "I'll be wearing my spectacles down."

Her mother blinked. Even their father lowered his book and looked up.

Lady Tarryton's lips thinned. "You will not."

"I require them to see."

Her mother waved one hand in the air. "Enough. I'll not be having this discussion with you now. We're expected below."

Imogen took a step forward, letting her fingers drift from her sister's. "We need to have this discussion, Mama. We've been putting it off for far too long."

"There is nothing to discuss. You won't be wearing them."

"I will," Imogen said firmly.

"Why do you choose now to vex me?"

"I'm not doing this to vex you, Mama."

"Please," her mother scoffed, turning to the cheval mirror in the corner and adjusting her glittering ruby necklace.

"I can assure you, it won't harm our family name a bit. Besides," Imogen continued, "it gives me a headache to be without them."

When her mother made no hint of having heard her eldest, Mariah spoke up in the tense silence. "Let her wear them, Mama."

Lady Tarryton looked at her younger daughter in the glass. "Has the world gone mad?" she asked no one in particular.

And then, to everyone's everlasting surprise, Lord Tarryton spoke.

"Dash it all, Harriett, let the girl wear the blasted things. They aren't doing anyone any harm."

Imogen's mother drew herself up straighter and raised her chin a fraction. "So this is it, then. You are all against me. Fine," she spat in Imogen's direction, her eyes shards of ice, "wear them. But if this affects Mariah's chances, it will be on all your heads."

Lord Tarryton sighed. Then, rising, he went to Imogen. He gave her a small smile and a pat on the shoulder. "Well then, that's settled."

Without another word, he left the room. Lady Tarryton followed. But before she rounded the doorframe, Imogen heard her mutter, "It won't improve her lot one bit anyway."

Chapter 9

Imogen felt a ripping in her chest. Her mother's words were muttered low, too low for either her father or sister to hear. But Imogen heard them clear as day. And in that moment she knew, deep down, her mother was right.

In the grand scheme of things, being able to wear her spectacles in public was ridiculously trivial. It would not change the course her life was destined to take. Her future would still be at the mercy of others. Her place was with her parents, and after they went to their reward she would go to her siblings. Like an ugly heirloom vase no one really wanted but felt obliged to put on the mantle.

Mariah smiled and linked arms with her, dragging Imogen from her maudlin thoughts. "Well done," she whispered. "I'm so proud of you."

Imogen forced her lips to turn up in what she suspected was a horrid imitation of a smile but seemed to appease her sister nonetheless. She should be happy, after all. She had won. But she wanted to cry. Never had she felt jealous of her sister, but in that moment she would have given much to trade places, to have Mariah's possibilities, the ease that she had with others.

She was well past the age of possibilities, however.

Perhaps, she thought as they made their way to the ground floor, if she had something to hold on to, some wonderful memory, she would be able to move on with her life with a bit more grace. Perhaps if she had thrown herself into experiences when she was younger, had not been so rigid, she would have remembrances to warm her at night.

But she had nothing. And it was too late for her now, wasn't it?

• • •

"I didn't know your Miss Duncan wore spectacles, Willbridge."

"She is not 'my' Miss Duncan," Caleb replied by rote. But the small burst of pleasure at the phrase shocked him. How peculiar, he thought absently as he followed Tristan's gaze toward the door. He stilled, for there stood Imogen, her eyes wide and luminous behind a delicate pair of spectacles.

She no longer wore the squinting, strained expression he associated with her. No, he thought in appreciation, the lines of her face were more relaxed now, softened. And even from his position across the room he could see how the thin wire frames accented her beautiful turquoise eyes.

He had thought her pretty before, but now she was, quite simply, lovely.

"They suit her."

Caleb frowned as Morley's voice broke through his thoughts. "I'm sorry?"

His friend waved one hand vaguely in front of his face. "The spectacles. They are not at all the thing, of course. But they suit her."

Tristan nodded thoughtfully, a faintly quizzical look on his face as he stared at Imogen. "They do. Funny how I never noticed those eyes of hers before now."

Caleb watched his two lifelong friends studying Imogen and fought the sudden and swift desire to slam their heads together. What the devil was wrong with him? They were only observing her improved appearance, not making lecherous comments about her.

He glanced in Imogen's direction once more. She had just noticed him, and as their eyes met she attempted a smile. But it was a pathetic thing at best. Forgetting his friends, his promise to take care with her reputation, even the room full of people between them, Caleb went immediately to her.

The first thing he noticed was how much larger her eyes were. Their color was intensified behind the lenses of her spectacles, and he was struck dumb. He simply stared down at her in silence, feeling that incredible blue-green loveliness clear to his toes.

But the sadness on her face finally broke through his muddled brain. She was striving to hide it, but it was there all the same.

"What is it?" he asked in a low voice.

She only shook her head, her throat working as she swallowed hard.

"Tell me."

"It is nothing," she replied. The slight frown marring her brow, however, told a different story.

"You are an abysmal actress, did you know that?"

She sputtered on a bit of startled laughter but sobered quickly. "I cannot talk about it here," she whispered. Her eyes slid to the side. Her mother was close by, talking animatedly with several other matrons.

All of a sudden Imogen's expression changed. She studied him with a peculiar intensity.

He leaned closer and raised one eyebrow.

"I need to ask a favor of you," she said in a low voice. "Will you meet me after dinner in the orangery?"

"Certainly," he answered immediately.

She smiled up at him, and Caleb found himself struck dumb for the second time that evening. And as he watched her walk away to join her sister, he had a feeling it would not be the last.

• • •

Caleb watched with barely contained frustration at dinner as course after course was brought out for the guests' enjoyment. Was it just him, he thought, or were people taking an inordinately long time in savoring their food this evening? By the time the women left the men to their port, he felt he would burst from his skin.

And then wouldn't one gentleman begin telling a drawn-out story about some opera singer he'd bedded, which led to another revealing he'd bedded the same woman last Season, which prompted a lively discussion on her technique. When it then turned to a general discussion on opera singers versus actresses, Caleb could stand no more. Determining that the group's attention was engaged, he slipped from the room.

When he reached the orangery, however, he found the glass-fronted room still quite empty. The warm, clean, tangy smell of citrus filled the air, and the glossy dark green leaves of the trees shimmered in the pale moonlight. He spotted a stone bench against one wall and sat to await Imogen's arrival. Had she come and left already? Would she still come? And why in hell was he so damned nervous?

Mere moments later, however, the door opened silently and she slid into the room. He stood as she approached him. She was grinning.

"I have never done anything like this before," she said a bit breathlessly, a small laugh escaping her.

"Not once?"

She shook her head. "It quickens the blood, doesn't it? This sneaking about and all."

He smiled. "Yes."

She breathed in deeply, no doubt taking in the wonderful scents of the room. Her eyes roved over the moonlit plants with interest.

"How long have you worn spectacles?" he blurted.

She glanced up at him in surprise. "Since I was ten."

"Why have I not seen you in them before?"

She shot him an ironic look. "My mother is not...partial to them."

"Partial? That's an interesting word."

"If you must know, she believes I'll be labeled a bluestocking and that the entire family's reputation will be damaged."

He laughed. "You're kidding."

"I wish I were."

He studied her for a moment in disbelief. "So you wearing spectacles in public is akin to the greatest scandal that could befall your family."

"Something like that." Her lips quirked, but he could see he wasn't too far off the mark.

She suddenly cleared her throat, all business. "But that brings me to the matter at hand. Thank you so much for agreeing to meet me, by the by. I realize it's a shocking business, for us to be here alone."

He fought the urge to laugh. With the utter earnestness on her face, he didn't think she would welcome it at this time. "No problem at all," he replied instead, attempting to adopt her serious mien.

"You're probably wondering what prompted me to act in so forward a manner. The truth of the matter is, I need you for something."

All manner of images flashed through his mind at that, not a one that he could possibly share with her. He cleared his throat. "Anything at all."

She drew a deep breath. "I need you to help me have an adventure."

"A what?"

"An adventure." She saw his blank look and sighed, the pain he had noticed in her eyes earlier returning. "You see, Lord Willbridge, I know full well my situation. I am aware I will never marry, that I will forever live on my parents' charity, and my siblings' after that."

Anger rushed through him at her words. He was vaguely aware that others thought of her that way. Hell, he had believed the very same thing when he first met her, which brought him no little shame now. That she believed it, however, made it all too real.

And she should not have to settle for such a life.

"Don't say that," he growled.

"Why not? It's true."

"It does not have to be. You could still marry, have a family."

But she was looking at him calmly. "It's fine. I've come to terms with it. I'm not afraid to face my future." She drew herself up, and he was touched by the quiet pride that shone from her.

"But I would very much like," she continued in a low voice, "to have some memories to bring with me into that future, my lord. To know that not all of my life has been planned and pre-scribed and…wasted." Her slender fingers gripped at the fabric of her skirts. "I want to know I lived a bit. I want an adventure or two to warm me. Nothing extravagant. Just to know that I had enough bravery to try something new and daring, before the chance was lost forever."

She only wanted a bit of an adventure? He would do that and so much more for her if it would bring a smile, even fleetingly, to that sad, too-serious face.

And who knew, maybe this was a way, however small, to begin making amends for his past sins. It would not bring Jonathan back, would not erase the pain of the past decade. But at least he could make a difference for the better in someone's life.

"Imogen, don't you think you had better start calling me Caleb? After all, a good adventuring would be stifled by such formalities."

It took her a moment. But when the realization hit her that he had agreed, her entire being lit up. Not just her face, which had broken into the most glorious smile he had ever clapped eyes on, but her body as well. She straightened, and it was as if a bolt of lightning had struck her, filling her with so much energy that she fairly crackled with it.

And then she did the thing he least expected. She rushed at him, flinging her arms about him. In his shock he automatically clasped her to him. He experienced a rush of awareness as he felt every curve of her pressed to him, the warmth of her through her thin gown. The clean scent of her drifted up to him, making him slightly dizzy. And he knew he wanted nothing more than to kiss her.

He stilled, his arms gripping her a bit tighter. He had no wish to ruin their friendship. He could imagine her shock if he followed through with the urge. He had gotten away with accidentally kissing her once; he did not think he could talk his way out of it a second time.

Gently pushing her back, he looked down into her flushed face, her eyes glittering like twin stars. There was that urge again, even more insistent. He ruthlessly buried it.

"Do you have any idea what you would like to do?" he asked her.

She spread her hands wide. "I haven't a clue," she replied breathlessly. "I have no notion how to go about adventuring."

If this were London, he would have all manner of outrageous things he could drag her to. But they were in the country, and there was dashed little he could offer her here.

Her eyes were wide and full of expectation. No, he thought, mad London adventures weren't what she needed, or indeed what she would even want.

What she needed was just to loosen up her boundaries a bit, to experience fun just for the sake of it.

He smiled wickedly. "What do you say to a spot of swimming?"

Confusion clouded her face. "Swimming?"

"I know of a pond not far from here. We could go tomorrow, while everyone else goes to town for the shopping expedition."

"Swimming in a pond in broad daylight? Oh, no, I couldn't." Her eyes widened considerably in shock, but he saw the lurking interest just below the surface.

"Do you even know how to swim?"

"Of course I do. Well, I did so as a child. I swam with my siblings. But ladies do not do such things…" Her voice suddenly trailed off. And then a slow smile spread across her face. "Very well, I'll go swimming. I shall claim a headache and ask to be allowed to stay behind."

He smiled at her approvingly. But as he saw the dawning excitement in her eyes and the way her body fairly hummed with energy, he had a moment of doubt. Swimming. With Imogen. What new hell had he foisted upon himself?

Chapter 10

It didn't take much work to convince her mother that she should be left behind the following day. And after looking in the mirror, Imogen knew why. Her color was high, her eyes bright. Her mother must have suspected a sickness much worse than a mere headache. A giggle escaped her and she clamped her hands over her mouth. Heavens, what was she doing?

She stood in the middle of the room, at a sudden loss. She had never in her life lied to her mother, had never even considered doing so. But, strangely enough, she had not been the least concerned about her mother believing her. No, it had been Mariah that had caused her apprehension. Mariah, who had always been able to read her like an open book. But, wonder of wonders, she had even managed to convince her sister that she was unwell.

Imogen felt a brief moment's guilt before the excitement that had been building in her all night and into the morning burned it away with a fire that would not be contained. Full of nervous energy, she moved about in agitation, donning her stoutest walking shoes, a bonnet, and a shawl. Taking up the small bundle she had readied the night before that contained a towel and spare chemise, she hurried out of the room.

Caleb was waiting for her at the end of the hall, leaning against the wall. He grinned when he saw her approach. "I thought you wouldn't come."

She held her bundle to her chest like a talisman. "Of course I will not back out," she said indignantly. Her voice warbled a bit and she clenched her teeth.

He straightened and held out his arm to her. "Well then, are we ready, fellow adventurer?"

She took his arm, gripping it tightly as he led the way down the servants' stairs and through a back entrance of the house into the gardens.

"You certainly know your way around," she said in surprise.

"I was here many times as a boy. The pond I'm taking you to used to be a favorite haunt of mine and my cousin's."

She was oddly touched that he would bring her to a place he held special. "And what is that you have there?" she asked, motioning to the wicker basket he held.

"All good adventurers need nourishment. And it is just our luck that Cook is quite fond of me. This lovely basket will prove a godsend after a morning of swimming."

Just then they reached the cover of the trees. There was a path here, though it was old and overgrown with disuse. She picked her way carefully through the brush at his side.

"As far as adventures go," she said, her voice sounding unnaturally loud in the confines of the dense foliage, "this must be tame compared to what you're used to."

Caleb chuckled. "Tame can be a good thing," he said, helping her over a fallen tree branch.

But Imogen stopped. Caleb stopped as well, looking at her in curiosity.

"What is it?" he asked, and then his smile turned sly. "Are you backing out?"

"Hardly, my lord."

"Caleb," he gently reminded her.

"Caleb," she repeated, flushing slightly. "I want to know why you're doing this for me."

"Why?" He tugged her on, and they resumed their walk through the trees.

"Yes, why? Why are you helping me? What are you getting out of this?"

He was silent for so long she thought he would not answer. And then, just as she was about to ask again, he finally spoke up.

"You ground me," he said, his voice so low she had to strain to hear him.

"I'm sorry?"

"You ground me," he repeated. "For so many years I've been living an existence of excitement and stimulation and excess. Then I met you."

"Why does this sound more like an insult?" she grumbled.

"No!" He stopped and turned her to face him. "You don't understand, Imogen. I was not living that life because I wanted to. I did it because I felt I *had* to."

"Had to? But why?"

His features immediately shuttered. A muscle worked in his jaw for a moment before he replied. "The 'whys' are not important. What *is* important is I found you. Or rather, you found me in that garden at the Morledges'."

Imogen blushed, fighting to make sense of his speech. "Me? What is so important about me?"

He gripped her hands tightly. Imogen nearly gasped at the contact, at the heat of him through her kid-skin gloves.

"There is *everything* important about you," he said, his voice so intense, so certain that she was struck mute. "You have brought a peace to me that I have not felt in ten long years."

She looked deeply into his pale gray eyes and was shocked at the very real pain there. What had this man been through? What had hurt him to such a degree that he suffered because of it even now?

She was about to question him further when he was suddenly off again, pulling her through the brush.

"But this is getting us nowhere if we wish to start your adventuring," he said briskly over his shoulder.

Imogen stumbled after him, just barely avoiding a low tree branch. "What is your hurry?" she gasped. "The pond is certainly not going anywhere."

"No, but there is no telling when someone will go looking for one of us. And I'll not have you say I have failed you on the first try."

Within minutes they broke through the cover of trees into a small clearing. Sunlight shone golden through the branches above them and sparkled on the still face of a small round pond. A large flat rock jutted out over the water, and it was here they stopped.

"Caleb," Imogen breathed, turning in a slow circle to take it all in, "however did you find such a place?"

Caleb placed the picnic basket down and shrugged out of his coat. "My cousin Ignatius and I spent many an idyllic afternoon here when we were children." He paused to waggle his eyebrows at her. "Sans clothing."

As he sat and pulled off his boots, Imogen sputtered a laugh. But it quickly died as Caleb rose and removed his waistcoat. Her eyes fastened on his long, tanned fingers as they went to his cravat. He pulled apart the intricate knot, and then the long, snowy white piece of fabric joined the growing pile of clothing on the ground.

Imogen stared in fascination at the small triangle of taut strong throat that had been revealed, her mouth suddenly dry as dust. She moistened her lips, adjusting her spectacles as he undid the buttons and the shirt went up and over his head, ruffling his copper hair so it fell in adorable disarray over his forehead. Her breath hitched as her eyes travelled over the smooth, tanned skin of his chest and arms and abdomen, at the well-defined muscles, cording every bit of flesh into firm perfection, at the faint smattering of hair that dusted his chest and trailed down, over his stomach, past his navel, into the waistband of his breeches. And then his hands were there, at the fastenings, and he was pushing the fabric down over his slim hips...

Imogen gasped, covering her face with her bag. "What are you doing?" she squeaked.

"Swimming," he replied patiently. She heard the faint whisper of more cloth hitting the pile, and then a splash as he entered the water.

"Damnation!" he swore, gasping. "I don't remember it being so cold. Oh, pardon me."

"Don't curb your tongue on my account," she muttered. "Though I'm not sure that's any way to actually get me in that frigid water." She peeked over at the pile of clothes he had left, his boots nearby. *Please*, she thought madly, *let him still have his smalls on.* She shifted her gaze to where he treaded water, chewing on her lower lip.

He stared at her, water streaming down his face and neck. "Imogen?"

"I cannot do it!" she burst out.

"Yes, you can," he replied with infinite patience.

"No, no I cannot." She began to back away. "Thank you for trying. Truly, thank you. But I cannot do this."

"Imogen," he said, swimming back toward her with strong, smooth strokes, "come here."

Imogen's eyes widened at the silken purr of his voice. "No," she answered. "I think I had best return to the house."

"Imogen," he repeated, placing his hands on the rock, "you will come into this water if I have to physically drag you into it." He saw her gaze dart to his pile of clothes and his eyes narrowed thoughtfully. "If you force me to leave this water, you will find out for certain."

Her gaze, wide-eyed in horror, flew to his face. "Find out what?" she managed on a croak.

He grinned wolfishly. "Whether I've taken my smalls off or not."

She gasped, then colored. "You are horrid!"

"If being horrid is what it takes to keep my promise to you, then so be it."

She stared at him for a long moment, at the determination that glinted like steel from his gray eyes, and she knew with certainty he would come after her if she turned and ran. An image of him, streaking after her through the trees, wearing nothing but what he was born with, came unbidden to her mind.

"Fine!" she exploded. "Turn around so I can get this gown off."

She blinked as his grin widened and he turned away. Seriously, he could make double his fortune if he were able to bottle whatever it was that made his smiles so potent.

After a long moment he spoke up. "I am waiting, Imogen. And I am not a patient man."

She started and dropped her bag. Her fingers flew to the buttons of her gown.

In no time she was down to just her chemise. She removed her spectacles and laid them down gingerly on her neatly folded pile of clothing. Only then did she approach the water, keeping a wary eye on him all the while. He was still facing the opposite bank, treading water. She sat down on the flat rock and gingerly dipped her bare toes in the water. The chill stunned her.

"It is freezing!"

He snorted. "You are not getting out of it that easy. Come along, Imogen. Once you start moving, you will adapt in no time."

She shook her head in disbelief. Well, she thought as she contemplated the smooth surface of the pond, she really might as well get it over with. If he could do it, so could she. Taking a deep breath, she plunged into the cool depths.

The water enveloped her, shocking her. She came up sputtering. The first thing she saw when she cleared the water from her eyes was his laughing face, mere inches from her own.

"Well done, Imogen," he said.

And that was it. She lost her breath entirely. It was not due to the cold water or even her daring. It was him. And she knew, with every fiber of her being, despite all her protestations, she had fallen in love with him.

She could see every detail of this moment, as if it had been stilled for the purpose of her memorizing it, bit by bit, when she had realized herself in love. She saw with unbearable clarity the beautiful curve of his lips, the water droplets caught in his impossibly long lashes, the hard arc of his neck and shoulders above the water line, the sleekness of his wet hair and how it made his cheekbones stand out more prominently.

But mostly she saw his eyes. Their pale gray depths were soft with affection. And then his smile faded and a heat filled them that warmed her body. She no longer felt the chill water, only a strange aching warmth that coursed from the core of her and through her limbs. She longed to reach out and place her hands on the hard muscles of his shoulders and let her body float against his. Even as she thought it, she saw his eyes travel to her lips. Subconsciously she licked them. His eyes widened, and the cords of his neck moved as he swallowed.

In a swift sweep of his arms he submerged, and the moment was lost. Shaken, she watched as his head broke the surface half the length of the pond away. He grinned at her, and even without her spectacles she saw it was the same easy grin he always wore. Had she imagined the entire thing?

"Come on, Imogen," he called.

Oh, this was not good, she thought as she watched him paddle easily through the water. She was not supposed to fall in love with him. This would make things so much more complicated, so much harder on her when it ended and she returned to that future of hers. She was a fool, an absolute fool.

But even as she thought it, as she treaded water and watched him swim about, she knew she would not give up her time with him, no matter the pain she would feel later. These moments were a gift, and she would not allow her feelings to ruin it.

Determined to enjoy herself though her heart was in turmoil, Imogen swam toward him.

Chapter 11

Caleb cursed himself ten times a fool. What the hell had he been thinking? Swimming? Truly?

It had all seemed innocent enough when he had first thought of it. Something children would do on a hot summer's day when they had a chance to escape their studies. Something fun and carefree that Imogen could enjoy. But he had forgotten one crucial detail: wet clothes plastered to a lusciously rounded figure.

His first glimpse of her body below the water, her thin chemise hardly a barrier as it floated against her flesh, had brought that glaring oversight into focus. Her arms were bare, her shoulders smooth and glistening with water. And her hair, an incredibly thick mass of light brown that streamed over her shoulders, swirling in sensual disarray about her. Seeing her hair down, wet and clinging to her skin, affected him in places he was glad she could not see.

When she licked her lips he had almost been lost. He had very nearly closed the distance between their bodies, pressing his arousal against her, pulling her wet, practically unclothed body against his own.

It had taken every bit of his control to swim away. Immersing himself in the coolness of the pond and having the utter quiet of being submerged, even for so short a time, helped him to pull himself together. He would not—*could* not—allow himself to lose control with her. By the time he broke the surface of the water again he felt he had taken the reins of his desire in hand.

Now he watched as she swam toward him, her strokes slow, a look of intense concentration on her face.

"So you do know how to swim," he teased.

She laughed. He was surprised to hear a peculiar tightness in it. But her voice, when she answered him, was as calm as ever, if a bit breathless. "My muscles seem to remember what to do, though my memories are a bit hazy. I haven't swum since I was a girl. My siblings and I went down to the lake near our property quite a bit in the summer with our nurses and governesses."

They reached the opposite bank and by silent agreement began to slowly swim back to the flat rock. "Just how many siblings do you have?" he asked.

Beside him her head bobbed along the surface, her hair flowing behind her like a veil. She smiled at the question. "Six. My sister Frances, who married the Earl of Sumner several years ago, is next in age to me. I miss her dreadfully." A look of pain crossed her face. But there was something else. Worry? It soon cleared, however, and she continued. "Actually, I miss them all dreadfully. Even the ones who drive me nearly insane with frustration." She gave a light laugh.

"Tell me about them."

"Well," she panted, her arms working at keeping her afloat, "after Frances is Nathanial. He is twenty-two, and has just completed his time at University. Mariah you know, of course. After her there are the three youngest. Gerald is sixteen, and the most serious of the group, already planning on becoming a great London barrister. Evaline is next. She could test the patience of a monk. Last is Bingham, just turned eleven and anxious to start at Eton next year. It has not been easy for him, being the youngest and so far behind his brothers." Her voice had become pensive and wistful, and she trailed off. When they reached the flat rock once more she grasped it and turned to him. "You have told me a small bit of your own siblings," she began gently, "and that you have lost a brother. Would you talk about it with me now?"

He felt a pain shoot through him that actually stole his breath. Quick memories that he fought to banish flashed through his head of blood, agony on his mother's face, the cloying scent of lilies in the house.

His smile felt plastered to his face in an uncomfortable way. "There is nothing to talk of, I'm afraid. My brother died. He was twelve. That is basically all there is to it."

"Losing your brother at that age must have been dreadful."

"Yes, it was dreadful," he muttered, looking out over the landscape, unable to bear the compassion in her eyes. He certainly did not deserve it. "But it is in the past."

There was a beat of silence before she spoke again. "At least you have your other siblings. Such support must be necessary in such a situation."

Again that pain, only more intense this time. In her ignorance of the situation she was cutting straight to the quick. "I'm afraid," he said through stiff lips, "that, as my life has led me to spend the majority of my time in London I am no longer close with any of them." No need to tell her why he was in town most of the time. Nor that it was the strain at home that had prompted the move, not the other way around.

Out of the corner of his eye he saw her bow her head and shake it slowly. "It must be like losing them all, then."

What could he say to that? It was the truth. He had lost much more than Jonathan that day.

"I hate the thought of you being so alone, Caleb."

He forced a laugh at that. "I am certainly far from alone. I have not exactly allowed myself to be without companionship in the past years."

He inwardly winced as the crass words left his mouth. It had been beyond the pale to bring up his reputation as Society's Lothario, and with Imogen of all people. But he had never before had anyone question him about his relationship with his family or probe into the unhealed wounds of the past.

Imogen ignored it. "That is not what I meant, and you know it. There is something sacred about the relationship between brothers and sisters. Especially having lost one, you should not have to go through the pain of losing the others. Surely there must be something that can be done to remedy your relationships with them. All cannot be lost."

He gritted his teeth, fighting the strange longing her words brought forth. He never allowed himself to consider regaining closeness with his siblings. It was not possible, not after what had happened with Jonathan. Imogen, however, was bringing to light these hidden desires: to have an easy rapport with his family, to not feel gnawing guilt whenever he was in their presence.

"Enough about me." As he spoke he saw her draw back, and he realized his words had been sharper than he'd intended. He smiled, softening his tone. "This afternoon is about you. We will not spoil it by bringing up the past."

Still there was worry on her face, creasing the space between her brows. He had to deflect her.

"I still don't know what you're capable of in the water," he mused. "I'm not quite sure you can hold your own with the likes of me."

His words seemed to do the trick. Her eyes cleared, a sly smile lifting her lips. "I do believe I'll surprise you."

"Very well then—prove it. What do you say to a race?" And before she could answer, he was off.

"No fair!" she called. She let out a wonderful peal of laughter, so enchanting in its exuberance that it seemed to unfreeze whatever pall had temporarily settled over the afternoon. She came after him, her efforts laborious but growing in confidence. By the time she reached where he was lazily treading water, she was grinning in triumph.

"I'm doing it," she breathed, letting out another laugh. "I really am doing it."

Her joy was infectious. He splashed her, which caused her to gasp and retaliate. Before long the clearing rang with splashing and laughter. And Caleb thought he had never been so happy in his life.

• • •

Well before Imogen was ready for the day to end, it was time to emerge from the water. Her fingers were wrinkling horribly and her lips, Caleb told her, were turning an interesting shade of blue. She grudgingly admitted he was right, and when his back was firmly turned she emerged first, ducking behind an obliging bush to dress. A blush suffused her face—and lower—when she saw how her chemise clung to her body, leaving absolutely nothing to the imagination. Thank goodness she had been fully submerged.

Before long she had a dry chemise on, her clothing over it and covering her from neck to foot once again. Caleb took his turn behind the bush, and then they moved to the blanket he had laid out for them. The sun warmed them, drying their hair and taking the remaining chill from their skin. Imogen dug with zeal into the willow basket Caleb had been so kind as to bring, surprised to see that he had been right about needing the nourishment after swimming. She was absolutely famished.

She was just finishing up a second leg of cold chicken when Caleb, his food long gone, leaned back on his elbow. He stuck a long blade of grass between his teeth and chewed it thoughtfully.

"You are a brave woman, Imogen," he said softly.

She nearly choked on her food. "Come now," she scoffed, wiping her mouth with a napkin. "That isn't the least bit true."

"No, I'm serious." He sat up, his expression intent. "You are inspiring. You know what your future holds, and though it's not to your liking, you aren't cowed by it. I mean, look at you. You're out here, having adventures. We most of us are slaves to our fate. But here you are, looking for joy and passion." He shook his head in admiration. "It is something to be proud of, Imogen."

She stared at him wordlessly a moment. And then she smiled, reaching out and grabbing at his hand. "It's because of you, you know."

"No," he replied, his eyes warm on her face as he returned the pressure of her hand, "it's because of *you*. You are braver than you realize. This here, this moment, is proof positive of that. Don't ever lose that."

He rose then, and helped her up. As she twisted her hair up, jabbing pins into it in an attempt to tame it, Caleb packed the basket. Before long they had their things ready and were heading back to the house in a companionable silence.

Caleb managed to sneak her back to her room with ease. As she was about to slip through the door, however, she paused. He looked at her quizzically.

"So what is next?" she asked, her voice eager even to her own ears.

"You will just have to wait and see," he replied mysteriously before retreating down the hall.

Imogen closed the door softly and leaned her head against the smooth wood. A wide smile stole over her face as his jaunty whistle, slowly growing fainter, reached her ears.

But as the glow of the morning began to fade, so did her smile. Perhaps she should put a stop to it. But at the mere thought of letting him go, her heart twisted painfully in her chest. Nearly gasping, she gripped the fabric over her breast tightly.

She thought suddenly of her sister Frances, of the daily heartache she suffered from loving a man who could not love her in return. Not that their situations were at all the same. She would never marry Caleb, after all. But she could now sympathize more with her sister, could now understand a bit of the quiet sadness that filled her face every time she looked on her spouse.

She could not stand the thought of having to live with such a grief. But she knew that, to some degree, she would. Just how much it would hurt when they parted for good, after her heart was even more embroiled than it was now, only time could tell.

• • •

The following afternoon Lady Tarryton deemed her daughter well enough to join the rest of the party. Imogen accompanied her, along with Mariah, to the library before luncheon in an attempt to locate Lord Tarryton. He was there, buried amidst a towering mound of books he had pulled from the shelves.

As her mother was engrossed in talking with him and Mariah was quickly cornered by several of her admirers, Imogen was left to her own devices. She wandered down the shelves, perusing the titles there. Her fingers trailed lightly over the leather bindings, noting with satisfaction the wonderful variety the Knowleses had accumulated over generations. She could get lost in a room such as this, she thought with a happy sigh.

Just then a person stepped in her path. She looked up to see Caleb standing before her. His eyes twinkled merrily, though his mouth was unsmiling. He held out a book to her.

"Miss Duncan," he said in a carrying voice, "perhaps you would enjoy this book. I highly recommend it." As she reached out and took hold of it, he leaned in and muttered darkly through stiff lips, "Turn to page one hundred and thirty-two."

Imogen's lips quirked. "Did you know you would make an appalling spy?" she whispered back.

He flashed her a mischievous smile before turning about and striding toward the door. After looking about furtively, Imogen flipped to the appropriate spot. A note lay there, written in a bold, messy scrawl.

Meet me at the entrance to the North Tower at midnight, it read. Below the words a small, detailed map had been copied out carefully, showing her the way.

How very gothic! She glanced toward the door. To her surprise, Caleb was still there. He waggled his eyebrows at her when he caught her eye. Imogen clapped a hand over her mouth to prevent a laugh escaping, but she only managed to make herself snort inelegantly. Several people glanced at her in some alarm, and she turned her faux pas into a coughing fit. Over the noise she could hear Caleb's laughter as he moved down the hall.

"Imogen," her mother hissed as she approached, "you came down too early. You should still be abed. Now you shall get on my nerves with that cough." Lady Tarryton glared at her and shook her head. "You had best retire early. I'll have a tray sent up." When Imogen did little more than stare open-mouthed at her, she sighed in exasperation. "Go on," she said, making shooing motions at her. "Off you go."

Imogen escaped with all due haste, the treat of an entire afternoon and evening with nothing more to do than read in blessed peace spread before her, followed by a mysterious assignation with a handsome man. A thrill of anticipation coursed through her, and she hugged the book to her chest. As she closed herself off in her room, however, a realization settled like a weight on her. She was looking forward to her time with him too much. She did not know if it was possible to love someone by degrees, but she knew that if this kept up she would be even more deeply in love with him, even more in danger of emotional agony.

But despite this knowledge, she could not quiet the rapid beating of her heart at the idea of meeting him late that night. No, she thought in dismay, there was no hope for her. She was truly lost, indeed.

Chapter 12

Hours later, Imogen followed Caleb up the winding stairs of the North Tower. He was carrying a lamp, and each time he turned to glance back at her it cast a ruddy glow over his face, making her heart twist in longing. He still hadn't told her what they were doing, but she didn't care. She was with him; that was all she needed.

He had managed to keep up a grave manner, but his eyes held all the mischief of a little boy. Occasionally they passed a narrow window and the pale moon shone on her face in a fleeting, thin shaft. The lantern threw dancing light upon the unfinished brick interior, and she got the distinct impression that this part of the house was rarely used, though it was as well-maintained as the rest of the manor. Finally they reached the top and Caleb opened a door, motioning her through. Imogen stepped out into cool night air, and as she pulled her shawl more tightly around her, she looked up at an inky black sky full to bursting with stars. She realized with a jolt that they were on the rooftop of Pulteney Manor, its many chimneys rising up like benign sentinels around them.

She gave him a questioning look.

He motioned to the sky in a broad wave of his arm. "Stargazing," he answered simply.

And then he stepped onto a blanket she had overlooked and that he had obviously placed there earlier. He sat, staring up at her with a small smile on his lips, his hand extended to her in invitation. If Imogen hadn't already realized she was in love with him, this would have done her in. In the lamp glow, he had to be the most achingly beautiful thing she had ever seen in her life.

"Stargazing?" she repeated stupidly, her voice oddly breathless. She moved forward, taking his hand and sinking down onto the blanket. A hot desire snaked through her at the contact, but she shook herself, trying to jolt some sense back into her brain.

She had done much thinking since they had returned from swimming the day before and had come to the conclusion that having him guess that her affection for him went beyond friendship would be an end to it. The last thing she wanted was for him to look on her in pity. Miss Imogen Duncan, aging spinster, in love with Caleb Masters, Marquess of Willbridge? There wasn't anything more pathetic than that.

He suddenly blew out the lamp, bringing her back to the present. "Have you ever just gone out at night to stargaze?" he asked as she settled her skirts about her.

She paused, thinking back. Now that she considered it, she couldn't remember a time she ever had.

He noticed her uncertainty and smirked. "I thought not. Now," he said, stretching out on his back, "just do as I do."

She looked at him in fond exasperation before complying. "Is there an art to stargazing?"

"There is an art to everything." he replied, utterly serious.

"Very well then. Lead on, tutor."

"You can be a sarcastic little baggage at times. Did you know that?"

"Of course," she replied in lofty tones. "But only with those I am closest to."

"Well," he murmured, his eyes smiling at her, "count me honored, then."

And then, because she couldn't stand the ache that was forming in her chest as she looked on his moonlit face, she swung her gaze to the darkness above her. Tiny pinpricks of light dusted the sky and she took a deep breath, forcing her muscles to relax as she took it in.

"Do you even know what we're seeing here?"

"Certainly. Well," he hedged, and she could hear the smile in his voice, "some. My tutor did attempt to teach me astronomy. I didn't have much of a grasp on it, I'm afraid. But," and here his arm swung up, his long fingers pointing to a spot to the right, "I do remember that the cluster of stars just there, those three in a line, is Orion's Belt. You can see the stars surrounding it are in the shape of a hunter with his bow. That would be the Orion constellation."

She gazed up, so very happy for her spectacles. Now that he had pointed the formation out, her mind was connecting the points, making the image he had described stand out amid what had seemed a veritable jumble of pinpricks. "Yes, I see it," she murmured.

"Now," he said, moving his arm to the left and up a bit, "do you see those two bright stars there?"

She followed his finger. "Yes."

"That would be the stars Castor and Pollux. They form part of the constellation Gemini."

She nodded. "The twin brothers from mythology, each born from the same woman but of different fathers. One mortal and one divine."

She sensed him glancing at her but kept her eyes firmly on the night sky.

"You know your mythology well, it seems."

She shrugged. "It was a passion of my father's for a time. I admit I found it fascinating as well. He would read me the stories when I was small." She sighed happily. "It is wonderful to imagine people hundreds, even thousands of years ago, gazing up at these same skies, at these same stars. What histories these heavens have seen."

"Yes," he murmured. "Wars and pain, romances and joys, all under these very stars."

And as she lay there, flat on her back and looking out into the great emptiness above her, she felt it. Clear to her toes she felt it, the smallness of herself, the vastness of the heavens above.

She let out a soft, awed sigh.

"It is amazing, isn't it?" he asked quietly.

"Yes," she breathed. "It makes you feel as if all your problems are tiny in the grand scheme of things."

"That it does," he agreed. And then somehow her hand was in his and everything else faded, and she felt the utter perfection of the moment go straight to her heart.

• • •

He did not know how it came about, how her hand wound up in his while they lay on that blanket, stargazing like two children. But he did know one thing—that it felt right.

He paused but a moment before lacing his fingers with hers. He felt her give his hand a small squeeze, and a contentment he had never known rolled through him. Her hand was so small in his own, the bones so delicate. And yet it radiated strength.

They lay there like that for some time. Suddenly, in the quiet of the night, he heard her give a sigh. It was a small sound, but the forlorn tone of it caught at him. He looked over at her and saw the moon reflect off her spectacles as she turned to meet his gaze.

"That sounded as if the weight of the world were in it," he said softly.

Her mouth twisted at the corner, but not in humor. "Tomorrow is the masquerade."

"Yes?"

"And then we will return to London. And this will all be over."

The very thought sent a chill through him. "We can still continue on in London."

The smile she gave him was full of sadness. "No, we cannot. Things will be different there, much more formal. And anyway," she continued, returning her eyes back to the sky, "it is time I began living my life. I cannot keep it at bay forever." Her expression relaxed then into one of true contentment. "But I have wonderful memories to bring with me. I will never, ever forget this. This moment, right here, I will carry with me always."

He got up onto one elbow and looked down into her face. Her

eyes were soft and luminous in the moonlight, a small smile playing about her mouth as she gazed back at him. And then, because he could not have stopped himself if he had tried, he leaned down and kissed her, softly.

Her eyes fluttered closed and she sighed against his lips, returning the pressure of his mouth. And though he felt desire trail along his skin, making him hot in every part of him, he felt something else as well. Something he did not want to look at too closely but that was there nonetheless, making his heart race like mad.

He pulled back and smiled. "Then we'd best make our last night one to remember."

• • •

"You are mad."

It was the day of the masquerade ball, and the entire Knowles house was in an uproar, with more guests coming in from London for the occasion than the manor should rightly hold. Not long ago, Imogen had received a message from Caleb instructing her to meet him in the storage room at the top of the house. She stood there now, surrounded by hulking pieces of furniture covered in sheets, paintings of Knowles ancestors propped against the walls, and wooden chests no doubt filled with all manner of treasure. At any other time she would have grabbed Mariah and dragged her up here, and they would have spent a wonderful afternoon exploring. But instead she was staring in disbelief at the bundle Caleb held in his arms, all sapphire blue silk and silver lace.

"Madness is a matter for interpretation," he said haughtily. "I promised you a night to remember, and never say I go back on my promises. This," he said, holding the diaphanous bundle out to her, "is the key to it all."

"But I already have a costume."

He lifted one eyebrow at her.

"I do," she insisted.

"Tell me," he drawled, "who picked it out?"

Imogen flushed. "My mother," she muttered reluctantly.

"And what exalted figure does she have you dressing as?" he prompted.

She grumbled something unintelligible.

"Sorry, what was that?"

"A sheep," she admitted with a grimace.

He stared at her a long moment, slack-jawed. "A sheep."

She heaved a deep sigh. "Yes. Mariah is a bucolic shepherdess, and I am...her...sheep."

They stared at one another for a long moment. And then they both burst into laughter.

"Well," he stated as their chuckles died away, "you will no longer be a sheep. In fact, Miss Imogen Duncan is no longer going to the masquerade."

She frowned in confusion at him. "But you just said—"

He held up one hand. "You are quite the smartest woman I know, so please strive to keep up. Miss Imogen Duncan is not attending. She will be in bed, fighting off a lingering cough. There will, however, be a mysterious woman there in a beautiful blue gown."

Her eyes widened as the magnitude of what he was saying sank in. "Oh no!" she exclaimed.

"Oh, yes." He pressed the gown into her hands. "I've taken care of everything. Here are the shoes, and the mask." He plunked both atop the teetering pile she was holding. "I have a lady's maid ready and waiting to do some minor adjustments. She shall be there as well later this evening to help you into the gown and do up your hair. All you need do is fake a cough and plead off going." He stepped back, giving her a smile that was very much cat-that-licked-the-cream.

Her mouth worked for a while silently, until she finally made out faintly, "You are mad."

"I believe we have already established that. Now, off you go. She will be waiting for you."

With that he shooed her away. She went obediently, her mind

in a confused haze. Before she knew it she was in front of her room. How she had gotten there, she never could quite figure out. And then the door was thrown open from inside by the borrowed maid and there was no more time to think.

She was poked and prodded, the strange gown pinned and tucked. It was whisked off of her, and the maid was telling her she'd have it done in a trice. And once again she was alone, and faced with the significance of what she'd agreed to.

Well, "agreed to" wasn't necessarily the correct terminology. She hadn't agreed to anything. But the maid was off now doing the necessary alterations. She couldn't very well have all that work go to waste.

And truly, did she really want to say no to Caleb, to put on her sheep costume and tamely go down like—well, like a sheep?

Or did she want to live for one more glorious night, to have that adventure she had craved so badly?

She removed her spectacles, then took up the mask and held it up to her face, turning to the looking glass as she did so. It was a fanciful silver concoction, with deep blue paste gems rimming the eyes. Several sleek white feathers curled over one brow and down the side of her face. Right away she felt transformed, no longer the placid Miss Duncan but another creature entirely. How would it feel, she thought, to wear the entire outfit? Would she look like herself anymore? Would she *feel* like herself anymore?

She felt a shiver of anticipation. To be transformed, even for one night, would be a heady thing, indeed.

Chapter 13

The moment Caleb saw the stunning creature in blue enter the room, he knew it was Imogen. The way she held herself and walked was the same. But that was where the similarities ended.

The woman who stood uncertainly in the doorway, her hands clasped together tightly, looked nothing like her. Somewhere the maid must have found the stays and hoops necessary for the construction of the eighty-year-old dress. The elaborately embroidered stomacher, with its silver thread and seed pearls, accentuated a narrow waist and high, full breasts. Her shoulders were creamy where they rose up over the wide, square neckline. Her light brown hair was a riotous mound of curls, piled high on her head, accentuating the length of her neck. Several long strands trailed in a teasing manner to brush her neck, her shoulders, the tops of her breasts. Caleb swallowed hard at the sight.

Her mask was firmly in place, but her color seemed high. Was that rouge she was wearing? The thought unsettled him. Imogen was simple, wholesome, utterly without artifice. This creature was not her.

But that was what he had tried to do for her, he reminded himself. He had wanted to give her the gift of being completely free of her future for one magical evening.

Looking on her now, however, at the stranger she had become, he felt he had erred, and horribly. She did not look like herself, the Imogen he had come to care for. Needing to see her, speak to her, know that she was still in there, he strode across the ballroom toward her.

It was crowded, quite a feat considering they were miles from London. It seemed no one had turned down the invitation. As he moved through the throng, he lost sight of her. But finally he caught a hint of sapphire blue shimmering through the crowd. And then the sea of people opened up, and there she was.

But what he saw made him stop dead in his tracks. She was smiling shyly at a young gentleman, who held his arm out gallantly to her. She took it, and he led her out as the music started up.

Caleb could only stare after her as she joined in the sets on the dance floor.

And that was the pattern for the next two hours. He would watch her dance, smiling and happy, her partner staring down at her with avid interest. Once she was led from the floor, Caleb would attempt to reach her side. But before he could, someone was already leading her out for another set. And each successive time found a frown pulling down on his face, his mood darkening until he was a seething ball of frustration.

By the time Tristan and Morley located him, he was ready to punch a wall.

"Ho there, Willbridge. You've been deuced hard to catch up to. You've been running back and forth across the ballroom like your shoes have caught fire." Tristan peered at him from behind his black and green mask. "You all right there, man?"

"I'm fine," Caleb snapped. He didn't miss the look that passed between his two friends. What the devil was wrong with him? He attempted to rein in his mood.

"Abominable crush," Morley commented, obviously trying to turn the conversation. "Can hardly move about the place. I did see Miss Mariah Duncan and her glorious shepherdess costume, however. Even managed to get a dance in." He paused. Then he asked casually, "Didn't see her sister, though. What is Miss Duncan disguised as, Willbridge?"

Immediately all thoughts of cooling his temper fled. "I believe she is ill and could not make it down," he growled.

"Dashed bad luck, to miss the ball."

Caleb grunted, his eyes back on the floor and Imogen as she twirled by in the arms of Ignatius Knowles. Obviously the man wasn't planning on settling down with Mariah any time soon if he was looking at Imogen like that. Caleb had never had a mean thought about his cousin before, but he did now. Several of them. Some involving a satisfying amount of violence.

Tristan seemed to have followed his gaze. "Don't know who that stunning one in the blue is. I've been trying to find out all night. Do either of you know?"

"Haven't a clue," Morley responded. "Quite a figure, though. That dress accents her assets perfectly. It looks like something my great-grandmother would have worn, but if she had looked like *that* in her portrait at home you can be assured I would have had some very interesting dreams about her in my youth." He chuckled.

Caleb saw red. Quite literally his vision went crimson. Luckily for his friends, however, it was at that moment that the dance ended and Imogen was brought to the side of the room not ten feet away from him. Without even a farewell glance at the two other men, Caleb stalked off toward her. She would not escape him this time.

• • •

Imogen's feet hurt from dancing in the heeled slippers, her cheeks hurt from smiling constantly, her head hurt from being without her spectacles again, and her back hurt from the uncomfortable corset. All in all, she thought, the evening was not turning out as she had hoped. It was all well and good to want to be the belle of the ball. But if this was what her sister had to endure night after night, she was glad for her own unpopular social status.

And she had not seen Caleb once. Granted, she thought she had glimpsed him from afar, or rather the blurry outline of some-one very tall with his color hair. But he had always been across the room, and she could never be certain.

And then there had been her family. She had spent an inordi-nate amount of time avoiding them, certain they would know who she was and out her for the incredible fake she was. But when she had inadvertently entered into the same set as her sister, she had not received more than a small, friendly smile.

Now she stood at the side of the room, her previous dance partner having just left her. She reveled in not having to laugh and smile for a moment. She eyed the entrance to the ballroom. It was not so very far away. Perhaps she could slip out before anyone else approached her…

"May I have this dance?"

The familiar deep voice sounded in her ear. A shiver ran down her spine. She turned to face Caleb, her face breaking out into what had to be the first real smile she had given all night.

His hand was outstretched, his pale eyes glittering behind the simple black mask. Without hesitation, Imogen reached out and took it, allowing him to lead her to the floor. At the touch of his fingers, all of her uncomfortable aches and twinges fled. This was what she had been waiting for all evening.

It was a waltz. No other dance could have made this moment more perfect. And she was determined to enjoy every bit of it. She closed her eyes and felt his hand press against the small of her back, his other gripping her own. She could even feel the heat of his body, though they were the appropriate distance apart. And then he began to move, and it was as if she were flying. Nothing else had ever felt so lovely as being twirled about in the arms of the man she loved. She was determined to forget about tomorrow. For now she would embrace every second.

"You seem to be enjoying yourself tonight."

She opened her eyes and looked up at him, smiling wide. "Now I am."

"You weren't before?"

She shook her head.

"You certainly gave the impression that you were."

The words gave her pause. A strange foreboding began to break through her joy. "No," she said slowly. "It was pleasant at first, I suppose, to be the recipient of so much attention. But it was getting tiring."

"You must be a better actress than I gave you credit for. It certainly looked as if you were enjoying yourself. Quite a bit, actually."

She stumbled before righting herself. "I'm sorry?"

"I don't believe I stuttered."

She stared up at him in disbelief. "Caleb, what is wrong with you?"

Something mean flashed in his eyes. "What is wrong with me? I could ask you the same thing. You have had every man here panting after you."

Anger lanced through her. "I've had enough of your abuse. I'd rather not cause a scene, but if you do not deposit me at the side of the room this instant I will leave you here on the floor, I swear I will."

He considered her, seemingly calculating whether she was bluffing. Finally, giving a small nod, he began dancing her away from the center of the floor. But instead of stopping at the side, he sailed right out the open doors leading to the garden.

Once out in the cool night air, he abruptly released her from his embrace. He then took hold of her hand and, dragging her along behind him, moved away from the lights of the ball and into the darkness of the garden.

"Wait," Imogen cried, "where are you taking me?"

He glanced back at her. "We need to discuss this, and we cannot do it in a ballroom full of people."

Imogen tugged ineffectively on his hand as she stumbled along behind him. "There is nothing to discuss. You are acting like a child, and I do not want to deal with your strange mood."

But he ignored her and continued on. She finally gave up trying to free herself and accepted the fact that they would have this out whether she liked it or not. Although what "it" was, she truly hadn't a clue.

Everything was a dark blur to her. In the distance she could see candles glowing brightly behind the mullioned windows of the house, obscure rectangles of golden light, but everything else was unidentifiable. They finally came close to the building and she was able to get an idea of where they were. From the moonlight sparkling off the many windows, she guessed they had come to the orangery. Caleb opened the door.

But the rustle of cloth, as well as the soft moans that reached their ears, told Imogen that the orangery certainly wouldn't do.

Heat suffused her face. Caleb swore softly and closed the door. Tugging again at her arm, he continued on. He ducked through a side entrance into the manor house, to a hall that was blessedly devoid of people, and began working his way down the vast expanse, trying doors as he went. Each room was either occupied or locked.

"Can no one control themselves at this blasted gathering?" Caleb muttered to himself as he tried yet another door and found that some other, more amorous couple had gotten there before them.

"I am quite through being treated like a pull toy," Imogen stated as he towed her along yet again.

Suddenly he stopped. Imogen ran into the solid wall of his back and glared up at him.

"Damnation, there's only one place I can think of that will guarantee us privacy." And with that they were off again.

Imogen had had just about enough. The elaborate little heels were blistering her toes and she had lost her breath long ago from the tight stays. The ridiculously large hoops swung about her, making the dress catch on everything within reach. And she had more pins jabbed into her scalp than had a right to be there. She was exhausted, and she wanted nothing more than a quiet room to scrub the rouge from her face and soak in a tub of hot water.

And now here was Caleb, acting as if she had offended him in some way. His grip remained firm as he pulled her through a hidden passage to the servants' hall. Skirting the busy throng of footmen and maids, he dragged her up several flights of stairs until they were on the guest floor. Soon he was pushing her through a door, closing it firmly behind him.

She moved further into the room once he finally released her. Rubbing her hand, she glared at him.

"Where are we?" she asked, glancing around, trying to make out any identifiable shapes. Moonlight filtered through a sheer curtain, but did not give her imperfect vision enough light to see details beyond a few hulking pieces of furniture. One of which was—a bed?

"My room," he replied. He stayed in the shadows by the door.

She turned on him, her mouth falling open. "Your room? I should not be here."

She could just make out him shrugging. "No one will know you're here. You're in bed ill, remember?" His voice held an edge to it.

"What is the matter with you?" she demanded. "Why are you angry with me?"

He paused, and she wished desperately she could see his face.

"I am not angry with you, Imogen," he replied in a low, intense voice.

"Then what is it? Why are you acting like this?"

He took a step toward her. "This isn't you."

She gave an exasperated sigh. "No, it isn't. But wasn't that the whole point? This was your idea, that I should have one night as someone else."

He took another step. "I made a mistake. I never should have had you dress like this."

"Why?" Her eyes strained, but his face evaded the light, remaining in shadows even as he came closer. "It was only for one night. Why are you reacting so strongly?"

He didn't answer. Instead he stepped into the moonlight, so close she had to crane her neck to look at him. He had removed his mask, and the expression on his face took the very breath from her lungs. There was a heat there, an intensity she had never seen before.

He reached out and pulled the ribbon securing her mask, removing it and throwing it aside. She could only stare at him mutely, her every nerve ending tingling with awareness. Gripping her arms, his hands were hot on her flesh. He dragged her against him, and even through the stomacher and stays and hoops she could feel the hard, muscled length of him pressed to her.

"You don't need this, Imogen. You don't need *any* of it."

With that he lowered his mouth to hers.

Chapter 14

This kiss wasn't like the first time, when he thought she was someone else. Nor was it like last night, when he had kissed her with a gentleness that had bordered on familial. No, this kiss was hard, and hot, and full of some desperate emotion she could not begin to name but that she wanted more of. So much more of.

His hands dove into her hair, pulling pins from it. Imogen could vaguely hear them hit the floor over the rushing in her ears. Her hair tumbled free, the great heavy mass falling like a wave down her back. He ran his hands through it even as his lips tore free from hers and moved to the column of her throat. She gave a shuddering breath, her eyes closing as she was bombarded with sensation. She arched her neck, her entire body thrumming and alive.

"Your hair is glorious," he said against her skin. "*You* are glorious. Every bit of you. I don't know why I fought it for so long."

Fought what? she wanted to ask. But then his lips moved down, over her collarbone, to the mounds of her breasts pushed up over the neckline of her gown, and her brain simply stopped working. She gasped, straining toward him as his lips and tongue played over her flesh.

He growled when he reached the fabric of the dress. Immediately his fingers were at the stomacher, fumbling at the material as he searched for access to her.

"How the hell did our ancestors manage to get these blasted things undone?" he muttered against her skin.

Imogen gave a breathless laugh. Without a second thought she began working at the clothing. Between the two of them they managed to get the gown, corset, and hoops undone. And then she was standing before him in just a thin shift, her hair free down her back.

She couldn't feel ashamed or shy. No, this was Caleb, and she loved him.

His eyes were hungry as they raked her body. He gave a tortured groan and stepped closer. She reached for him, beyond caring that this went against every one of Society's rules, that after tonight she would be ruined beyond saving. Never before had something felt so right and pure and...*good*.

Her hands gripped the soft thickness of his hair as his lips claimed her own. She sighed into his mouth at the intimacy of the embrace. Now she could feel him, the thin material of her chemise doing nothing to hide the hardness of his aroused body against her own. He reached down, grasping her bottom, and she could feel the insistent length of him pressing against her belly.

But it still wasn't enough, she realized hazily as his mouth devoured her own. There was a tension, an ache building inside her, and she knew she had to feel more of him, to see more of him.

Her hands took on a life of their own, working at his cravat, loosening the material and tossing it aside, moving to the buttons of his coat, his waistcoat, his shirt. His hands left her body long enough to shrug from his clothing, his mouth lifting from her own only as he pulled his shirt over his head. And then he hauled her back against him, and her hands were on his skin, that same smooth skin she had so longed to touch at the pond just days ago. Now she took her time, delighting in the way it bunched and flexed under her questing fingers. He felt hot, and tense, and absolutely wonderful.

He moved her further into the room, and soon something pressed against the backs of her legs. Her world momentarily tilted as he lowered her to the bed, the softness of it embracing her like a lover. He left her lying amid the blankets and pillows. She felt bereft without him, chilled.

But a moment later he was back at her feet, and to her shock she could see every lovely bare inch of him exposed to her view. He was beautiful, all lean muscle. A trail of pale hair dusted his chest, down across his stomach, and to that part of him that was swollen and straining toward her. She swallowed hard, focusing on his face instead, suddenly nervous. But the ache in her had not gone away at the sight of him aroused and ready for her. It had only grown. She needed his arms about her, his lips on hers again, more than she needed anything.

She reached out for him. Instead of coming to her, however, he leaned down. She gasped as he reached up under her shift, his warm fingers on her legs, slowly rolling her fine silk stockings down over calf, heel, toes. And then, to her shock, he took the hem of her shift in his teeth. He began to pull it up, inch by inch. Her breathing grew ragged and she bit her lip to keep from moaning as he worked his way up slowly, baring every bit of her.

In one swift move his hands joined his teeth and the shift was gone, up and over her head. Caleb held himself above her for a time, looking down at her naked body, pale in the moonlight. Imogen gripped the blankets in her hands, stunned at the raw need she saw on his face. And then he growled low in his throat and covered her body with his own.

Imogen shuddered at the feel of his skin on hers. Nothing was between them now, not even a breath of air. Never did she think such a sensation existed. Surely nothing could feel better than this.

He proved her wrong in the next moment.

"Imogen," he groaned. "Do you have any idea what you do to me?" His lips worked their way down her throat, across her chest and to her straining breasts. Imogen's breath caught in her throat, her back arching toward his questing mouth. He claimed her nipple, his mouth hot and moist. She cried out, nearly coming off the bed in her shock.

His hands went to her hips, holding her still beneath his onslaught. And then the fingers of one hand loosened their grip and trailed across her stomach. When he reached between their bodies and touched her, that intimate center of her that she hardly even touched herself, she instinctively clamped her legs together.

"Open for me, Imogen," he rasped. He pushed at her legs, and she let them fall open to him. His fingers caressed her, swirling over her swollen flesh, making her gasp and writhe beneath him. Her hands gripped his shoulders for support.

When his finger entered her, her body coiled unbearably. She was so close to something, desperately wanting it.

"Caleb," she gasped, a plea.

"You're so ready for me." He raised his head then and looked down at her. His eyes were almost wild from desire. But he paused.

"Imogen," he said, his voice low and taut as the string of a bow, "if you want me to stop, you have to tell me now. There is no turning back after this."

She gazed up at him, at the torture he was putting himself through to make certain she understood. He would stop this very moment if she asked him to. She knew it with every bit of her. She would still be a virgin, would still have her honor.

But she didn't want him to stop. If he stopped now, she felt she would break into a million pieces and would never be able to put herself together again. She could no more leave him than stop breathing.

"Don't stop, Caleb," she whispered. "Please."

He groaned, his body coming down hard and heavy on hers, his mouth claiming her own. His hand left her, and a moment later he was moving between her legs, his lean hips fitting between her thighs. His hands gripped her hips.

Imogen clung to him, her fingers digging into his sweat-slicked back as he poised himself at her entrance. He began to push forward slowly, and she felt an unbearable tightness as he filled her.

He suddenly stopped, seeming to gather himself. And then he surged forward in one smooth thrust.

The breath left her, more from shock than pain. But in the space of a heartbeat it dissolved away, and all that was left behind was sensation. He began to move within her, and the strange tension she felt before came back tenfold.

She threw her head back, gasping. Her feet dug into the mattress, her hips moving with his. She was aware of his breath, ragged in her ear.

"That's right, love," he rasped. "Let it come."

His movements quickened. The tension became a nearly unbearable ache.

"Caleb, please!" she cried, not understanding what she was asking for.

"Imogen," he groaned.

And then she shattered. Caleb's mouth covered hers as she cried out. Golden stars burst behind her closed lids, her every muscle taut, her breath strangling in her throat. As she began to float back to earth she felt him tense, give one final thrust. She captured his own shout of completion as he had done for her, her limbs cradling him as he collapsed atop her.

And then there was only a wonderful lethargy, and peace, and happiness as her eyes shut and she drifted off in his arms.

Chapter 15

Imogen awoke slowly, aware of a wonderful contentment filling her. Caleb lay next to her, his strong arm cradling her to his side. Her head rested on his chest, and his heartbeat sounded steadily in her ear. The faint sound of music drifted to her. There was a soft white sheet pulled up over them, and she realized Caleb must have tucked them both in. It was a heavenly thought that made her smile. She sighed softly, happily, her arm stealing about his waist and holding him tightly.

"I'll go to London tomorrow for a special license," he murmured, his voice rumbling in her ear.

Her eyes flew open. A feeling of dread began to uncurl in her belly. "Special license?"

His cheek was resting against the crown of her head, and she could feel him nod. "We can be married by tomorrow evening if you wish."

This could not be happening. She could not marry Caleb. There was a sudden flash in her mind, of her sister Frances's pale, drawn face, her eyes filled with more misery than they should rightly be able to hold. That was what happened to a person when they married someone they loved and who did not love them in return.

"No," she said out loud. It was all she could manage.

She felt him shrug. "If you would like to postpone it a day or two, that's fine. But I warn you, I won't take kindly to waiting much longer than that." He chuckled low, his hand doing wonderful things to her back. She shuddered, and then with great force of will she wrenched out of his arms.

She rose to a sitting position, pulling the sheet up over her nakedness. He regarded her from the pillows with a small smile on his face, his eyes soft in the dim light. He put one arm behind his head, and the position brought his muscles into beautiful relief. Her heart ached at the sight. In that moment she almost lost her resolve. Almost.

"I won't marry you, Caleb."

"What are you talking about?" He reached for her, but she scooted off the bed, bringing the sheet with her. Which was a mistake, for now he had nothing covering his glorious nakedness. She swallowed hard, willing her eyes not to stray from his face.

"I won't marry you," she repeated, hoping he missed the quaver in her voice.

He rose, and every beautiful inch of him began a slow and steady advance on her. "But you will," he said, his voice full of a certainty, a maleness that suited him deliciously.

She held a trembling hand out, and he stopped.

"I will not marry you," she said once again, inserting as much steel into her voice as she could, praying he would leave it alone.

But of course he did not. "We have no choice," he said patiently. "Imogen, we just lay together, as a man and wife would."

"It makes no difference. I shall never marry, so there is no man I need to remain pure for. No one will know, and we can go on with our lives."

"But I will know," he said quietly, intensely. "And you will know. Our bodies know each other now. You can never change that."

She shivered from the emotions his words brought her. She clenched her hands until the knuckles showed white. "We can't, Caleb." *It will destroy me*, she wanted to say. But to her relief, her throat closed up before the words slipped free.

"We have to," he insisted. "Imogen, I am a gentleman. And a gentleman does not make love to an innocent lady without marrying her. My honor will not allow me to do otherwise. Besides," he added quietly, "there might be a child."

She blanched. "We'll deal with that if it happens. There is no use rushing into anything until we're certain. Otherwise, I release you from what you perceive as your responsibility toward me. You need feel no duty toward me, nor feel your honor is being impugned. I refuse to marry you. And so, you see, there is no cause for all of this talk of honor and duty." Her voice had become frenzied, and she fought to calm herself.

He regarded her in silence, his eyes showing his confusion. Suddenly his expression changed, became intent, focused. He took a slow, measured step toward her, for all the world as if he were stalking her. Imogen felt frozen as he advanced.

Coming close to her, he reached up, gently dragging his knuckles down her cheek. His thumb rubbed her lower lip. She gave a shuddering sigh, the fire inside her leaping to life once again.

"Marry me, Imogen," he whispered, his eyes hooded and hot. He leaned toward her, his gaze fastened on her mouth. And, God help her, she wanted to say yes, to melt back into his arms and take everything he offered.

With a cry she pulled away from him. Turning about, she fled from the room, the sheet flying behind her like a specter.

• • •

It was only much later that Imogen was able to think back with horror at what she had done. Not lying with Caleb. No, that she would never regret. But fleeing from him wearing nothing more than a sheet, running down a hallway in a house that was full of people—that made her cringe at the very recollection.

Somehow she made it back to her room unseen. And after she dressed herself in a nightgown with shaking hands and ducked down into her bed, she experienced what turned out to be the longest night of her life.

For a long while she expected Caleb to come after her, to

pound on her door and demand answers. But he didn't, and Imogen wasn't sure what she felt more, relief or despair. She told herself that she should feel only relief. She had turned down his marriage proposal and certainly did not want him renewing it. Even so, there was an ache in her chest that she could not banish.

She *had* wanted to accept. She could imagine nothing so wonderful as marrying Caleb, living her life with him and giving him children and growing old with him. More than anything she had wanted to say yes. Her very bones ached with the need.

But...

That was the one word that had stopped her, the one word that brought to mind every reason why she couldn't accept him.

But he didn't truly want to marry her.

But he'd only asked her because of what they had done.

But he didn't love her.

No, he had never mentioned feelings at all when he had proposed. But she knew he didn't love her. And she could not stand a life beside him knowing he had shackled himself to her, and that his feelings would never be the same as hers. For in the end it would destroy her. As it had destroyed Frances.

And Imogen knew, deep down, that if she were to marry Caleb, she would find herself just the same as Frances, a pale copy of herself, her heart breaking daily until it was in fragile pieces, never to be made whole again.

Some time in the night there was a quiet knock at her door. Imogen gasped and clutched at the sheets, a horrible hope blooming in her breast.

"Imogen," came the soft call from the hallway. And Imogen felt a fissure appear in her heart when she realized it was not Caleb, but Mariah. She kept still, listening, until the heels of her sister's shoes could be heard heading away from the door and all was quiet once more. It was then that Imogen's tears finally came. They poured like a torrent down the sides of her face into the pillow and ran unchecked till dawn broke and she finally fell into a fitful sleep.

She was woken by a pounding at her door some hours later.

She opened her swollen eyes to peer blearily out the window. The sun was well up in the sky now. It must be nearing noon.

"Imogen." Her mother's strident voice came through the door. "Are you up? Imogen, open this door at once."

With a groan Imogen threw off the covers, fumbling for her spectacles and night robe and making her way to the door. She winced as her body ached in unaccustomed places, bringing to mind the previous night in full force. She shook her head to dispel the memories and opened the door just as her mother was about to knock again.

"Oh!" Lady Tarryton exclaimed. "My heavens, you look worse than you did yesterday." She shook her head. "No matter. I'll send a maid to you shortly to help you dress and finish packing. Try to clean yourself up a bit. We leave within the hour." With that she turned and marched away.

Imogen closed the door quietly and leaned her head against it. Back to her life, she thought in weary resignation.

• • •

"Imogen."

Caleb stood behind her in the front hall. All about them people were preparing to leave, their bags and trunks being packed into their carriages for the return to London. He ignored all the commotion. Instead he watched her solemnly as her shoulders stiffened and she slowly faced him.

He immediately noticed the changes to her since the night before. Her eyes were red-rimmed and puffy, her mouth turned down at the corners. But most of all he could see the lack of emotion in her eyes. It was as if her soul had fled the shell of her body.

He took her elbow and pulled her off to the side. "Have you changed your mind?" he asked in a low voice.

She gazed at him a long moment. And then she shook her head no.

His lips tightened. "I wish you would, Imogen." When she

made no response, he sighed. "Now is not the time, I suppose. I will visit you when we return to London so we can continue this discussion more privately."

"I think it would be best if you did not." Her voice was thin and brittle.

"I will see you in London," he repeated firmly before turning and striding away. The look in her eyes, the fragility, made him want to howl. He felt that if he were to stay and watch her climb up into her family's carriage, if he witnessed her mother verbally beating her down again, he would break and hit something.

He stomped unseeing though the throng that filled the entrance hall. Several people greeted him as he went by, but he paid them no heed, instead heading for his room.

However, though he felt an uncommon need for solitude, he realized immediately that it had been a mistake to return there. The dress and shoes were no longer there; he had risen early and returned them to the attic where he had found them. But he had not been able to part with her mask. He had hidden it away in his trunk, and it called to him now.

He went to the trunk and opened it, taking up the mask from where it rested amidst his clothes, running his fingers lightly over the silver thread and paste jewels and delicate feathers. He sat on the bed, but that too carried memories, these even more vivid. He remembered with an ache Imogen tumbled amidst the covers, her skin pale and perfect in the moonlight, opening herself up to him.

When she had left him the night before, he had been sorely tempted to run right out after her, sans clothing and all. But she had needed time, he knew. Time to come to terms with this great change her life had taken. And so he had forced himself to stay in his room. He had returned to his bed and lain amid sheets that still smelled of her.

But sleep would not come. Instead his mind had worked furiously throughout the night, trying to make sense of her reaction. He could not understand her refusal. Wasn't he a sight better than waiting hand and foot on her mother for the rest of her life? After all, he wasn't an ogre, he thought with no little bitterness. He had a full head of hair and all his teeth. He was youthful and titled and rich. And they got on famously. He had never got along with another female as he did with her. And he believed he had just proved to her that their union would not be without passion.

Ah, such passion and utter abandon she had shown him. He was not an inconsiderate lover. But with Imogen he had reveled in her body, in her pleasure, as he never had with any other woman. And he *still* ached for her.

She was all unaffected sweetness, a balm for his soul. He should never have had any right to her, even as a friend. Most especially as a lover. He, with his hidden demons, could easily extinguish whatever burned in her that made her who she was.

He always knew one day he would marry. It was his duty as eldest. But he had assumed it would be a society marriage, one with a woman who would be content with the veneer he showed the world. A woman who would not try to look behind the cheerful, carefree façade, would not question his past, would leave his heart and mind untouched. A woman he couldn't destroy by what lay within him.

Imogen was the opposite of all that. She saw *him*, and would not be content with just the surface of him. No, she would seek, and find, his soul.

The thought terrified him. But there was a kernel of relief somewhere inside him at the thought of not having to hide that part of himself from her any longer. No matter what it did to her when she discovered it.

Was he a selfish bastard? Yes, for he would marry Imogen despite all of that. She was his now, and he'd be damned if he'd let her go.

Chapter 16

"I have never been so insulted in my life," Lady Tarryton huffed over dinner at their London townhouse that evening. "For Lord Willbridge to not even acknowledge your presence at that ball, Mariah, and you looking so becoming in your costume."

Mariah glanced quickly at her sister, worry knitting her brow. Imogen caught the action and attempted a look of unconcerned calm. She could sense from Mariah's manner that her younger sister had been only too aware of her depressed spirits since their departure from Pulteney Manor. Imogen knew she was curious, that she not only worried about her sudden seemingly declining health, but also about the apparent tension that had cropped up with Caleb that final morning. Mariah had attempted to question her about it upon their return, but Imogen had managed to shrug noncommittally and escape to the privacy of her room, claiming a need to rest from the journey. She knew, however, that she could not put her sister off for long.

"Mama," Mariah said soothingly, "there was no reason to suppose Lord Willbridge should ask me to dance."

"Of course there was," their mother scoffed, rolling her eyes heavenward. "What is more important than courting his prospective bride?" She sniffed. "Well, I, for one, will no longer mention his name. And none of you are to mention it, either. If he does not know the gem he could have had in our darling Mariah, then I have no more use for the man."

Imogen kept her eyes on her plate and her hands clasped tightly in her lap. She knew if she were to reach for her fork, her hand would tremble violently. She could sense something coming, like a teakettle at a rolling boil, about to spill over.

In the next moment it did.

"And you," her mother hissed at her, "you had to wear those spectacles, had to pull your little act of rebellion. I am certain Lord Willbridge would have proposed but for that."

A moment of shocked silence left everyone else in the room frozen. Finally, her husband found his voice. "Harriett, you must be joking."

"Of course I'm not. Do I appear to be joking?"

Imogen glanced up then. Her mother's mouth was pinched into a thin line, her eyes tight and hard. No, Imogen thought, she certainly did not. She felt a bubble of hysterical laughter well up inside her but swallowed it down. Ah yes, her spectacles, instruments of doom.

"Harriett," her father said, his voice reflecting decades of practiced patience, "of course Imogen's spectacles did not scare away Lord Willbridge's suit. The boy didn't have designs on Mariah in the first place." He looked at his younger daughter, an apologetic smile on his face. "Not anything against you, my dear."

Mariah was quick to jump in. "Of course, Papa. I am fully aware Lord Willbridge never considered me for a bride. And I am glad of it, for I never desired him as a husband."

"Never desired him as a husband!" Her mother's voice carried through the room in a shriek. "Lord Willbridge is a marquess. I think you must agree that available men of his status are in short supply." She closed her eyes, pressing her fingers to her temples. "I warned you all. I told you that it would be a mistake, that Imogen being seen as a bluestocking would taint our family name. But you would not listen to me. Now we will be lucky if we can nab a baron for you."

And that had been that. By some miracle it seemed her mother had finally given up all hopes for Caleb to come up to scratch, for in the days following that tirade she made no mention of him. Not so much Mariah. Several times she had cornered Imogen and demanded to know what had happened between Caleb and herself. Finally Imogen could stand it no more.

"Please," she had begged, holding up her hand to ward off her sister on the afternoon of the second day, "leave it alone, Mariah."

Mariah had stopped in her tracks, a look of hurt and worry flashing across her lovely face. Imogen felt a bone-deep regret. But she could not confide in her. Not only was the truth something she should not burden an innocent with, but she feared saying it aloud would well and truly break her.

Mariah must have seen something in her face, for she reached out and clasped her hand warmly. "I am sorry, dearest," she said quietly. "Only know that should you require a confidante, I will be here for you."

Imogen had attempted to smile in gratitude. But she knew in her heart that, though this was the most important matter in her life, she was utterly alone in it.

Determined to put Caleb from her mind, Imogen threw herself into the schedule her mother had mapped out for them in the search for a husband for her youngest, chaperoning Mariah on outings, attending evening revelries and the like. She expected to see him everywhere she turned, but there was no sign of him.

But as busy as she kept her days, her nights were another matter entirely. With nothing to do but contemplate the ceiling above her head, memories of him assailed her. Even in sleep he invaded her thoughts, filling her dreams with all the desperate desires she kept buried deep otherwise. More than once she awoke, hot and gasping. The dreams were so vivid that she expected to turn her head on the pillow and find him next to her, reaching for her.

It was then the tears came, the only time she was so vulnerable that she could not keep the pain at bay. She clutched the pillow to her face to muffle her sobs, knowing that if Mariah heard there would be no hiding the truth from her. She could only hope that as time went by the memories would fade and she would be able to sleep easy. But in her heart she feared that would never be the case.

On the third morning Imogen accompanied her sister in a walk to the park. The day had turned out to be a fine one and Mariah nattered on about anything and everything. Everything, that was, except Caleb. Imogen was grateful for the reprieve. For, though her mother had determined never to mention his name again, her increasingly dour attitude and caustic comments on spectacles and lost chances brought Caleb to mind more often than not. But they could not put off the inevitable for long, and so, at the end of an hour, it was with a small sigh of resignation that the two girls turned for home.

On their return they found their mother waiting for them in the entrance hall, fairly buzzing with excited energy.

"Thank goodness you are come!" she exclaimed when she saw them. "Mariah, go freshen yourself immediately, and make haste."

"Mama, what is it?" Mariah hurried forward and took up her mother's hands as Imogen removed her outerwear and handed it to the butler.

"You are being offered for this very minute. He is with your father in his study. Oh, Mariah, you will outshine even your sister Frances in status." Lady Tarryton looked as if she would burst out of her bodice, her chest was so puffed up with pride.

Mariah looked over at Imogen in confusion before turning back to their mother. "But *who* is with Papa?"

"Lord Willbridge. I knew that man would come up to scratch eventually. I just knew it. Oh, my darling girl, you've landed a marquess. A marquess!"

Mariah gaped in horror and her eyes swiveled frantically to Imogen and back again. "But Mama…"

Imogen didn't hear the rest. A loud ringing had started up in her ears, drowning out all else. The entrance hall suddenly began to tilt about her. She reached out toward a table to keep herself from toppling.

Immediately Mariah was at her side. She put an arm about her to steady her.

"Imogen, are you all right?" she whispered frantically in her ear. "You know he is not here for me."

Lady Tarryton hurried over, oblivious to Imogen's near collapse. "Mariah, get upstairs at once. Lord Willbridge will be out any minute and you need to look your best."

Just then, however, they heard a door opening and the sharp click of boots on the polished marble floor. They all turned in the direction of the sound just as Caleb strode into view.

"Ladies," he said, gifting the group with a melting smile. He approached, bowing over Lady Tarryton's hand. "My lady, I thank you for your hospitality."

"You are not leaving so soon?"

"I'm afraid so. Though I hope to see you all tomorrow."

Imogen watched the exchange mutely. Her memories were nothing to seeing him in the flesh. Her eyes drank him in, travelling over his slightly mussed hair, his broad shoulders, the long, lean length of his legs. But no, she could not do this again. He should not be here. She had told him to stay away. She clutched onto Mariah, dreading when he finally turned to her.

"Oh, my lord," their mother was saying, "as you see my daughter Mariah is here. She has just returned from her walk, and so your timing is impeccable."

Caleb dutifully bowed toward her sister. "Miss Mariah, as always it is a pleasure." He then turned toward Imogen. And everything stopped. The heat in his eyes stole the very breath from her lungs.

"And your eldest as well," he murmured, advancing on her.

"Oh, yes, Imogen. Say hello to his lordship."

But Imogen could only stare as Caleb came and stood before her. She was vaguely aware of Mariah's arm slipping from her waist as her sister moved away. And then Caleb took up her hand, bending over it. His lips brushed her knuckles, the barest of touches. But the feel of his mouth on her skin made her knees weak with wanting.

"Miss Duncan," he murmured, his pewter eyes fastening on her mouth as he straightened. "How lovely to see you again."

And then he was gone. Imogen felt her lungs expand as she took a breath for what seemed the first time since the exchange started.

Caleb accepted his hat and gloves from the butler and bowed to them. "Until tomorrow." With one final heated look at Imogen, he departed.

The three women were silent a long while after he left, staring blankly at the door.

"Well, my word," Lady Tarryton said faintly. "That's an odd way to greet your future wife."

Mariah returned to Imogen's side, linking arms with her. "Oh, I don't know about that," she said, giving Imogen a small smile.

Their mother looked lost for a moment. Suddenly she straightened her shoulders. "Well, I will not sit around waiting for your father. Come along, girls."

She sailed from the hall. When Imogen made no move to follow, Mariah tugged her along.

"No," Imogen said.

"Yes," Mariah replied forcefully.

By the time they reached their father's study, their mother was already storming through the door.

"Well?" she demanded.

Lord Tarryton glanced up from the papers on his desk. "Well what, my dear?"

She rolled her eyes in exasperation. "What did Lord Willbridge say?"

He smiled then, and looked directly at Imogen. She felt her heart drop into her toes.

"Why, he asked for Imogen's hand."

There was a moment of quiet in the room before Lady Tarryton shook her head impatiently. "You must be mistaken, Ernest. Surely he said Mariah. You misheard."

"No," Lord Tarryton replied calmly. "He was quite specific. He wants Imogen."

The room went completely still before exploding into action.

Mariah, that most wonderful sister, squealed loudly enough to attract every dog in the capital. Her arms went about Imogen with surprising force, knocking the breath from her body—if Imogen hadn't already lost it in a large exhale of shock.

Her mother swiveled her head between her husband and her two daughters, her mouth working silently. Finally she managed, "But…Mariah…"

Lord Tarryton rose and went to his wife. "Harriett, did the boy ever show a bit of interest in Mariah?"

"Of course he did—"

"No, he did not," he interrupted. "He wants Imogen. You shall have to pin your hopes for Mariah elsewhere."

He turned from his stunned wife to his daughters. "Imogen," he said, "I leave the matter up to you. Do you accept Lord Willbridge's offer?"

Imogen looked at his face, feeling a modicum of strength from the kindness there. Refusing to meet her mother's eyes, she swallowed hard. "No, Papa," she whispered.

He nodded. "He told me you would say as much."

"What!" Her mother finally came to life. "You refuse him?"

Imogen could only nod.

"Have you gone mad?"

Lord Tarryton held up his hands. "Calm down now, Harriett."

She turned on him, her eyes blazing. "Calm down? He is a marquess, Ernest. A marquess! She is lucky to get an offer at all at her age, and from a marquess, no less. A man of Lord Willbridge's youth, position, and wealth could get any girl for a wife, and he has offered for our obtuse daughter, who would not know good fortune were it to slap her in the face."

"Imogen has the right to accept or refuse any man, no matter his social status or fortune," Lord Tarryton said quietly. Imogen had not loved her father quite so much as she did in that moment.

Her mother sputtered and raged. They all let her, until finally she lost steam and stood there looking defeated.

"Now," her father said once the room went blessedly silent, "If Imogen was to decline, Lord Willbridge informed me that she and I are invited to his country house for a fortnight."

"No," Imogen said. "I won't go."

Once again her father nodded. "He thought you would say that as well. He said to inform you that he has already sent word ahead to his family, and will be here with his carriages tomorrow morning despite your wishes."

Imogen stared at him. "And you agreed to this?" she asked in disbelief.

He went to stand in front of her and took up her cold hands in his. "I brought you up to be more fair than that, my girl. Give the lad a chance. If at the end of our visit you still won't have him, I shall support your decision."

If he had threatened or bargained with her she might have been able to stand her ground. But his quiet and sensible reasoning obliterated her defenses. "Fine," she muttered, her shoulders slumping in defeat.

"Well, don't just stand there," her mother said. "If you are to leave tomorrow you must get packed at once. I'll send Mariah's maid with you; she can share Paula with me for now. You cannot visit the Marchioness of Willbridge looking like...well..." She flapped her hand vaguely in Imogen's direction. "It really is too bad he did not give us more time. I could have had your dresses altered to look a bit more...ahem..." She trailed off, then shooed Imogen from the room.

Mariah followed in her wake. "Imogen," she whispered, "did Lord Willbridge ask you to marry him at the Knowles's house party?"

Imogen blushed and kept her head down as she hurried to her room. "Yes," she replied tightly.

"And you turned him down?"

"Yes."

"Why didn't you tell me, Imogen?"

Imogen stopped on the landing and looked at her. Not

"Why didn't you accept him?" but "Why didn't you tell me?" Her heart swelled.

"I couldn't, Mariah," she said helplessly.

Mariah studied her for a long moment before nodding sagely. "Well, then," she said briskly, "let's get you ready to go."

Chapter 17

The following morning began the longest day and a half of Imogen's life.

She should have known Caleb planned on making things difficult for her the moment he stepped from his carriage. Ignoring everyone else, he approached her. Which was mortifying on its own. But then he reached out, gripping her fingers in full view of her family. While her cheeks burned he leaned in close, his lips brushing her ear, and whispered, "You left me no choice. You are mine now, you know, and I wasn't about to let you go so easily."

The words had made her shiver, and not just from apprehension.

She had done her best to pretend he did not exist during the long journey. But it seemed the harder she tried, the more aware of him she became. A bump of his leg here, a brush of his hand there, and the plush interior of the carriage seemed to shrink with each passing mile. His heated glances and small smiles told her more than words that he was fully aware just how he affected her. Even now, as he rode alongside the carriage for the final leg of the trip, she was not immune to him. He passed into view, and though she had determined to keep from seeking him out her traitorous eyes had other ideas. He caught her looking and gave her a roguish wink. She jerked her gaze from him, but even so the damage had been done to her already taut nerves. She squirmed in her seat.

"Are you well, Imogen?" her father asked over his book.

She blushed and adjusted her spectacles. "Yes, Papa."

He glanced out the window, squinting at the bright landscape. "Lord Willbridge said we would be arriving late this afternoon.

How lovely that Northamptonshire is not even two days out of London. And who knew it was so close to Frances's home? It really is too bad she's in Rutland just now. It would be wonderful to see her; we get that chance so rarely these days." His voice trailed off, his brow lowering before he turned back to Imogen with a bracing smile. "We should be seeing the start of Lord Willbridge's property shortly."

Sure enough, the carriage rumbled to a stop and Caleb rode up to the window. "The gatehouse to our land is just a mile ahead of us, and then it is a mile to the house. I'll ride on ahead to give them news of our approach and will see you there."

Though his words sounded relaxed enough, cheerful even, there was a certain tightness to his eyes that gave her the impression all was not right. Not for the first time on the journey, she recalled their conversations regarding his family, and wondered why he was bringing her here. It was obvious it would be a difficult situation for him, given his strained relationships with his siblings. So why was he insisting on this trip?

Before she could think on it further he was off at a gallop and the carriage lurched forward to rumble at a more sedate pace in his wake.

"Splendid," her father said with a happy sigh. "Cannot wait to stretch my legs. Never did like travel." And then he was back to his book, and Imogen was able to stare at the passing scenery in peace, even as her insides roiled.

Only two more miles, she thought, listening to the carriage wheels eat up the distance. Two miles until she would see his home, the home she could be mistress of if only she could ignore her instincts and go along with her desires. Two miles until she would meet the family that could have been hers.

She had come to a sad realization after miles of road with nothing to occupy her mind except some novels that did not hold her attention. Though they had been traveling for the better part of two days, though her legs were cramped and her body was stiff from the confining—albeit, sumptuously appointed—interior of the carriage, she was still not ready to see Caleb's home and meet his family. And she would most likely *never* be ready. To see these things, to have them in her memories, would only make the future all the more painful for her. Even though she was saving them both from an imprudent match and unhappy union, she would always know that, had she been any more selfish, she could have had these things for her own. And now the time was upon her, and there was no delaying it.

A short ten minutes later and they were passing the gatehouse. Then they were on his land, the distance between her and Caleb's home closing by the second. Was it just her, she thought as panic began to set in, or were the horses going uncommonly fast? She was vaguely aware of her breath speeding up and her hands clenching at the seat beneath her. With utmost will she slowed her breathing and loosened her grip. Trying to distract her mind, she studied the passing landscape. The trees were enormous oaks, lining both sides of the road and shading the gravel drive as they no doubt had done for centuries. Beyond them she caught brief glimpses of open areas warmed by the sun, the hills green and rolling. And then the tree line opened.

Imogen had known his home would be a place of beauty. But she was quite unprepared for the scene that greeted her wide eyes. Beyond two soaring carved stone columns and a circular drive lay the house, the late afternoon sun lighting on the pale limestone of the Jacobean exterior. The mullioned windows sparkled under gracefully shaped gables. Front and center stood a small portico, and there was Caleb, smiling as they drove closer. Imogen felt an immediate welcome, a homecoming, and ruthlessly tried to squash the feeling. No good could come of being enamored with the house. It was bad enough she'd fallen in love with its owner.

The carriage made a circuit of the drive, rocking to a gentle halt before the entrance. Then the carriage door was thrown wide.

"Welcome to Willowhaven," Caleb murmured, offering her his hand.

Imogen paused before she placed her shaking fingers in his

and descended the steps. The gravel crunched under her boots, and then Caleb led her forward toward an intricately carved, heavy dark oak door that stood ajar. She was vaguely aware of her father being helped down behind her before Caleb guided her into the entrance hall.

The walls were paneled in the same beautiful dark wood as the door, giving an impression of intimacy and warmth. The floor was white marble interspersed with black marble diamonds, the ceiling painted white with dark beams running throughout. She walked as if in a trance by Caleb's side, taking it all in. He moved them beyond the small entrance into a bright room with arched windows opening onto what seemed to be an interior courtyard. Delicate tables were set in alcoves, topped with vases overflowing with blooms. The heady aroma was a delicious addition to her senses. Against one wall stood a huge marble fireplace, a portrait of James I gracing the space above.

Imogen swallowed at the grand richness of it all. She could only be glad that her mother was not there. For Lady Tarryton would have been an embarrassment of fawning attention in the face of so much wealth and grandeur. Their family was aristocracy, and far from poor, but her mother had been a mere baronet's daughter, and a snob for social position, and this would have sent her into raptures.

Lord Tarryton, on the other hand, stood silently beside his daughter, smiling affably at their host. Though her father was absentminded in his best moments, he would provide a silent support for her through this and would not embarrass her.

As the butler relieved them of their outerwear and instructed the footmen on the removal of their luggage from the carriage, as well as directions for their servants that had followed in a second, smaller carriage, Caleb spoke.

"Billsby will show you to your rooms now. We can meet before dinner in the small drawing room. I shall have a maid show you the way at the appointed time."

Imogen felt a frisson of uncertainty travel down her spine. She could not place it until, as she turned with her father to follow the butler, she realized what it was.

She stopped and turned toward Caleb. He immediately went to her. "What is it?" he asked in concern.

"Is your mother Lady Willbridge in residence? I was given the impression that she was."

To Imogen's surprise, Caleb's mouth compressed and the corners of his eyes tightened. "Yes, my mother is here, along with my two younger sisters. However, I thought you would be more comfortable meeting them after you had a chance to rest a bit from the journey. You will see them before dinner."

"I would like to meet them now," she said quietly.

Caleb frowned. "After we get you settled. You must be tired."

"No, we should meet them now. It would not be polite to delay." Her voice held an undercurrent of steel that seemed to give Caleb pause.

"Very well," he said slowly. He offered his arm to Imogen and she took it. He then bowed to Lord Tarryton.

"My lord, if you are amenable, I will show you to Lady Willbridge."

Lord Tarryton smiled broadly. "Of course, of course. Lead on, dear boy."

As they started off, Caleb was strangely subdued beside her. One would almost think he had no wish for her to meet his mother. But she was nervous enough without having to worry about that as well.

It seemed the house was built around the open courtyard she had viewed upon first entering. Caleb brought them off to the left and through a limestone arch to a highly polished oak staircase. They travelled up a floor and through several richly appointed rooms before reaching the small drawing room. The butler was there before them, opening the door and bowing as they entered.

"Thank you, Billsby," Caleb murmured, and guided Imogen in.

A dainty woman sitting on a pale green settee looked up from her embroidery in surprise when they entered. From Caleb's initial insistence on delaying her meeting his mother, Imogen was taken aback at the positively frail-looking creature before them. She had expected a harridan, a woman who terrorized all in her midst. Instead, the woman looked more nervous than she herself did. As they approached the marchioness, Imogen saw her look to her son with a longing that was almost painful to behold.

She had Caleb's coloring, though there was a generous sprinkling of gray dusting her copper hair. Her face was softer, more heart-shaped, and lined around her mouth and eyes.

"Mother," Caleb said, stopping before her, "may I present Lord Tarryton and his daughter, Miss Imogen Duncan. Imogen, my mother, the Marchioness of Willbridge."

Imogen curtsied, her knees shaking. As she rose she was surprised to see the marchioness had risen as well and stood before her.

"My dear," she said gently. There was the same tension in her face as her son, but her smile was kind and genuine as she looked at Imogen. "I am so glad to meet you, that you have deigned to visit us."

Imogen was taken aback at the strange turn of phrase. She searched the woman's face for any sarcasm or insincerity but found only an uncertain friendliness.

"Thank you, my lady," she replied, smiling tentatively. "I am honored to be here."

"And Lord Tarryton," the woman said, turning to her father, "I have heard you are a learned man. I do hope you make extensive use of our library during your stay. I believe you will find much to please you. I have been told it is the finest collection of books in Northamptonshire."

Her father's eyes positively lit up, and suddenly Imogen knew the draw this visit had for him, how Caleb had used her father's passion for books to guarantee their presence.

"Thank you, my lady," her father replied, "I look forward to it."

The marchioness turned then, and for the first time Imogen noticed the two young women seated off to the side. One, a subdued-looking young woman in a slate colored gown with Caleb's copper hair, had her face resolutely turned to the side. The other, obviously the younger of the two, had curling strawberry blond hair and a fetching lime green gown. She was staring at the newcomers with avid interest.

"And may I present my daughters?" the marchioness went on. "This is Emily," she said, motioning to the more sober of the two. "And this is my youngest, Daphne."

Imogen curtsied once more. Lady Emily stayed seated, and somehow, without looking directly at Imogen, managed to incline her head in her direction. The younger, however, sprung from her seat and took hold of Imogen's hands. Her eyes were a brilliant green that almost matched the hue of her gown and filled to the brim with excitement.

"Miss Duncan, I am so thrilled you are here. You have come straight from London?"

"Y-yes," Imogen stuttered. Lady Daphne was all bounding enthusiasm and energy, a daunting force indeed.

"Please come and sit here by me." Without waiting for an answer, the girl pulled Imogen to the couch her sister occupied.

"Daphne," Caleb said in a warning voice.

"It is quite all right, my lord," Imogen said, not wanting to be the cause of further strife between them.

"Yes, Caleb," Daphne chimed in. "Calm yourself. Imogen and I will be the very best of friends. I may call you Imogen, mayn't I? And you must call me Daphne. None of this 'Lady Daphne' business, if you please. We mustn't stand on ceremony here, after all."

Imogen drew breath to reply, but the girl launched on and Imogen closed her mouth with a snap.

"And I simply must hear all about London. Imogen, you must tell me about all the latest gossip and fashions. Mother says we may go to London next Season for my come out, and it seems ages until we do."

The marchioness cut in. "I must apologize for my youngest, Miss Duncan. We do not get many visitors here, you see, and she is quite keen to go to the capital."

Imogen smiled reassuringly. "Please, there is no need to apologize. I understand. In fact, your daughter reminds me not a small bit of my own dear sister, Mariah, who is in London for her own first Season now."

Daphne jumped on this. "Oh! Is she quite popular? Has she permission to waltz? Has she any prospects as of yet?"

Imogen broke into a startled laugh. "Oh yes, she is quite popular. And when I receive word from her, for she has promised to write, I shall share with you any news I receive of London."

"Oh, how delicious," Daphne gushed. She twisted with impressive speed to face her sister, who sat silently on the other side of her. "Emily, isn't that simply wonderful?"

Lady Emily turned then. Imogen was suddenly very glad she had practiced her careful, calm expression so often. For when she caught sight of the other side of the girl's face, she very nearly gasped aloud. An angry looking scar ran from her left temple and across her cheek, ending at the corner of her mouth. It seemed an old wound, but how it must have pained her when it occurred. What could have caused such a violent injury?

"Yes, wonderful," Lady Emily murmured. She stared at Imogen, as if testing her reaction to her appearance.

Imogen smiled gently at her. "And have you been to London, Lady Emily?"

"No."

And that was it. Lady Emily gave Imogen her profile once again and said no more.

Imogen had no time to ponder her strange attitude, however, for the marchioness spoke up. "Is not Lady Sumner your sister as well?"

"Yes. I was pleased to hear your estate is so close to her own, though she is not at home just now. They are visiting one of her husband's estates in Rutland."

"That is too bad. It would have been lovely for you to have a chance to visit with her while you're staying with us. Though perhaps she might return in time. We do like Lady Sumner exceedingly."

Daphne, who had been bouncing impatiently in her seat for this short exchange, captured her attention again and held it until Caleb moved to her side and interrupted. "It is time Miss Duncan and her father retired so they can rest before dinner. They have been travelling the better part of two days and will want to get settled."

He put his hand under her elbow. Imogen rose obediently, but she chafed at his management of her. She was surprised at how readily she had taken to Caleb's family, how much she enjoyed their company, and would have liked to stay a bit longer.

Though, now that she thought on it, perhaps it was best not to get too attached. As she allowed Caleb to lead her father and herself to their rooms, however, she saw that particular battle had already been lost. For she liked his family very much, and knew that she would only grow to like them more during her stay, which would make her final break from Caleb all the more painful.

Chapter 18

"Where is the rest of my gown?" Imogen cried as she looked at her reflection in the mirror.

Kate, her sister's maid and for the time being her own, studied her handiwork, looking quite pleased with herself. "It's all there, miss. Well," she conceded, "most of it, anyhow."

Eyes wide, Imogen stared at the lowered neckline of her pale yellow silk gown. She had never had so much of her bosom exposed in her life. Though perhaps that was not precisely true, she thought, recalling the night of the masquerade ball and the stunning sapphire gown she had worn. That dress had been much more revealing, with its tight stomacher and square neckline, the tops of her breasts and shoulders bare for all the world to see. But she had been able to pretend she was someone else that night, not shy, plain Miss Imogen Duncan. Right now she could see it was just her, horribly exposed and uncomfortable. She flushed crimson, watching in fascination as the color spread down her neck and over her now obviously ample chest.

"Who gave you orders to butcher my dress?" she demanded. But the second the words were out of her mouth she knew: her mother. That woman would do anything in her power to ensure her daughter became Marchioness of Willbridge. Even if that daughter was Imogen.

"Lady Tarryton gave the orders, miss," the maid verified. "I've been working my fingers to the bone since we left London, adjusting all your gowns. And I don't mind telling you, sewing in a moving carriage is no picnic. Actually," she amended, reaching out to adjust the small capped sleeves of the dress, "most of the gowns we brought weren't yours at all, but Miss Mariah's. Course, she's taller than you. But you've both got the bosom, so it only took hemming up the skirts to get them to work on you."

Imogen's mouth opened and closed several times. So this was it, then? Her mother meant to have her paraded before Caleb like a prize mare. She tugged at the bodice, hoping to hide a bit more of the flesh swelling above. When that proved fruitless she gave a frustrated huff. At least her hair looked pleasing. She was wholly unused to having anyone dress her hair. She had always pulled it back in the simplest way possible, believing the severity of her efforts the only way to tame hair as unruly as hers.

But Kate had wrung magic from her unmanageable light brown locks. Tonight her hair was a mass of intricate braids woven in a coronet about the crown of her head. Several long strands curled teasingly down her neck, a neck made much longer, she had to admit, by the low cut of the gown. Though the yellow of her dress still lent a slightly sickly cast to her complexion, the entire look made her appear much softer, more feminine. Perhaps, dare she say, even a bit pretty? If she could continue to keep her color high by blushing through the night, one might even be able to look past the horrible color choice.

That, she reflected wryly, giving her chest one last disbelieving glance, would not be a problem one bit in her estimation.

• • •

Caleb was posted at the window in the drawing room, staring out, unseeing, into the darkening night sky. Both of his sisters and his mother were perched like flighty sparrows on the couch behind him, quietly chatting amongst themselves. Well, his mother and Daphne were. Emily was, as ever, silent and withdrawn. He could not remember a time she had not been like this in his presence.

No, he thought with a frown. That was not true. There had been a time she was full of life, a shy but cheerful young girl. If he thought very, very hard, he could even remember her laugh, something he had not heard in more than a decade.

But he would not remember. He tugged sharply at his cuff, banishing the wispy memory. Such thoughts were not welcome, especially now. He glanced at the clock above the mantle. Imogen and her father should be joining them any moment. It would not do to be distracted by visions from the past that would only bring him pain.

He wondered, not for the first time, the wisdom of bringing Imogen here. He had needed to get her away from London to someplace she would feel comfortable, more herself. She had bloomed at his cousin's house party in the country. It had been a simple leap to come to the conclusion that bringing her to one of his estates was the answer.

He did not know why she had refused him. But at least in this setting he would be able to prove to her more easily how wonderfully they would suit. If he could claim back some of the ease they had shared at the house party, he was certain she would accept his proposal.

He had briefly considered opening up one of his lesser homes for this. They were all well-maintained places, beautiful each in their own way. But in the end he had dismissed them all. Not only was Willowhaven spectacular, but he also required the presence of his family.

His family. He shook his head, his jaw clenching almost painfully. Yes, he needed his family, as he had not in many, many years. He could not invite Imogen to visit him at one of his country residences, being the bachelor that he was and with the reputation he had, regardless of her father accompanying her, without his own family in attendance. It was essential to protect her reputation, as well as to make her see he was serious in courting her.

But was it wise? His mother, he knew, would do everything in her power to see the match was made. He was thirty, after all, and needed to marry and produce an heir. He was certain that, had they been closer, she would have been badgering him as unmercifully as his peers' mothers did to find a bride and set up a nursery.

Daphne, as well, would not prove a problem. Indeed, with her enthusiastic nature, she might even be a help in making Imogen feel at home.

But then there was Emily. He fought the urge to look over at her, seated beside their mother, staring as she always did at nothing in particular, her posture stiff and unwelcoming. He could not know how she would play into this whole business. Would she ignore Imogen as thoroughly as she ignored him? Would her reserved manner hinder his suit?

Just then he heard a commotion at the door. He turned—and found he forgot to breathe for a moment.

He had only seen Imogen arrayed thus once before, and that was the night of the masquerade ball. He recalled his anger at the sight of her then. She had not been his Imogen, but someone else entirely.

Now, however, he felt none of that. This was his Imogen, there was no question about it. There was no tight corset, no outrageous pile of curls, no rouge. Her hair had been softened in a quietly elegant style, her gown cut to enhance her figure. And the blush that stained her cheeks was entirely her own.

He had never seen anything so beautiful in his entire life.

He strode to her, forgetting everyone else in the room, including her father, to whose arm she was clinging. Taking up her hand, he brushed his lips against the backs of her trembling fingers. Her eyes were huge and an unbelievably clear turquoise behind the delicate wire frames of her spectacles.

"Imogen," he murmured, knowing he was staring at her like a starving man confronted with the most delicious food in the world and not caring a bit. "You look…"

Her lips thinned. "I know," she muttered as her father moved discreetly away to greet Lady Willbridge and her daughters. "It is too much."

"No," Caleb hastened to assure her. "That's not it at all. It is just right."

Just right? What was he, some green boy fresh out of University?

At her puzzled glance he attempted to repair the breach. "What I mean to say is, you look beautiful beyond words." He had lowered his voice to an intimate rumble, and was rewarded with the glazed look in her eyes and her slight shudder. Her tongue flicked out nervously to moisten her lips and his eyes were captivated by the movement. Had he ever seen anything more erotic than that quick flash of her small pink tongue?

Just then Billsby entered, announcing supper. Caleb silently held out his arm to Imogen, and felt her fingers, as light as a bird, alight on his sleeve. As he guided her from the room, he smiled to himself. Goodness, but his Imogen was full of surprises. And he was eager to uncover every single one.

• • •

It seemed that sleeplessness was just something she would have to get used to.

Imogen lay in the wonderfully soft, large bed that was hers for the next two weeks, staring up at the intricately detailed stucco ceiling above her, seeing only a hazy moonlit mix of swirls and curlicues. Her mind, however, was several doors down, where Caleb slept. If she had only said yes to his proposal, she would be there with him even now, wrapped in his arms. Instead she was here, in this strange bedroom, positively aching for him.

She sighed and turned onto her side. She would not allow herself to visualize him in bed. Determined to get some rest so she would not be a bloodshot ogre in the morning, she purposely closed her eyes and tried to think of something, anything, but Caleb.

Except now that her mind was not full of him, it was replaying the entire evening over. After her initial nervousness at her state of dress—or undress, as the case may be—had faded, she had been better able to study the Masters family. Caleb was still the same charming rogue, smiling and making jokes. But he held himself back from his family with a distinction that seemed so out of character. There was no friendly banter, no affection. He treated them as he would strangers.

His mother, on the other hand, looked at him with such longing and worry that more than once Imogen had to turn away. The woman obviously loved her son, wanted his attention, and yet he would hardly look at her.

His sisters were opposites in every way. Lady Daphne was a bubbling ball of delight, finding something to please her in everything that was said. And despite what Caleb had said about being estranged from all of his siblings, Daphne did not seem to see it that way, often joking with her brother despite his seeming determination to stay aloof. Lady Emily, however, sat stiffly in her chair for most of the evening, her entire bearing unwelcoming and cold, only giving the barest answers to any inquiries put her way. Several times Imogen caught her looking with a hooded gaze on her brother. For the life of her, she could not interpret it. But it was obvious that there was something wrong here.

Giving a low growl of frustration, Imogen threw off the sheets and rose, finding her slippers and night robe. She slipped them on along with her spectacles and then, lighting a candle, made her way out of her room. She would go to the library, she decided, having exhausted the books she'd brought with her for the journey. Perhaps she'd be able to find something to calm her galloping mind.

She made her way down the long hallway, moonlit rectangles of light shining on the floors and wood-paneled walls. Willowhaven was old, but obviously well-loved. It was not drafty, as so many of these old houses were, or a showplace for ancient family heirlooms, but comfortable and warm, a place you could truly call home. She made her way down the main oak staircase, letting her fingers trail over the silky railing, and through the long entrance hall. She remembered the way to the library vividly. Her father had insisted on being shown the room before they retired so he might get an early start the following morning, and she had committed the path there to memory, knowing he would be spending the majority of his time there.

She found her way with ease, and once inside walked over to a towering bookcase, bringing the light close to peruse the titles. As she made her way down the row, she gave a wry smile. Her father would be unlikely to make it out for meals if even this one shelf was anything to go by. It seemed to be an eclectic collection of botanical tomes, including several catalogues of specimens that Imogen knew her father had a particular interest in.

She sighed and moved on. Before long she came to a section she knew to be much newer. She grinned. It seemed that one of Caleb's sisters was an avid fan of gothic novels. She let her fingers skim the bindings, finally deciding on volume one of *The Romance of the Forest* by Ann Radcliffe. She had pulled it from its place and was about to return to her room when Caleb walked through the door, a small lantern in his hand.

She started. He saw her in that very same moment and stopped dead in his tracks.

"Imogen," he said in surprise.

She clutched the book to her chest. The light from her candle wavered as her hand shook, making shadows dance over the walls. She remembered all too vividly the last time they were alone at night. She swallowed hard, even as heat rushed under her skin.

"I'm sorry," she said, her voice a wisp of sound. "I could not sleep and thought a book would help."

He smiled wryly and Imogen felt her stomach do a flip. "I was in quite the same frame of mind." He came closer. Imogen pressed her back to the bookcase as he loomed over her.

"What have you got there?" he asked.

Wordlessly she held it out to him. He chuckled.

"A gothic novel? I did not know your tastes ran in quite that direction."

She flushed under his amused gaze. "They do not. I mean, I do not typically read them. But I was restless and thought it could provide a bit of amusement."

"It will at that, I'm sure," he murmured, his eyes warm.

"Do you know who they belong to?" she blurted. "I would not want to borrow them unless it was right to do so."

He frowned. There was a flash of something—pain? Regret? In his eyes. He quickly wiped it from his face and pasted on a bland look instead.

"I truly don't know. But I'm certain whomever they belong to won't mind in the least."

Imogen felt a tinge of wrongness at that. Shouldn't he know who in his family took such an interest in things of this nature? From the collection of titles that filled the shelf, it was obvious that the person who had attained such a quantity of these books had quite a passion for them. Perhaps more than one person in the household read them and that accounted for his lack of knowledge.

Imogen nodded. "Well then. I'd best be off." She went to go around him. The feel of his fingers on her arm, however, stopped her. His hand was hot through the thin material of her night robe.

"No, please don't go," he said softly. "We have not been alone since…well, since. Come and sit with me." At her uncertain look he smiled faintly. "I promise to behave and keep my hands to myself, if that is your worry."

Averting her suddenly hot face, hoping he would not see the desperate longing there, she gave a quick nod. He led her over to one of the comfortable overstuffed chairs that faced the large fireplace. As he busied himself with building a fire, Imogen tried to compose herself. Instead, however, she found herself studying the play of muscles under the fine lawn of his shirt and the way his hair shone in the budding firelight.

He sat beside her when the fire was roaring. "I would like very much for us to be comfortable with each other again, Imogen."

"I'm not at all certain that is possible," she muttered.

"Why?"

She gave him a long look. "What happened between us—" Her throat closed up and she cleared it. "Things can no longer be the same between us. It's not conceivable."

"And why not? What happened between us was completely natural."

"But not in our society. We cannot take it so lightly."

He leaned in. "I do not take it lightly. You know what needs to be done now. We need to marry."

"No, we do not."

He apparently saw something in her eyes, for he leaned slowly back in his chair, the intense look fading from his face. "I will not fight with you on it, Imogen. For now I just want you to enjoy your stay. Do you like Willowhaven?"

She blinked at the sudden change in subject and demeanor. "Of course," she answered cautiously. "It's a beautiful home. I see that you love it here."

He nodded, his eyes softening. "I do."

"And yet you aren't happy here."

It wasn't a question. He had attempted to keep up a front since their arrival, but it was plain as day that he had been tense the moment he had entered Willbridge land.

He shrugged, turning to the flames dancing in the fireplace. A line formed between his brows.

"Why did you return then?" she asked.

His skin glowed golden in the warmth of the blaze, his pewter eyes reflecting its orange light as he looked at her. "For you."

The breath left her body in a slow exhale. "Me?"

"Yes."

She shook her head. "Why?"

"Because," he said, reaching for her hand, "I knew I could never get you to agree to marry me in London. I needed you in a place where you could be free to be yourself, out from under your mother's thumb. And I knew you would love it here."

She remained silent, as he must have known she would. His thumb absently rubbed over her knuckles, the small intimacy softening her spine and relieving the tension in her head. How she had missed this ease with him.

When he finally spoke again, his voice was uncertain, as if

afraid to break the tenuous peace. "You never did tell me why you will not marry me."

Frances's face flashed into her mind. She wanted to grip his hand tighter and tell him exactly why, that she loved him and was afraid he would never love her in the same way, that he would one day wake up and realize he had been burdened with a socially inept wife who had no business being a marchioness, that she would die a little inside every day until she was a mere shell of a person and he resented her presence in his life.

Instead she gently withdrew her hand from his. "We won't suit," she answered softly. "Not in that way."

"I think we can both agree that we do, Imogen." His voice was a purr, washing through her in a delicious way. She steeled herself against it.

"That is not all there is to marriage," she replied firmly.

He was silent for a moment. "No. You are right in that. But we have developed a wonderful friendship in the past weeks."

She had to say something. She had to know, once and for all, if there was more possible for them. "But," she managed, even as her blood pounded loud and hard through every part of her body, "couldn't you eventually want, or feel, more?"

She wanted to recall the words the moment they were from her mouth. What had possessed her? How could she have been so bold?

He smiled at her then, and it was so tender that she felt a spurt of hope. His next words, however, dashed that all to pieces.

"Have no fear on that score, Imogen. I'm not the kind to ever fall in love. I've never felt anything even remotely like what the poets and dreamers talk about. So you may rest your mind—I will never fall in love, will never be unfaithful to you, will never leave you."

He looked for all the world as if he'd just gifted her with something infinitely precious. She tried to return his smile—after all, what else could she do? So there was an end to it. She felt the hot press of tears but fought them back.

"And we do have passion, as I think you've seen," he continued, his voice suddenly dipping lower, making her remember things she had no wish to. "To have that, along with friendship, is more than I ever hoped for in a marriage."

She could not stay here with him a moment longer. He thought he was making things better, convincing her of their suitability, not knowing that he was only pushing her further away.

Standing, she made to leave. "I must get some rest."

He rose and again caught her arm, forcing her to stop. "You do care for me a bit, don't you, Imogen?"

She nearly blanched. "You know I could not have lain with you if I did not...care for you."

He moved closer. "Then give it a chance, Imogen. Give *us* a chance."

She should refuse him, remain stern and unyielding and let him know in no uncertain terms that she would not accept him. Especially after the revelations of the past several minutes.

But even after his verification that he would never love her, the words would not come. She tried to force them out. But her throat closed up and her lips would not form the words. Instead she found herself pleading, "I need till the end of my visit. Please."

He studied her for a long moment. Then something changed in him. His face took on a determination that frightened and thrilled her, and his lips quirked in that lazy, cocksure smile that melted her very bones. His gaze fastened on her lips. She could do nothing but stare up at him like a rabbit in a snare.

"I think you will find, Imogen," he practically purred, his hand cupping the back of her head, his deft fingers massaging into her hair, "that at the end of these two weeks we will suit. Very much indeed."

Chapter 19

Imogen spent more time than usual readying herself the following morning, but it was not by choice. Kate had insisted on giving her hair a softened look, framing her face with curls.

Her sister's dress had given Imogen pause when it had been brought out. The pale blue gown, with its wide satin sash under her breasts and delicate embroidered white flowers, was feminine and sweet, and unlike anything Imogen had ever worn.

She stared at herself in the glass when Kate was done. She didn't look much like herself anymore, though she admitted reluctantly that the changes wrought were positive. The blue of the gown gave an alabaster look to her skin and brought her eyes out in a startling way. Truly it was a lovely color, and Imogen knew that, had she been allowed to choose her own clothes, this fabric would have been just what she would want.

Then the thought occurred to her that perhaps Caleb would see these changes as her trying to please him. But a moment later she shook her head, straightening her shoulders and following the maid who was sent to show her down to the breakfast room. How she looked and what he thought would change nothing. At the end of this trip they would still go their separate ways. Then she could go back to her life as if nothing had changed.

Sorrow washed through her at the thought. But it was what had to be done, and so there was no point in wishing it otherwise. These two weeks would be a pleasant interlude. But when they were over she would put it behind her and soldier on, as she always did.

The breakfast room was on the ground floor, on the east side of the building. Pale yellow fabric covered the walls, and with the sun streaming in through the windows, Imogen found it to be a wonderfully cheerful space. Lady Emily was there already, seated at the rosewood table, her plate of food and the *Times* before her. She froze when Imogen entered, a bite of egg hanging suspended on her fork before she lowered it to her plate.

"Lady Emily, good morning," Imogen said brightly. The girl merely nodded before pushing back from the table and heading for the door. She slid past Imogen without a word, leaving her to stare after her in confusion and dismay. Had she offended Lady Emily the day before in some way? But no, the girl had been unpleasant from the moment she had met her.

Shaking her head, Imogen went to the sideboard. It was fairly groaning with food, surely more than six people could reasonably eat. She decided on toast and coddled eggs and took a seat. Just as the footman placed a cup of chocolate before her and she was spreading honey on her bread, Caleb entered the room.

He was exceedingly handsome in his buckskin breeches and burgundy tailcoat. The color highlighted the copper tones in his hair and made his eyes appear even more pale and striking. He smiled broadly as he entered. Her spoon slipped and she smeared honey on the back of her hand.

He came directly to her. "Imogen, you look utterly ravishing this morning," he murmured, taking up her hand and pressing a kiss to her knuckles. His tongue darted out and slowly licked the honey from her skin. If she had been standing she was sure her knees would have gone out from under her. When he released her and moved to the sideboard, she clenched her hands in her lap to keep them from trembling.

He returned a short time later with a plate piled high with food. Though the table was a large piece of furniture, well able to hold a dozen people or better, he took the seat next to her, brushing against her leg as he did so. Feeling the need to busy herself, Imogen reached for her chocolate, gulping it down. She just kept herself from gasping as her tongue was singed by the hot liquid.

Instead of starting on his food, however, Caleb reached out, tugging at a curl that was hanging down the side of her neck. His long fingers just barely skimmed her skin as he did so, and Imogen swallowed hard.

"I like your hair in this fashion," he murmured, his voice husky. "It is very becoming on you. You should not hide it away, you know. You have amazingly beautiful hair."

His words were deliciously intimate. Too intimate. Imogen glanced frantically at the footman stationed nearby, relieved to see he was busy rearranging the dishes on the sideboard. She could only hope his ears were as much engaged elsewhere.

"And this gown," he continued, and his fingers trailed feather light down the side of her neck to the sleeves of her dress. "The color compliments your eyes beautifully. I do believe it is my favorite color on you thus far."

Imogen cleared her throat. "Thank you, my lord. It is my sister's maid, you see. My mother sent her along with me. It was very generous of her, but I am afraid Kate is much more used to attending to Mariah. I was not at all certain about the changes she has made, but she was quite insistent, and as she knows what she is talking about in regards to fashion and the like, I felt it was not prudent to argue with her. I am much more used to seeing to my own hair, you see. And this gown is not mine, but I do like the color as well." She knew she was babbling, but she could not seem to rein in her tongue.

"Caleb," he cut in softly.

Her eyes flew to his in confusion. "I'm sorry?"

"We agreed to use our given names," he reminded her.

She feared the slender bones in her hands would snap, the pressure of her fingers gripping each other was so great. "I think it best if we forgo that for now."

"Why?"

"It might give your family the impression that we have come to an…understanding." She flushed, eyeing her untouched plate.

He was silent for a time. "Would that be so very repugnant, Imogen?" he asked quietly.

There was no possible way to answer that truthfully without showing her feelings, so she remained silent.

"Now, let us see what Cook has to offer this morning," he went on in a cheerful voice that was completely at odds with his previous tone. "You are in for a treat. Cook's food is my very favorite thing about returning to Northamptonshire. She does have a habit of preparing all of my favorites when I am in residence. I believe that if I were to stay here for any length of time I would soon be as big as the house."

He grinned at her and then dove into the mound of food on his plate with gusto. Imogen watched him in disbelief for a time before reaching for a piece of toast from her own and biting into it absentmindedly.

Her father chose that moment to join them, a book tucked under his arm. "My lord, Imogen, a fine day isn't it?" he said happily.

He moved directly to the sideboard, filling a plate and seating himself across from them. The book came up and his head went down, and Imogen knew with wry amusement that a herd of elephants could have tromped through the room and her father would not have noticed. His presence, however, allowed her to relax a bit. There was something unnerving now about being alone with Caleb.

Which was a sad thing, really. For some of the most pleasant moments she had ever spent were times when she and Caleb had been alone, far from judgmental eyes. One night of intimacy had changed all that.

"Do you have a preference for your first day at Willowhaven?" Caleb asked, pulling her from her thoughts.

"I haven't a clue."

A decided gleam entered his pewter eyes. She was suddenly, achingly reminded of their days of adventuring.

"What do you say to a bit of exploring?"

"Exploring?"

He waved his hands about expansively. "This house is nearly three hundred years old. There has been an incredible amount of history in those centuries." He waggled his eyebrows. "Some of it quite unsavory, indeed."

Imogen felt a smile tug at her mouth and the stirrings of excitement in her blood. There was nothing she would like more than to delve into every nook and cranny of this amazing house. "That sounds wonderful."

The happiness that suffused his expression was blinding. Her pulse leaped, but she shook it off and turned to her father. "Papa," she said loudly.

He looked up, obviously reluctant to leave his book. "Yes, my dear?"

"Lord Willbridge is generous enough to bring me on a tour of the house this morning and tell me some of its history. Would you like to join us?"

Beside her she could hear Caleb give a soft growl of frustration. She hid a smile. Point one for her.

"That sounds magnificent!" her father exclaimed. "Why, I do believe there's a house of similar design not far from here. It belonged to Queen Elizabeth when she was quite young, and to King James after. I wonder, my lord, if…"

As her father expounded on historical details, comparing the two houses and questioning Caleb relentlessly, Imogen settled back in her seat and finished her food off with much more enthusiasm than before. So this was the secret to self-preservation in the coming weeks, was it? Now if she could only engage a third person on most of their outings and refrain from being in solitary company with Caleb, she just might come out of this with her sanity intact.

• • •

She could not, however, hope to keep her father's attention forever, despite the great draw a house such as Caleb's commanded.

As soon as they reached the last room and Caleb suggested a

walk in the gardens, her father excused himself and scurried off to the library once more. It was with much more reserve than she had shown throughout the pleasant morning that she took hold of Caleb's arm and allowed him to lead her out of doors.

The sun shone warmly on her as she stepped into the small sunken garden just off the house. A stone pool graced the center, and as they approached, a number of birds took flight, the flapping of their wings like a hush on the still air. A small, simple fountain stood at the center of the pool, water breaking over its top and trickling down with musical grace. Tall, manicured hedges surrounded three sides of the space, giving it a feel of privacy and otherworldliness. At the far end was a fanciful walkway built through the hedge itself.

Caleb silently guided her down one side of the garden, their boots crunching on the gravel path. It was a lovely moment, and though she knew it would pain her in the years to come, she memorized every bit of it, tucking it away to pore over later.

His voice broke through the magical silence, and yet only seemed to enhance it, the intimacy of his deep baritone shivering through her. "Do I dare hope that you like Willowhaven, Imogen?"

It was the first either of them had spoken aloud since they had parted from her father. She continued at his side, trying to formulate a reply to his question, something he seemed to ask with heartfelt curiosity. How could she even begin to vocalize how she felt about his home?

Because the truth was, she absolutely adored it. Every bit of decorative plasterwork, every tile, every inch of silky wood. Even the ridiculous stories he had told that morning about dissolute monarchs and noblemen, the strange histories that had taken place inside these walls; she held it all in her heart. She could see herself living here. She felt at home. And the thought of leaving this place, of leaving him forever, made her want to weep.

Finally, she could delay no longer. "It is wonderful here," she said with a small sigh.

They reached the opening in the hedge. Caleb stopped and

turned her to face him, gently taking hold of her arms. "Could you learn to love it, I wonder?"

She wanted to cry out that she already did, almost as much as she loved him. But she reined in her tongue and stepped to the side, effectively extricating herself from his loose grip.

"This avenue is lovely," she said firmly, waving her arms toward the oak trees that lined each side of the path stretching on ahead of them. Their heavy branches reached out over the walk to protect whoever should happen to stroll in their shade.

He came up beside her, not touching her, and yet she could feel the heat of him across the small space that separated them. His voice was casual, as if to put her at ease.

"Beyond this avenue is the River Spratt. Well, it is so narrow here that it resembles more of a brook, really, unless we get a torrential downpour. There is a stone bridge there as well as some truly beautiful willow trees that I would love to show you, if you're amenable?"

She nodded, placing her fingers on his offered arm. Just as they were about to pass through the hedge, however, a figure came around it, colliding with them and nearly toppling Imogen to the ground.

Chapter 20

Caleb steadied her. "Imogen, are you hurt?"

"No, not at all. No harm done," she said, waving him off. He had put his arm around her, and that along with the confusion from the impact was making her feel decidedly dizzy.

She looked up to see who had caused the commotion and was surprised to find Lady Emily standing before them. Her face was pale, her scar standing out in vivid relief on her cheek. Her eyes seemed puffy and slightly red-rimmed, as if she'd been crying. She had her shawl clasped about her shoulders with a white-knuckled grip. Within the cage of her fingers Imogen thought she caught sight of a snowy handkerchief.

"Lady Emily," Imogen exclaimed. "Are you well?"

She reached out a hand, but the girl recoiled. Her pale eyes, so like Caleb's, swiveled to him, regarding him with a strange sorrow.

"I'm fine, thank you," she muttered through stiff lips. She glanced briefly behind her. Caleb tensed as he followed her gaze, the same grief that had been etched on Lady Emily's face flashing across his own.

"I am so sorry for having bumped into you," the other girl managed. Not waiting for an answer, bobbing a quick curtsy, she pushed past them. Imogen watched her go in confusion until she disappeared from view into the house's interior.

Caleb's hand was on her arm in a moment and he was pulling her along without a word, through the hedge and along the gravel path toward the avenue of oaks.

Imogen looked up at him in surprise. Shouldn't there be some concern for his sister?

"We should go after her," she said. She tried to tug free of him, but his fingers only tightened.

"She is fine," he murmured. "Our presence would only cause her more distress."

Imogen stopped abruptly. "But surely we should find out what is wrong—"

"I know what is wrong," he broke in. As Imogen stared up at him in bewilderment, his face transformed, losing the tightness that had momentarily overtaken it. "Trust me, Imogen. This is nothing we can help with. If we go after her she will only grow more anxious. She needs time alone."

Now that was something Imogen could understand. Her own need for peace and quiet, away from even those she loved, caused her to be particularly sensitive to such needs in others. Finally, she gave him a quick nod, and he smiled, tucking her hand in the crook of his elbow, and continued on.

But Imogen was not easy. She longed to ask him what was going on here, what lay between him and his family to cause such tension. She had a sense, however, that he would close himself off completely if she questioned him in a direct manner.

They walked in silence for a time. The oaks on either side of them stood like silent sentries, their immense size showing them to be a century or more in age. The leaves above their heads rustled as if in a whisper as a slight breeze passed through the branches. Typically, she would have reveled in the quiet beauty. But there was a disquiet in her now. She racked her brain, and yet she could think of no way to scale the immense wall Caleb seemed to have put up about himself.

Finally, they reached the river. It gurgled merrily beneath a gracefully arched stone bridge. Willow trees dotted the grassy bank on either side, their long, trailing branches dancing in the breeze, brushing the water like the graceful fingers of a dancer. Caleb and Imogen walked to the bridge, stopping when they reached the middle. Taking the chance to release his arm and distance herself from him, she went to the stone railing, placing her palms flat on the sun-warmed surface and leaning over to watch the water rush by. Caleb came and stood near her, his lean hip resting casually against the railing.

"If I recall from previous conversations of ours," she ventured, "you have three siblings. Where is the third?"

"Andrew is between Emily and Daphne in age. He has just finished at University, like your brother Nathanial, and is staying with friends."

His voice was casual, disinterested. She took that as a good sign and plunged on. "Daphne is lovely, very vivacious. She reminds me of Mariah in many ways. Is your brother more like her, or is he quiet like Lady Emily?"

She held her breath to test his reaction. There was a slight pause, barely noticeable, before he answered. "He is definitely more like Daphne. I expect I'll be getting a request for a commission soon from him. I cannot see him in the clergy, leading a flock with his upright behavior." There was a hint of wistfulness in his voice.

"Lady Emily seems very different in personality from the rest of your family."

She glanced up at him as she spoke. Was that pain she saw in his eyes? He turned his head to look out over the water, however, hiding the emotion from her view.

"No," he finally said, quietly, "she's quite different from us all."

"However did she get such a scar? It must have been exceedingly painful for her."

His jaw worked for a moment. "You recall me telling you of my brother, Jonathan? The one who died young?" His voice was so low she had to strain to hear him.

"Yes."

He took a slow, deep breath. "She got that scar in the same accident that killed him. There was an outcropping of rocks, close to the fishing pond. They were at the top when it gave way. They were twelve at the time."

"Oh, how horrible for her," she exclaimed. "It must have been a violent fall indeed to have caused such an injury." She frowned. "I had no idea Lady Emily and Jonathan were twins."

"Yes. They were very close, did everything together. She was forever trailing about after him…" His voice faltered.

Imogen could think of nothing to say. She watched the play of emotions over his face. It was obvious he still felt deeply about it. And Emily too must relive it daily whenever she looked in the mirror.

Perhaps this was the reason for the tension and estrangement between them all? Though surely not. How could the accidental death of a twelve-year-old boy cause this horrible distance between family members a decade after it happened?

"Perhaps," she attempted, "you would show me his portrait some time."

He finally looked at her, and she saw the shutters go up behind his eyes. Perhaps she had pushed too hard.

He smiled, but it was hollow somehow.

"Now, why would we wish to visit such memories when I have but two weeks to convince you to marry me?" He pushed away from the railing and offered his arm. Imogen took it, strangely sad that the town mask was back. What was this hidden part of him that he refused to show to the world? And why couldn't she seem to let go of the need to find it out?

• • •

The following morning Imogen managed to make it down to breakfast at an even earlier hour, hoping to avoid Caleb. As she was rising to leave, however, he entered.

He took her hand and pulled her off to the side of the room. "Come riding with me today, Imogen."

She tried to pull her hand from his grip, but he only tightened it. She gave a small huff of frustration. The night before she had done all in her power to engage Lady Willbridge and Daphne into conversation, all but ignoring Caleb's attempts at drawing her focus to him. Apparently, however, her efforts had been all too obvious. And they had not deterred him at all.

She gave up trying to free herself and glared up at him. "Let go of my hand."

He grinned unrepentantly. "No." He tried tugging her closer. Her gaze shot meaningfully to the footman in the corner, who was attempting to ignore them. Caleb's grin only widened. He leaned toward her, his face near her ear, and let his breath fan the curls on the side of her neck. "Have I told you today that your sister's maid is a wonder with hair?" he asked in a low rumble that she felt straight to her toes. "And this pale green gown is even lovelier than the blue." With his free hand he idly traced up her arm to the tiny cap sleeves.

Imogen glowered at him and slapped his hand away.

He chuckled low. "Come ride with me, Imogen."

"Fine," she snapped, finally pulling herself free.

"You know, I don't remember you being quite so difficult to manage."

"Keep pushing me and you shall see just how difficult I can be," she muttered.

Caleb laughed, clearly not put off at all. Dare she say he even looked delighted?

Just then Daphne entered. She caught sight of them, standing much closer than what was proper, and a grin, a mirror of Caleb's own, spread across her face. "Brother, Imogen," she said, fairly bouncing across the room to the sideboard. "Good morning to you both."

Imogen had a sudden inspiration. "Lady Daphne," she called to the girl. "Your brother has asked me to go riding with him this morning. Would you like to join us? I would love to have the chance to get to know you better, and what more perfect way than a brisk ride through the parklands?"

"Oh, what fun!" the girl exclaimed. "Just let me eat and I shall join you directly."

As Daphne went back to filling her plate, Imogen turned to Caleb with a serene smile. "Wonderful. I shall go up and change after I seek out my father."

She bobbed a quick curtsy to Caleb before walking off. And then it was her turn to grin, for the thunderous frustration on his face had been a sight to behold indeed.

• • •

Imogen easily kept her mare in pace with Daphne's. As they crested a hill and paused to take in the view, Caleb once more tried inserting his gelding between the two girls' mounts. With a beautiful bit of synchronization, however, Imogen and Daphne were able to put a stop to his endeavors.

It had been like that all morning. Daphne, bright girl that she was, had quickly understood Imogen's invitation and had gone about helping her with an impish delight. And so, despite his best efforts, Caleb had been unable to get Imogen alone.

It was actually a bit fun, though she felt a faint qualm every time she caught sight of the frustration on Caleb's face. But truly, did he think to get her alone and seduce her into accepting him? If the expression in his eyes whenever he looked at her was any indication, she was tempted to believe that was true. Never mind that the idea made shivers dance up her spine.

She told herself that his passion would fade and the thrill of chasing her would disappear. And then where would she be? Worse off than before.

"I believe it is time to return to the house," Caleb called out as they nudged their horses off to admire the fields laid out before them, separated by low stone walls and resembling a large patchwork quilt. "Luncheon will be ready by the time we arrive."

Imogen glanced at him. He looked perturbed, his voice harsh. She felt a pang of guilt but quickly abolished it. It was his own fault, after all.

They turned their horses toward Willowhaven, and a short

time later cantered into the stable yard. As they handed over their horses, the head groom approached.

"Lady Daphne," he said, "Lady Willbridge said to tell you when you returned that she needs you to join her in her sitting room directly."

"Oh dear, I wonder what Mother wants," she muttered. "Thank you, Joseph." She turned to Imogen, giving her an apologetic smile. And then she was off.

Imogen watched her depart in frustration. Suddenly Caleb was at her side.

"Shall we?" he murmured, indicating the path before them that trailed toward the west side of the house. His expression, she noted in consternation, was downright cheerful.

Without bothering to acknowledge him, she swept down the path, leaving him to trail after her. She kept her pace brisk, hoping she could reach a populated area before he had a chance to catch up to her. She was to find, however, that he was a much more determined man than she gave him credit for.

Chapter 21

Imogen was proving incredibly slippery in regards to this courting business. Caleb still could not understand why she was refusing him. But he had come to the conclusion that he might never understand it. The female mind was an incomprehensible thing. But it *was* changeable. And that was just what he would concentrate on.

He was not a rake for nothing. For though a woman's reasoning was well beyond him, a woman's body was another matter entirely. And if you played the body just right, the mind quite often followed. He saw the way her eyes softened when he touched her or whispered something inappropriate in her ear. He could see the way she shivered when his breath fanned her cheek, or the tiny flame in her eyes that she tried to douse when he came close to her. All Imogen needed was a bit of persuasion.

Right now she was hurtling ahead of him as if the hounds of hell were at her heels. A few long strides on his part, however, and he was beside her. And as they rounded the house and were fully out of view of the stables, Caleb took his chance, the only chance he knew he was to have for some time if she continued to expertly avoid him.

His arm stole about her waist and he pulled her past a row of tall topiaries leading into the knot garden. She didn't have time to do more than gasp before he claimed her mouth, devouring her like a starving man at a feast, his tongue delving into her mouth. He pulled her tightly against him and felt the soft curves of her give to the hardness of his body. Moving one hand to the back of her head, he held her captive to his onslaught. His frantic fingers dislodged her small riding hat, knocking it to the ground amidst the lavender and sage and rosemary.

She felt like heaven in his arms. Her scent enveloped him, that wonderful, clean, innocent scent of soap and citrus and her own sweet musk. There was a fullness to her that made him want to drag her to the ground and sink himself into her and never emerge. If he did not get her to marry him, and soon, he felt he would go mad with wanting her.

Imogen trembled in his embrace, her fingers digging into his riding jacket. Her body arched into his, her mouth moving beneath his own. She did not try to break his hold on her. And yet he could sense her hesitation, as if she were waging some violent internal battle. She stilled and began to pull away. Desperate not to lose the ground he had gained, he pulled her deeper into the garden, the smell of lavender wafting to him as he trampled a small bush with his boots. One of his hands moved to her riding jacket, flicking the buttons open with practiced fingers. And then his hand was at her breast, its heaviness filling his palm. He rubbed his thumb over her nipple, felt her shudder as it puckered under his touch through the linen of her blouse.

She groaned softly, going pliant in his arms and bowing into his touch. He felt a wild thrill at her reaction. Yet it was not enough; he desperately needed even more from her. Tearing his mouth from hers, he bent over her, his lips finding her breast. His tongue laved her through the thin linen and she cried out softly, her fingers digging into his hair and holding him to her.

"You make me wild for you, Imogen," he rasped.

A moment later he knew he had erred. She turned rigid, and before he could renew his efforts, she tore from his arms. Giving a small sob, she gripped the jacket closed over her chest and raced back for the house, her hair trailing loose behind her.

Breathing hard, his body a tightly coiled mass of desire, Caleb could only watch her go. Damn it, he had pushed her too hard. It had been such a heady thing, to have her back in his arms, that he had quite forgotten the slow seduction he had planned.

Cursing violently, furious with himself, he stalked back to the house. Perhaps if he wanted her less it would be easier. But he desired her with an intensity that left him as eager and impatient as a boy.

She had gone from a mildly pretty friend to quite the most desirable woman he had ever encountered in the space of weeks. How had it come to pass that he could not get her from his mind, that he thought of her day and night, that his body turned hard just remembering the feel of her soft skin?

He had been with scores of women, all of them seductive and stunning, knowledgeable in giving pleasure as well as receiving it. Each of those affairs had been a partnership in sensuality, gone into for the physicality and never with any intention of emotional entanglement. He had never made any promises and had wanted none in return. They were usually over with quickly, it being understood that a swift exit from the affair was essential for it to begin in the first place.

But with Imogen he had not wanted that kind of cold arrangement. Her innocence made him desire her all the more. He wanted her as he had wanted no other. Was this desperate burning because he was her first and only lover? Or was it simply because she was the first woman he had desired who had refused him?

Whatever it was about her that had him so enthralled, however, he knew well that passions faded eventually. Caleb had been witness to that more times than he cared to count, as wild lust for past lovers simmered down to nothing. This thing with Imogen was bound to abate eventually, as strong as it was now. He wondered for a moment why he was so determined to change her mind on marriage, knowing that harsh fact.

Yes, he had ruined her, and no gentleman took a woman's innocence and didn't offer marriage, but it was more than that. The truth was, he cared for her. Never had he thought he would marry a woman he respected and liked. Romantic love, of course, was completely out. All that nonsense that turned men and women into emotional idiots. But to have a wife he wouldn't mind seeing over the newspaper in the morning, a wife who made him laugh and smile—not to mention one who made his body burn, for however short a time he was blessed with that passion—was a boon indeed. He had believed his future marriage was to be one of polite disinterest at best. Now that he had caught a glimpse of the happiness life with Imogen would bring, however, he would not settle for less.

But if her reaction to him, that mad flight back to the house, was any indication, he had not set out on an easy task. He shook his head, frustrated, his body still taut with need. It seemed he was in for a long wait for her to come around. But he would need to learn patience if he was to make her his.

• • •

"Imogen, here is your cup, dear."

Imogen accepted the tea. "Thank you, Lady Willbridge." She sipped her beverage, trying to concentrate on the women before her and not on the brooding sentinel across the room. Caleb watched her with a silent intensity at all times now, though he never did more than offer her his arm to go into meals and such. She was grateful for the respite from his advances, but she found she also felt a certain loss as well.

It had been three days since Caleb had kissed her in the knot garden. No acknowledgement of the scene, or her subsequent escape from it, had been made by him, save for several sprigs of lavender tied with a pale green satin ribbon that had been left on her pillow later that night. At the scent she had been vividly reminded of their kiss, when his hands had roved her body and his lips had plundered her own. It made a longing for a renewal of the scene curl in her belly. She had wanted to toss the small bundle straight out the window. But at the last moment she had gripped it tight, instead hiding it away in the depths of her trunk.

No more was he attempting to get her alone. The invitations to go riding or walking were always accompanied with a twin invitation to another member of the household. Daphne, who was only too eager to be included, went along on most excursions, providing a vivacious centerpiece to each event. Imogen found more and more to like about the girl every day. She wished Mariah were here, for she was certain she and Daphne would become fast friends.

She had also come to respect and admire the marchioness in those three days. She was all that was gracious and kind and seemed so happy to have her son in the room with her, even if it was only due to Imogen's presence.

Lady Emily was still distant, often hiding off in a corner to embroider or locking herself in the music room for hours at a time, from which the most lovely, if mournful, songs issued. Imogen would have been happy to let her go her own way, unpleasant as she was. But the sight of the girl's face that first morning, white and tense, her eyes puffy from tears, would not erase itself from Imogen's mind. She wished there was some way to get through to her. But, alas, it seemed the girl was determined to stay as far from Imogen as possible.

The idea that Jonathan's death had been the cause for the strain in this family had whispered to her again and again in the past days. The more she watched the tense manner in which Caleb dealt with his family—and most especially the mutual avoidance between Caleb and Lady Emily—she couldn't help the encroaching thought that her conclusion was correct.

Just then Lady Willbridge spoke, pulling Imogen from her maudlin thoughts. "And how did you enjoy your time boating this afternoon, Imogen?"

Imogen flushed and adjusted her spectacles. She had a fair idea from Daphne's amused glance that the marchioness was repeating herself. Lady Willbridge, however, showed no signs of exasperation. A small, kind smile curved her lips.

"I enjoyed it very well, my lady," Imogen said, her embarrassment easing under the woman's mild gaze. "Your son is a fine rower. We did not tip over even once."

"It was not from lack of trying, I assure you," Daphne said, laughing.

"Oh, I can well imagine the mischief you brought about," her mother admonished with fondness. She turned to Imogen, her eyes fairly dancing with humor. "My younger son Andrew is indulgent with Daphne and often brings her out on the river. There have been several occasions when they have come back to the house dripping wet, due to my daughter's propensity for not sitting still in a boat."

Imogen joined Lady Willbridge in her laughter. She could well imagine the picture the woman had painted. Daphne had been full of boundless energy during their trip, and more than once Caleb had been forced to haul her back into her seat for fear of her tipping them all over into the River Spratt.

"You should come out with us sometime, Mama," Daphne said.

The marchioness held up her hands. "As I've told you many times before, no thank you. I leave such adventures to the more stout-hearted of you. For anyone who heads into open waters with you on board is either very foolish or very brave. As I am certainly neither, and Caleb and Imogen fall into the latter category, I leave them to it, with a grateful heart."

Mother and daughter shared a chuckle. Imogen smiled, her heart warming at their banter, though underlying it was the smallest twinge as she thought of her relationship with her own mother.

Just then Billsby arrived. To Imogen's surprise he approached her, holding out a silver salver. "These have arrived for you, Miss Duncan."

Imogen took the letters, giving a quick gasp of delight when she saw the returns.

Daphne was at her side in an instant. "Who has written, Imogen?"

Imogen smiled, fingering the envelopes. "My sisters, Frances and Mariah."

Daphne bounced on the balls of her feet in her excitement. "Your sister in London, and Lady Sumner? Oh, read them, please do!"

"Daphne," her mother admonished. "We should let Imogen read her correspondence in peace."

"Actually," Imogen said with a wry smile, "I find I cannot wait to return to my room. Would you mind terribly if I read them now? And I did promise to share any details of London with Daphne."

Lady Willbridge smiled. "Of course. Please feel free to use my desk."

Imogen hurried to the small white escritoire in the corner. Sitting down, she quickly opened the first letter, her gaze skimming the short missive eagerly.

"What news, Imogen?" Daphne called out.

"My sister Frances and her husband have just returned early from a trip to his property in Rutland. She is asking us to visit." She turned to Lady Willbridge. "Could my father and I take a carriage to call on her tomorrow afternoon? We see each other rarely now that she has married."

"Certainly, my dear. What a wonderful bit of chance that they should arrive while you are in the area."

Imogen could barely contain her excitement. To see Frances, to garner some strength from her, was a chance she could not ignore.

Daphne spoke up. "Perhaps we can make a party of it. I would love to see your sister."

"Yes, it has been some time since we visited with her," Lady Willbridge mused. "I do hope it is not an imposition, but do you think your sister would mind if we joined you, Imogen?"

"Not at all. Frances would love it, I'm certain."

As Lady Willbridge and Daphne discussed the trip, Caleb moved closer.

"Shall I accompany you?" he asked quietly.

Imogen regarded him. To have Frances meet Caleb, to have the chance to get her sister's impressions regarding him, would be valuable indeed.

"Certainly, my lord," she murmured. His eyes, to her surprise, flared with relief before he bowed and moved away. Had he feared she would deny him?

She broke the seal on the second letter, giving it a quick read before going back to the beginning to pore over her sister's words more slowly.

Daphne was at her elbow the moment she lowered the paper to the desk. "And what news from London?"

Imogen laughed. "My sister Mariah has attended four balls since we have been here, and received an invitation to Lady Seymour's afternoon gala for next week. She also talks a great deal about a dance that is taking the ballrooms by storm, one called the Andrew Carey."

"I don't believe I have heard of that one."

"It was new around the time of my come out. But now it seems to be having a resurgence in popularity. I've witnessed it done, but have not done it myself."

Daphne's eyes lit with what Imogen was beginning to recognize as mischievous purpose. "Would you teach me? If I am to be in London next Season, I wish to know all of the most popular dances ahead of time."

"Certainly," Imogen said with warmth.

"But surely we cannot learn the dance without a proper amount of couples." Daphne looked to her mother. "We should invite the Sanderses, and cousin Mottram and his family as well. And Lord and Lady Sumner, of course."

Lady Willbridge lowered her teacup. "What exactly are you hatching in that mind of yours, Daphne?" she asked with amusement.

"Nothing extravagant. Perhaps a small dinner party and casual dancing after."

Caleb spoke up from across the room. "Absolutely not. Imogen does not like crowds or strangers."

Daphne stuck her chin out mulishly. "They are not strangers. Besides Imogen's own sister, half coming would be related to us and the other half would be Vicar Sanders and his family. Hardly the scum of the earth. Even if they all accept, we shall have only seventeen people, surely nothing grandiose or objectionable."

Imogen fought the urge to laugh at the sarcasm dripping from her voice. Caleb, on the other hand, only grew angrier. "Most of them are not known to Imogen, and thus strangers to her. I will not allow it."

At once Imogen felt a frisson of ire travel down her spine. "On the contrary, my lord, I have no objections whatsoever. It sounds like a lovely evening."

Daphne beamed. "There, you see? Imogen has no objections, and so it behooves you to agree." She turned to her mother. "I shall send invitations out directly. If I warn Cook now of the extra guests for dinner, we can have them here as early as tomorrow evening!"

The girl bounded up and out of the room with her typical energy. Imogen stared after her with a small smile. That is, until she realized what she had agreed to. Daphne wanted her to teach the dance steps to everyone present. She would be getting up in front of strangers and instructing them. A queer sickness settled in her stomach.

She was just about to run after Daphne, to tell her to forget the entire thing, when she happened to glance over at Caleb. He was staring at her again, but with a hint of wry admiration in his eyes. Pressing her lips together, she settled back into her seat. She could no more lose face in front of him after that display than she could waltz at Almack's in nothing but her shift. She would grin and bear it…even if it killed her.

• • •

"Imogen! I am so glad you have come, dearest."

Frances embraced her, and Imogen found herself holding on a bit longer than necessary. The turmoil of the past days seemed to still. Here was reason. Here was why she had fought so hard against Caleb's pull.

As Frances greeted their father, followed by Caleb and his family, Imogen greeted her sister's husband. "Lord Sumner, thank you for having us."

Frances's husband smiled benignly at her. "Not at all. We are family, after all."

Imogen kept her placid expression from slipping, but inwardly she rolled her eyes. He hardly ever showed himself during the visits her family made to his homes, and never deigned to visit his wife's relations at all.

She knew what made the difference now, however. She watched as he moved toward Caleb. The earl's fawning smile and over-eager attitude told her all. The man was highly ambitious. To have someone with the status of the Marquess of Willbridge visit his home was a coup, indeed.

But enough. It was not him she had come to see, after all.

"Won't you all have a seat?" Frances said, motioning to a circle of highly fashionable, highly uncomfortable seats. No doubt Lord Sumner's choice. The man made certain every aspect of his residences, from the wall coverings to the silverware—even to his wife—showcased his status in the very best light.

"I must thank you for allowing us to accompany Imogen and Lord Tarryton on their visit," Lady Willbridge said to Frances. "It is most kind of you. I do hope we are not encroaching on your private family time."

"Not in the least, my lady," Frances said.

"No, indeed," her husband chimed in. "We are happy to have you. Please know that your family is always welcome here." He glanced from Caleb to Imogen. She could practically hear him wondering what this peculiar visit by his sister-in-law meant in the grand scheme of things. And how he could benefit from it.

Lady Willbridge nodded politely to Lord Sumner, her expression serene, before she returned her attention to his wife. "It has been such a pleasure having your father and sister visit with us. It was so generous of your mother to spare them while the Season is in full swing. She must have her hands full with your younger sister's schedule."

"Oh, have no fear on that score," Frances replied. "Our mother would put any military general to shame. She quite delights in that sort of thing."

Not a person present could fail to hear the hint of coldness in Frances's words. Imogen ached for her sister. Frances, she knew, had never forgiven their mother for her ruthless maneuverings during her own Season.

Lady Willbridge spoke up, breaking the uncomfortable silence that had settled like a pall on the group. "Daphne comes out next year, and I am quaking in my shoes at the mere thought. It has been many a year since I have been to London. My husband was not fond of city life. To be truthful, I'm not that keen on it myself. And you, Lady Sumner? Do you enjoy time in town?"

The distraction worked, for immediately talk turned to safer subjects. Imogen could only be grateful for it, and though she had gained a deep respect for Caleb's mother, she now found her heart swelling with affection as well.

Tea and a light repast came then, and when everyone had their fill, Frances suggested a walk in the gardens. The group set out, Imogen making sure she hung back in order to be paired off with her sister. They linked arms and followed slowly after the rest. The sun was warm on their backs, the air smelling heavily of roses and rich earth.

Imogen watched as the others pulled ahead a bit before speaking. "You are well, Frances?"

"Very well."

And, to Imogen's surprise, Frances did look well. There was a bit more weight on her and a certain fresh blush to her cheeks. Could it be that things were improving for her sister and her husband?

"I am glad you are here," Frances continued, squeezing Imogen's arm and smiling at her. "What a treat this is."

"I am sad you won't be able to make it to Lady Willbridge's dinner party this evening. Can you truly not change your plans?"

Frances gave a small sigh. "I'm afraid not. James has been trying to convince Lord Finch for ages to sell his property to him. It rests against the west fields, and would double the grazing area for our cattle. He has a very limited time in which to meet with the man. It was the reason we returned from Rutland in such haste. No, James will not change his plans, even for a marquess." She turned to Imogen with a speculative look. "Speaking of which, what was Lord Willbridge's reason for inviting you and Father to his home? It does seem peculiar."

Imogen blushed but couldn't find the words.

"He is devilishly handsome, Imogen," Frances went on, a slight smile lifting her lips. "Of course, you are looking much improved yourself. That dress is lovely on you. And your hair. I cannot believe the difference it has made."

Imogen could feel her face grow hotter. "It was not of my doing, I assure you."

"It is nothing to be overwrought about." Frances patted her arm comfortingly. "Though I do wonder at the change, especially as I see you are now allowed to wear your spectacles in public. What was that battle like, I wonder."

Imogen gave a wry smile. "Not pleasant."

"And now to have captured the attentions of the Marquess of Willbridge? Does he mean to court you?"

Again Imogen could not speak. She knew her sister would take her reticence for the answer it was.

They walked on in silence for a time, and Imogen allowed her gaze to rest on Caleb. Daphne's arm was tucked into his, and he responded to something that Lord Sumner was saying. He looked toward her then, gave her a small smile. Her body reacted immediately, her draw to him unmistakable. Yes, he was handsome. Quite the handsomest man Imogen had ever seen. But there was so much more to him than that. There was kindness, and gentleness, and a deep hurt that she wished with all her might she could mend. What, she wondered, did Frances see?

As if reading her mind, Frances spoke. "He seems a good man, Imogen."

"He is," she murmured.

"You care for him." It was not a question. And again, silence was the only answer Imogen could give. She had acknowledged it in her heart. If she said it aloud, it might be her undoing.

"Take care, dearest," her sister whispered.

The rest of the party joined them then, and there was no more chance for talk. But Imogen observed. And what she saw surprised her.

Here was Lord Sumner, actually showing care for Frances. She had noticed it earlier in the drawing room, but now it was more pronounced. He made certain his wife rested, that she not over-exert herself, that she was shaded from the hot afternoon sun. Frances for her part seemed happy with the change.

Something uncurled in Imogen's chest. If things could alter for the better in Frances's marriage, wasn't it possible for a relationship to work between Caleb and herself?

A short time later she made her farewells of her sister and her husband. She placed her fingers in Caleb's to allow him to hand her up into the carriage for the journey home. As the now familiar electric shock from his touch sizzled through her, she vowed not to make her decision too quickly. But the surge of hope in her chest told her exactly what her heart's say in the matter was.

Chapter 22

Imogen stood up before the assembled couples and swallowed hard. This was proving even more difficult than she had imagined.

The evening had progressed surprisingly well—as long as she hadn't allowed herself to think of what was expected of her after supper. There had been a wonderfully casual feel to the party from the start. The good Reverend Elijah Sanders and family had arrived first, as his vicarage was just a short walk from the manor house. He was a jolly, rotund gentleman with an equally jolly, rotund wife. They had two daughters, the Misses Rebecca and Hannah Sanders, both of whom were sweet, bright girls, as well as a younger son, Gabriel, who it seemed would be following in his father's pious footsteps. The reverend and his family did not fawn over Lady Willbridge, as so many vicars with wealthy patrons did. Instead they had a comfortable way of talking with the marchioness that showed years of true friendship.

Sir Alexander Mottram and his family also seemed quite close to those at Willowhaven, related to Lady Willbridge on her mother's side. The two families lived but an hour from each other, and from the conversation that circled around the table it seemed they got together often. Sir Alexander and his wife had two sons, tall and witty Mr. Daniel Mottram, who was not long out of University, and Mr. Christopher Mottram, a younger son who was vocal in his desire to buy his commission and join the Horse Guards.

Imogen liked them all immensely. They were neither unfriendly nor pompous, but instead had a wonderful openness that allowed her to relax and converse with surprising ease.

Dinner had gone splendidly. Never had she been surrounded by so much gaiety at a meal before. Everyone laughed and joked, with none of the separation of status that was so apparent in London. Even when they had invited local families to dine with them at Hillview Manor, there had been a pronounced hierarchy. Imogen found that, though meeting new people and conversing in large groups was something she avoided at all costs, she could not help but enjoy herself.

She was achingly aware that Caleb watched her closely throughout the night. He knew her feelings on socializing. And with the informal seating, he made certain to sit by her side at supper. Imogen tried to feel annoyed at his hovering, but found she was oddly touched at his sensitivity to her preferences.

Trying to banish the small hitch in her breathing every time his gaze landed on her, she ignored him as best she could. Mr. Daniel Mottram was seated on her right, and was engaging as well as funny. But she was drawn again and again to Caleb at her left. He'd brought forth his town persona for tonight. But it did not feel forced, as it sometimes did, and as it had ever since they had arrived at Willowhaven. He charmed everyone in the room; seemed to genuinely like them all; and it was clear that the two visiting families held him in the highest esteem.

When the time came to retire to the formal drawing room for dancing, however, Imogen found herself nearly paralyzed with fear. She had succeeded in putting the coming event from her mind, but now that it was here she was overwhelmed with anxiety. The gentlemen had eschewed staying at the table and imbibing in the traditional after-dinner drink, instead joining the ladies as they exited. Imogen watched them all go, unable to follow for fear her suddenly trembling legs would give out.

Caleb was at her side in an instant, reaching for her cold hand. He secured her arm through his own, and she felt a modicum of sanity return. She could not lose face now, not when she had purposely crossed him in the matter of this party.

He leaned down close to her ear. "Are you certain, Imogen?"

"Of course."

He raised one copper eyebrow before leading her forward.

And now here they were, collected before her. All the young people, with the exception of Lady Emily, who had stationed herself at the pianoforte, were standing about. Daphne had paired everyone off in her energetic fashion and directed their eyes to Imogen at the top of the room.

Caleb had not left her side. She glanced up at him, taking a measure of strength from his calm demeanor. Imogen cleared her throat nervously and adjusted her spectacles. Perhaps if she could imagine she was helping her younger siblings out, as she had so often done back at home.

With that in mind, she plowed on, her voice faint at first but growing in strength as she talked. "The Andrew Carey is done with a fleuret step, with three equal steps and a plié, and then repeated. You'll be gliding, not skipping. We'll do it with four beats, as it is easier to follow."

She began to hum the tune, surprised and relieved as Caleb's baritone joined hers. She gave him a grateful smile, which he returned with an encouraging one of his own, and they started to move. She slowed in certain sections, explaining the other couples' parts in the movements. When they had got through the dance, the others began talking excitedly.

"Let's give it a go, shall we?" Daphne said over the din. She grabbed her cousin Christopher's hand, shoving him into the proper position across from her. The others followed until they were in a line down the center of the room.

Imogen was prepared to hum again when the sound of the pianoforte started up, copying the melody she and Caleb had been singing perfectly. She looked over to the corner and saw Lady Emily at the keys. Imogen smiled broadly at the other girl, and was heartened when she received a tentative one in return.

She turned back to the assembled dancers. She and Caleb began to move into the steps, the others following their lead. She gave instructions as they went, telling each couple how to weave about the other when it was their turn. There was much stumbling at first, with giggles and raucous laughter all around. Toward the end it seemed everyone had begun to catch on to the steps. They attempted the dance once again, this time with much more grace and success.

When the music came to a stop, everyone broke into enthusiastic applause. Imogen felt flushed and mussed, and yet when she looked up into Caleb's laughing, admiring eyes, she felt a burst of true happiness.

Daphne took the lead then, much to Imogen's relief. She chose several more dances, of which the party was more than eager to perform. Everyone paired off in a casual manner, exchanging partners with a relaxing ease. First Imogen was pulled into a cotillion with Mr. Daniel Mottram, followed by a quadrille with the very young but very charming Mr. Gabriel Sanders. Mr. Christopher Mottram, with his laughing blue eyes, was next to claim her for a stately minuet. The elder members of the party were unable to keep away when a good, energetic Scottish reel was brought forth.

Imogen laughed along with the rest of the young people. Seeing her father paired off with jolly Mrs. Sanders, his legs cutting through the air as he moved in a way she had never seen before, was a sight indeed, and by the time the older people dropped with inelegant gaiety back into their seats and the younger partygoers took control of the floor again, she felt she had never been part of such a wonderful night in her life. Erased were the memories of the London balls she had attended, sitting at the edge of the room and watching the elegance of the attendees as they paraded before her. In its place was this, an evening of fun as she had never known, with people who did not treat her as if she were a pariah, but welcomed her.

Laughing, she turned to claim her next partner in the revelries. The laughter died on her lips, however, when her nose nearly collided with a starched white cravat. She needn't look up to know who it belonged to. Only one man in the party was as tall as he, only one with shoulders so wide or dress so elegant.

But look up she did. The expression in Caleb's pewter eyes almost undid her. There was a softness there, an admiration that was altogether new. He looked as if he'd never seen her before now.

He held out his hand, and wordlessly Imogen took it, unable to tear her gaze from his. It was only after she gripped tightly to his fingers that she realized Lady Emily had changed the tone of the music. A gentle melody poured forth from the keys, and too late, she found herself pulled into Caleb's arms as a waltz played.

Only once had she danced the waltz with Caleb, the night he had pulled her off to his room and made love to her. It came back to her now in a rush. Her skin was suddenly feverish and sensitive. His hand at her back burned through the thin gown, the fingers of his other hand wrapped possessively around her own. Kate had outdone herself with this evening's dress choice, for the bodice of Imogen's gown had been altered lower than anything she had ever worn. The tops of her breasts were pushed up over the cream-colored silk of the dress, and the evening air along with the feel of the sleek material on her skin were making her feel decidedly inflamed.

But affecting her more than the daring dress, more than her memories of their one night together, was Caleb in the flesh before her. His eyes were on her now, the heat in them unmistakable. And, God help her, she could no more look away from them than stop breathing.

He didn't speak. He didn't need to; his expression said everything. He wanted her. She felt herself swaying closer as he swung her about and around the others. His hand pressed into the small of her back, drawing her a fraction closer than was proper. Her breathing sped up as his gaze fastened on her mouth. She tilted her head up a bit more, swept along in the music and him, forgetting that they were surrounded by others.

"Imogen," he whispered.

The music stopped then, the couples around them breaking apart and applauding. A second too late, Imogen realized just where she was. She quickly tore free from Caleb's arms, backing up a good distance and applauding with the others. She had been lost in him, and in a room full of people. Her face was hot as she glanced surreptitiously about, wondering if anyone had seen. Everyone was busy conversing. All but Lady Emily, who looked at her with a strange curiosity before turning quickly away.

The party broke up soon after, Sir Alexander declaring he felt in his bones they were due for a storm and that he wanted to make the trip back home before it broke. Imogen stood with Caleb and his family as the guests departed, waving her goodbyes along with the rest.

With a vividness that took the very breath from her body, she pictured herself standing here in years to come at Caleb's side. And she found she wanted it. With every fiber of her being, she wanted it. Without meaning to, she let out a sharp breath.

"Imogen, what is it?"

She looked up, dazed, into Caleb's face. He cared for her; there was no doubt as to that. Did it really matter that he did not love her as she loved him? Couldn't they somehow make things work, despite the difference in their feelings?

She needed time and space to think. Her emotions were in turmoil when he was near. Though her entire body strained toward his, she forced herself to take a step back.

But she needn't make a decision this moment. She had until the end of her trip. That was plenty of time to think on all the frightening, wonderful possibilities that loomed before her.

"Goodnight, my lord," she said, her voice sounding far off and dreamy to her own ears. Bobbing a quick curtsy, she turned and fled to the safety of her room.

• • •

Imogen was roused abruptly. She lay utterly still, uncertain why she was suddenly so very awake. Her eyes took in the unfocused darkness of the room before she turned her head in the direction of the window. She had left the curtains parted when she had retired for the night; though Sir Alexander had declared a storm had been brewing, the sky had been beautifully clear, with the moon plump and bright in the sky, illuminating her room in a soft silver.

Now, however, it was black as pitch, nary a bit of light breaking through the veil of night that seemed to have fallen over her eyes. The air had an electric anticipation to it, and she found herself clutching the blankets to her chin.

Then, suddenly, the whole of the room was illuminated in a bright flash. Light burst in, sending the shadows running, leeching everything of color. And then it was gone as fast as it had come. Imogen began to count as she used to as a child, slowly and softly. When she reached ten, a low rumble started, shaking the very windows in their frames, rolling on and on.

Now she sighed softly and sat up in bed, reaching over to light a taper. There would be no sleep for her until the storm had passed, so she might as well make the most of her time. She reached for the well-worn copy of *The Romance of the Forest* from the library and began to read. It was quiet for a time, the gentle fall of rain starting up against the glass panes of her window, providing the perfect backdrop for dark forests and ruined abbeys. And then another flash, followed more quickly this time by a sharp clap of thunder. The storm was moving closer and would be directly over their heads shortly.

A peculiar shuffling in the hall caught her attention just before a rumble boomed with enough force that it seemed to shake the very foundation of the house. She looked up quickly as a faint cry followed by a muffled thump reached her. As silence settled once more, Imogen heard the shuffling again, what she could now determine as the muted sound of footsteps passing directly outside her door.

Someone was out there, perhaps in some distress. Imogen put the book aside and threw off her covers, quickly lighting a candle and throwing on her spectacles and robe. She had seen firsthand the terror such a storm could invoke in a person, her young brother Bingham being deathly afraid of them. If there was any way to help someone through this, she would try.

She opened the door and looked down the hall. At the very end was a golden shimmer of light that bounced on the walls and grew fainter. Someone had just turned the corner. Imogen hurried forward on bare feet, the rug that covered the floorboards helping to dull the sound. She rounded the corner and peered into the open door that she remembered led into the Long Gallery.

Down at the far end was a silent figure in white. Dark hair trailed in a long plait down her back. The candle the woman held before her flickered over the walls, casting a feeble light on one painting in particular. She stood before it with a stillness that sent a chill up Imogen's spine.

It was a scene straight out of a gothic novel, she thought as another burst of lightning bathed the room in its harsh, brilliant illumination. It was followed immediately by a violent crack. The figure at the other end of the gallery jumped, the light from her candle careening across the walls.

Imogen shook herself. The woman in the gallery was obviously of flesh and blood, no specter come to haunt her former home. She had been reading too much of Mrs. Radcliffe's novel. There was no reason to be afraid.

Squaring her shoulders, she slowly moved into the room.

Chapter 23

At Imogen's approach, the silent figure tensed and whirled about. Her white night robe billowed out, her heavy braid swinging in an arc. The flame from her candle nearly guttered at the movement but struggled back to life, shining on the face of Lady Emily Masters. The glittering trails of tears shone like diamonds on her cheeks.

The two women stared at each other for a shocked moment. Lady Emily was the first to react.

"Miss Duncan, what are you doing up?"

"The storm woke me," she answered gently. "I thought I heard you in some distress, so I followed. Forgive me. I thought I could be of help."

Emily shook her head and wiped hastily at her cheek. "I apologize for disturbing you."

Imogen regarded her carefully. This was the longest conversation she had ever shared with the other girl, and she feared breaking this unexpected truce with a wrongly placed word.

"There is nothing to apologize for," she said softly. Emily turned from her, back to the portrait. Hesitating for a fraction of a second, knowing she would not get a chance like this again to reach out to her, Imogen slowly stepped up beside her.

The painting was of a young boy, perhaps ten or twelve years of age. His copper hair curled endearingly over his forehead and hung a bit overlong to shoulders still narrow under his deep blue coat. He had a wonderfully assured look in his gray eyes, with a spark of mischief that was only enhanced in the slight quirk of his lips. He had one hand in his pocket, the other holding the lead to a black and white spaniel that lay obediently at his feet.

With a shock, Imogen realized the young lad looked eerily like Caleb. But with a sad certainty Imogen knew deep in her heart that this boy was Jonathan, the brother Caleb had told her of who had perished so cruelly and at such a young age.

She felt a wave of grief for this boy she would never know. She could not imagine what Emily had gone through, being so young when she lost her twin, nor what she must still feel with her face as a daily reminder of it.

"This is Jonathan?" she asked quietly.

Emily swung sharply to look at her. "How do you know about Jonathan?" she rasped. Imogen could hear no animosity in the question, only shock.

"Caleb told me," she answered.

Emily's mouth fell open. "He told you? About Jonathan?" Her voice broke slightly on his name; she frowned and cleared her throat.

"A little. Just that he died quite young, and that you were injured in the same accident."

Emily regarded Imogen in silence for a long moment.

"Yes," she finally answered. "Yes, that is true."

"I imagine it would be difficult to get over losing a sibling in such a way," Imogen said softly.

Emily turned back to the painting. "It is not something you *can* get over."

Imogen regarded the portrait with a respectful silence. Another burst of lightning, this time not quite as bright. The rumble of thunder that followed was slow in coming and muted with distance. Rain began to hit the long windows with more force.

"Would you like to talk about him?" Imogen asked gently.

She glanced over at Emily in time to see her close her eyes, a look of such painful longing on her face that Imogen felt inclined to look away again from the sheer private nature of it.

Emily's voice was a mere whisper. "He was amazing. So brave, so funny, so clever. He never turned me away when I insisted on following after him, never grew cross with me or refused my company. When he went off to school I felt I'd lost a part of myself. Every time he drove away for the new term, I couldn't breathe for a week after. He was my very best friend."

"He sounds an incredible brother," Imogen said softly.

"He was. Oh yes, he truly was." She opened her eyes and turned to Imogen. "I wasn't always like this, you know. When I was young I was mischievous, and daring, and lively. My brother brought those things out in me, you see. He made me strong."

"I suppose," Imogen said carefully, kindly, "that those things are still inside you. They would not have manifested at all if you were not capable of them from the start. You can still draw strength from your brother, though he may only be with you in spirit, and find that part of yourself again if you so wish it."

Emily's expression seemed to lighten at that. Her mouth tugged up a fraction, and she turned back to look at Jonathan once more. Imogen watched her for a moment, the sudden bond she felt with this sad girl surprising her. It sounded as though Jonathan had brought out different qualities in Emily than anyone else had, ones that had perhaps made her more daring and outgoing. What, then, was the difference between this girl and herself? In Caleb's friendship she had found the strength to try new things, to stand up for herself and find her voice. Even having the willpower to refuse him was a direct result of that. So what would happen to her if she decided to reject his offer of marriage? Would she, too, lose that part of herself, allow it to shrivel until it had all but vanished?

She stared at the flame of her candle, which danced in the faint breeze from her breath. The bright golden glow of it was so fragile. The slightest effort on her part would have it gone, snuffed out forever. Her newfound strength, too, could easily be extinguished if she allowed it.

She cupped her hand around the flame, protecting it. It glowed orange on her skin, the heat seeping into her, warming her chilled fingers. Yes, Caleb had brought out the best in her. But perhaps her best had already been within her, slumbering, waiting for the spark to waken it. The trick was to never let the flame go out.

• • •

After Imogen had returned to her bedroom, she had been unable to sleep. Each time she closed her eyes, she saw Jonathan's innocent face as Emily must have seen it last, bloodied and still, all of the life gone. Imogen attempted to imagine what she must have gone through in that horrific moment, tried to imagine herself in a similar situation with one of her siblings. She couldn't do it. Her mind recoiled from it with a violence that shocked her. The thoughts haunted her even after she finally fell into a fitful sleep, disturbing her dreams so much that she was glad to awake the following morning and escape them.

She had an understanding of Emily now, one that made her feel connected to her in a small way. She had the distinct feeling that the girl had a difficult time opening herself up to others, especially an outsider such as Imogen, and felt touched that she had chosen to share even a small bit with her. Perhaps, though, it had just been the vulnerability of the moment. And so, uncertain of her reception by Caleb's sister in the bright light of day, she entered the breakfast room with trepidation.

Emily was already seated at the table with a small plate of food and the *Times* before her. At Imogen's entrance she looked up from the paper. Imogen tried for a smile and was relieved when Emily returned it.

"Lady Emily," Imogen said, moving to the sideboard. "I do hope you slept well after the storm last night."

"I did, thank you." She laid the paper aside, the reserve from before all but gone. "And please, call me Emily."

"Emily," Imogen repeated happily, pausing in spooning eggs onto her plate. "And you must call me Imogen."

"I'm afraid I do not sleep well in storms. But last night I

admit I dropped right off upon returning to my bed." She sipped at her chocolate.

"That's a relief to hear," Imogen responded, taking a seat at the table with her plate. "You played beautifully last night, if I may say so. You have a natural talent."

"Thank you. I admit it is one of my joys in life. Do you play?"

"I do, though I have not had occasion to practice for some time."

"I should love to hear you," Emily said before turning back to her food. After a moment, the hand holding her fork stilled and she looked at Imogen as if about to ask her something. Imogen tilted her head expectantly.

"Do you also sing?" the girl asked haltingly.

Imogen made a face. "Some."

Emily laughed a bit, but it did not relieve the look of uncertainty that had taken root. "You do not seem as if you enjoy it."

"No, I enjoy it very much." She smiled wryly. "But I'm afraid natural shyness and singing in public do not go hand in hand."

"I do know what you mean. Though, perhaps," she ventured, "you might make an exception for me?"

"I'm afraid I don't understand."

Emily leaned forward. "I have so longed to sing a duet, but my sister, though talented, shows no interest."

Imogen looked at her in some alarm. "Do you mean in the evening, in front of your family?"

"No!" Emily recoiled, her eyes widening in almost comic surprise. "No, I merely mean to suggest that you join me at my practice. I do so daily after breakfast, and it would mean much for me to have your presence there."

"Oh!" Imogen exclaimed, warming at the request. "That sounds lovely. It would be my honor to join you."

Emily's entire visage lit up. She was truly a beautiful girl. When she smiled like that, with her entire being, one could easily forget the scar that marred her features.

"Do you think you would be open to joining me this morning?"

"I would like that above all else."

It was at that moment that Caleb entered. Imogen watched, surprised, as the smile fell from Emily's face and she shrank down into her seat. Imogen looked up at Caleb, saw his steps falter when he saw them.

"Emily, Imogen," he acknowledged, and began piling a plate high with food. Imogen was aware of a sudden tension that had come over the room. She had already determined that Jonathan's death was at the crux of the strain in the family. But what had happened during that long ago accident that affected everyone even now? Grief she could understand. Something so horrific would leave its mark well after the event itself. But what went on in this family seemed something else entirely.

Just then, however, the heavy unease seemed to lift as he came and sat beside her. His gray eyes regarded her warmly.

"You were incredible last night, teaching everyone that dance. You amaze me more and more every day." His voice was a low murmur that vibrated intimately through her body. She flushed and cleared her throat, acutely aware of Emily's silent presence at the table. From the rustle of the paper she guessed she had gone back to reading the *Times*.

"Thank you, my lord. I admit I was a bit overwhelmed at first. But I have often done as much for my siblings, and so it was an easy matter to pretend that was the case in this instance as well."

"What an inspired way of viewing it. I, for one, have never enjoyed dancing more. Well, perhaps one other time..."

Imogen just kept herself from gasping, and instead kicked him under the table, hard. Caleb grunted, reaching down to rub at his shin.

"How fortuitous I am wearing boots," he muttered for her ears alone, "or that might have done far more damage than it did."

"What a pity, then," she replied flippantly, turning back to her plate and taking a small bite of ham.

"Touché," he said, and she could hear his grin. "Seeing as I am not grievously injured, however, I thought perhaps this morning we could ride into the village. You haven't been yet, and there are several sweet little shops we can visit in which you may be able to pick something up for your siblings."

Imogen shook her head. "I am sorry, but I cannot this morning. I have plans, you see."

"Plans," he repeated blankly.

"Yes. Emily and I will be practicing some duets this morning." She turned to look at Emily, who had forgotten her paper and gaped at Imogen. "Isn't that so?"

Emily nodded mutely. Her eyes darted between Imogen and Caleb in an uncertain fashion.

"Perhaps we may go into the village tomorrow?" Imogen asked Caleb.

"Certainly," he replied immediately.

"Wonderful." She turned to Emily. "Are you done with your meal? I should love to begin presently. I have some lovely songs that I think may interest you."

At Emily's stiff nod Imogen rose. The other girl followed suit, and soon they were heading out the door for the music room. Just as she was about to duck into the hall, however, she glanced back. Caleb was sitting at the table, his back straight, a frown marring his forehead. Chewing on her lip thoughtfully, Imogen followed after Emily.

• • •

Caleb felt as if he had walked into some strange, otherworldly place. By the time he regained his senses, the two women were gone from the room. He stared down at his untouched plate, suddenly finding he had no appetite.

He couldn't understand it. When had Imogen and Emily become familiar with one another? He had seen no sign of friendship develop between them in the week they had been there.

An uncomfortable weight seemed to have formed in his chest. Pushing away from the table, he rose and strode from the room.

Imogen was innately kind; her attempts to befriend his sister surprised him not one bit. He had seen her distress at Emily's aloof attitude to her, her confusion at the reserve she had found. But he had not thought much of it at the time. Emily was naturally reticent with strangers, after all.

Now, however, there was something forming between the two. And he hadn't a clue how to deal with it.

His steps slowed as he neared the closed door of the music room. He could just make out their light chatter, the gentle sound of a melody being tested out on the keys of the pianoforte. There was a bout of quiet laughter before the music started up in earnest.

He stared for a time at the door, listening. As their voices joined together in song, he frowned and strode further down the hall. Why did this bother him so much? He should be glad Imogen was finding a friend in Emily. He had seen a bond develop between Imogen and Daphne, seen how she respected and cared for his mother. Wouldn't it be in his best interest then to have her become attached to the final person in the house? It would connect her even more firmly to them, make it harder for her to refuse him when it was time once again to ask her to marry him.

But what if Emily talked of his part in Jonathan's death? She was one of the few who had been there, who would be able to tell the whole ugly truth. How would Imogen feel about him then, knowing he was responsible?

Agitated, he headed toward the stables. He should not have brought Imogen here. But blast it all, he had not been able to see another way to get her to accept him.

He glanced back quickly at the house. Now it seemed there was every chance he could lose her forever.

Chapter 24

After an enjoyable morning singing followed by a walk in the gardens with her new friend, Imogen took leave of Emily and retired to her room to rest and read. But she could not concentrate on the words. Instead her mind was full of energy after the changes in the past day. How strange and wonderful to finally have made a connection with the other girl, especially as Imogen was now considering marrying Caleb.

Emily was wonderfully sweet. She was not at all like her siblings, whom others instinctually gravitated toward. No, Imogen found the other woman was much like herself. The both of them were shy, had difficulty around strangers, and tried very hard to blend into the plasterwork. People such as they had a tendency to be eclipsed by those of a more outgoing nature. She was so glad, however, that she had been able to unearth the true person within.

A knock sounded at her door, breaking her from her thoughts. A maid entered, bobbing a quick curtsy. "Miss, Lady Sumner is here to see you. She's in the small drawing room."

"Thank you, I'll be there momentarily."

The treat of having her sister here for a visit was too good to miss even a moment of. She rushed through the house, her feet fairly flying. What would Frances say if Imogen were to tell her she was considering Caleb's offer of marriage? They would be close enough to visit one another every day if they wished. Joy burst in her chest, and the sensation caused her to skid to a stop just outside the drawing room door.

Had she decided, then? Was she going to marry Caleb? She rather thought the answer was yes.

A grin spread over her face, relief pouring through her veins. She had to tell someone. Of course, Caleb should be the first to tell. But he was off to places unknown, and Frances was here. Surely he would not mind if she confided in her sister first.

Throwing open the door, she rushed in. "Frances, I am so glad you are here."

Imogen went to her sister and embraced her. But as she pulled back she saw, even through her euphoria, that something was not right.

There was that misery again that she was so used to seeing in Frances's eyes. But now it was etched even more deeply, almost a raw pain.

Frances's voice was full of false bravado. "Nothing could stop me from coming to see my dear sister. Especially as she is so close."

Imogen's excitement vanished in an instant, and worry settled in her belly like a stone. She guided Frances to the sofa. "Sit with me for a bit and we can have a nice talk."

Frances frowned. "I would like a nice, simple conversation with you above all things, dear. But I'm afraid my visit has a purpose, and I dare not delay in bringing it up."

Alarmed, Imogen sat straighter in her seat. "What is it?"

"Mother wrote to me. She's told me what you've done, that you've rejected Lord Willbridge."

Imogen flushed. "Yes, I did reject him."

"Why? I saw you together when you came to visit. You care for him, Imogen, deeply."

"It doesn't matter why."

"Of course it matters why. Tell me, Imogen."

"He doesn't love me." In the next moment she slashed her hand through the air. "But that is neither here nor there. I have decided that when he asks me again I will accept."

Frances reached out and squeezed Imogen's hand. Her eyes

took on a feverish gleam. "No! You cannot do that. Have you learned nothing from me?"

It was the most intense tone Imogen had ever heard from her sister. She pulled back in surprise, breaking the contact.

"I don't understand," she mumbled through numb lips. "You and Lord Sumner seemed so happy yesterday. I thought things were finally turning around for you both."

Frances's face crumpled. Her hands flew to her mouth. But not before a sob escaped her lips.

Imogen leaned forward. "Frances, what is it?"

"I was such a fool," Frances whispered. "I knew he didn't love me when we wed. I told myself he would love me eventually, that my love would be enough for us. But I was wrong."

Imogen felt sick to her stomach. "But...yesterday..."

"An act," Frances spat. "Do you honestly believe James wanted the Marquess of Willbridge to see him in a negative light? That and the babe."

Imogen could well imagine the shock that took over her face. Frances caught sight of it, her lip curling. Even so, her hands came protectively over her abdomen.

"Yes, I'm with child. After so long married, it is a surprise to me as well."

"But this is good news, is it not?" Imogen wanted to embrace her sister, to congratulate her. But the bitter look in her eyes stopped her.

"Good for James, perhaps. He will finally get his heir after years of failure on my part. As he has told me on numerous occasions in the past week." She gave a sharp, humorless bark of laughter. The sound sent a chill up Imogen's spine. "You are stronger than me, Imogen. How I wish I had your strength all those years ago when I overlooked my better sense and agreed to marry a man more concerned with status and position than with the comfort of those in his care. I would give anything to go back in time and change things."

Imogen swallowed hard, fear rearing up. Her sister's words hung thick in the air. "But surely Caleb is cut from a different cloth."

Frances sagged back against the sofa. "That is just what I told myself. I was blinded; I loved him too much to see him for who he was." She shook her head, closing her eyes wearily. "My love for him died long ago. I am no longer blind."

Imogen looked at her sister's face, misery plain in every line. Would that be her in a few years?

She had very nearly given in. When next he asked, she would have accepted him. But this one brief meeting with Frances—no longer guessing what she endured, but seeing for the first time the true depth of her pain—Imogen knew she could never marry Caleb unless he loved her in return.

The joy of mere moments ago snuffed completely out. And with it every hope for her future with Caleb.

• • •

Imogen did not see Caleb until late that night. He had been called away to help with some difficulty with one of his tenants and was quiet and tired when he returned shortly before supper was served. He ate dinner in a strangely subdued manner, asking her about her day, conversing with her father on his findings in the library, deflecting questions Daphne put to him. When the meal was over he asked their pardon, saying he wished to retire early.

As Imogen turned to follow the others to the drawing room, however, he stopped her with a hand on her arm. She looked into his face, ignoring the jolt of desire that singed her nerves, deeply aware of the sorrow that had settled in her breast since her talk with Frances. There was a strange reserve in his eyes that had not been present before.

"Would you still like to visit the village tomorrow? I know we had talked about it this morning, but I thought perhaps you might have changed your mind." His baritone voice was quiet and neutral, giving away nothing of his feelings.

Imogen frowned and searched his face, forgetting her own worries, wondering at his peculiar mood. "Of course, I would love that."

He seemed to give a soft, almost inaudible sigh of relief. "Shall we leave right after breakfast then?"

Before she could answer, Daphne bounded up to them. "Where are you going tomorrow after breakfast?"

A muscle twitched in Caleb's jaw. "To Ketterby. I thought Imogen would like to do some shopping for her siblings."

"Wonderful, I shall join you. I would like to see Rebecca and Hannah Sanders. We can call for them at the vicarage on our way there."

She bounced off, and Imogen and Caleb were left staring after her in disbelief.

"She is a force to be reckoned with," Imogen muttered without thinking. Her hands flew up to cover her mouth in horror a moment later. What was she thinking, to say such a thing to Caleb about his own sister?

But he only smiled, his pale eyes crinkling at the corners. "She is that. I shall have to endeavor to get you alone another way." He leaned toward her, his head dipping so quickly that she had no time to react. His mouth captured her own.

But this was no kiss of possession and desire. It was brief but gentle, and so achingly tender that Imogen found she could not breathe for the emotions it caused to well up in her. His lips were firm and warm against hers. She tasted wine on his mouth, felt the soft stroke of his fingers on her jaw line. Just as she began to return the pressure of his lips and lean in to his body, he pulled away.

One more look, his eyes soft and almost sad, and he left the room. She stared after him dumbly for a long moment.

Suddenly her father was at her elbow. How had she had not heard him reenter the room? He eyed her in some concern.

"Are you ready to retire with the others, my dear?"

She forced a smile. "Of course, Papa." She placed her hand on his sleeve and allowed him to lead her from the room, though her mind was still with Caleb.

• • •

Imogen, for all her quiet ways, had never known such a loud quiet as when Daphne left her and Caleb alone on the dirt road leading to the village to fetch the Misses Sanders at the vicarage the following morning.

She had thought that a good night's sleep would return him to his usual cheerful self. But he seemed even more pensive than he had the evening before. He kept casting her hooded sidelong glances that more than once had her stumbling along the well-maintained road.

Imogen struggled for a topic to draw him out. Conversation had never been her forte, and that, combined with this strange awkwardness that had unexpectedly sprouted up between them, had her even more tongue-tied than usual.

"I do like the Misses Sanders," she finally said with false brightness. "They are both sweet girls."

"Indeed."

She cast about yet again. "Have you known them long?"

"All their lives."

"Ah, that accounts for Daphne's closeness with them."

He merely nodded.

Her lips compressed in frustration. "And Emily?"

He paused, giving her an inscrutable look. "What about Emily?"

"Is she friends with them?"

"I've no idea," he replied.

But she is your sister, she wanted to shout.

Just then, however, Daphne returned, followed by the Misses Sanders. The three girls chattered like magpies, dispelling the peculiar atmosphere. Imogen concentrated on their conversation, determined to enjoy such a glorious day. The sun was warm, the sky a clear azure. They reached Ketterby after a short while, and

Imogen forgot Caleb's strange reaction, instead finding herself utterly enchanted by the picturesque scene.

They entered the main road of the town via a wide stone bridge that spanned the River Spratt. Small cottages lined the road, all made of ochre-colored stone, their roofs recently thatched. One ruddy-faced woman tended the garden at the front of her property behind a low stone wall, several freshly scrubbed children playing and screeching at her heels.

"Mrs. Larstow," Caleb called, making his way to her gate. "I see young Thomas is fully recovered from his injury?"

Mrs. Larstow smiled in delight and walked over, dropping a curtsy. "Lord Willbridge, what a treat this is. Aye, my Thomas, as you can see, is back to his typical self. The arm doesn't bother him a bit now it's healed right and proper." She smiled at the other women and greeted them as well.

Caleb put his hand at Imogen's elbow. "And may I present Miss Duncan. She is visiting with us, along with her father Viscount Tarryton, from London. Imogen, this is Mrs. Larstow and her children Thomas, Julia, and Susan. Mrs. Larstow's sister, Miss Randall, was governess to my sisters."

The speculation in Mrs. Larstow's eyes was enough to make Imogen blush as she greeted the woman.

"And how is Miss Randall?" Daphne asked with real warmth. "Ah! I am sorry, she is Mrs. Fuller now."

Mrs. Larstow chuckled. "Aye, she's doing wonderfully. Just returned from visiting her husband's family up north. You may be able to find her home if you've a mind to later."

"Oh, that would be splendid! Caleb, perhaps Rebecca, Hannah, and I may do so after luncheon."

"Of course," he said, his eyes settling on Imogen with intensity. "You can be certain that Imogen and I will be fine for a short while on our own."

Imogen blushed furiously and looked away, trying to gather her scattered wits, hoping no one saw her distress. Thankfully, Miss Rebecca Sanders chose that moment to pull a jar from her basket, holding it out to Mrs. Larstow and thus gaining the woman's sharp-eyed attention.

"For Mr. Larstow, compliments of my mother." Miss Sanders said. "A liniment for his back. It should help to ease the strain he suffered considerably."

"My thanks," Mrs. Larstow said. "Can I entice you inside? I've made fresh muffins just this morning."

"Alas, no," was Caleb's reply. "I'm afraid we have to pass, though it is a tempting invitation."

"Another time, perhaps," Mrs. Larstow said jovially. They took their leave, and she waved them off before turning back to the house.

Imogen was thoughtful as they continued down the main street of the small village. Everyone they came across was full of greetings and goodwill, and she could not help but wonder at this man at her side. It seemed he came home only rarely, and yet the people here truly and honestly respected him. The houses and roads were in good repair, the tenants happy, the children healthy. He knew everyone by name, and they all were comfortable, even friendly with him. It was obvious he cared a great deal for the people under his care.

Which made the discontent and tension with his own family all the more pronounced. And all over the accidental death of his brother? No matter how hard she thought on the matter it made no sense at all.

Chapter 25

After Imogen had chosen a length of creamy lace for Mariah, as well as several small presents for her younger siblings, she and the rest of the party made their way to the local inn. It was a large two-story building bustling with activity and made from the same ochre stone as the rest of the homes and shops in the village. Caleb maneuvered the women past a restless team of horses and a lad unloading a coach and into the cheerfully whitewashed and immaculate interior of the establishment.

"Lord Willbridge," came a booming voice. Imogen jumped, spinning to face a large man striding toward them. He grinned and held out a beefy hand to Caleb, who shook it heartily. "I see you are here right as promised. I've got that hamper you requested all set to go. I'll have young Evan bring it out." The man turned and bellowed instructions through an open door. A moment later a thin boy bustled out, nearly bowing under the weight of a heavily laden basket.

"I thank you, Donald. I look forward to your wife's delectable cooking more than you know. Nothing in London compares." Caleb plucked the hamper from the lad's hands, peering down at him in amazement. "Why, Evan Samson, have you lost another tooth?"

"Aye, milord," the boy chirped proudly with a gap-toothed grin. "This makes five now."

Caleb ruffled the boy's hair. "Best watch out. Soon you won't have any teeth left to chew with." He threw the boy a coin with a smile. Evan caught it with a practiced move before scurrying off, his cheerful "Thanks" trailing behind him.

Caleb chuckled. "Donald, that boy of yours is growing up much too fast."

"Don't I know it." The innkeeper turned to peer down at Imogen. "Now, Lady Daphne and the Misses Sanders I know. But who might this young lass be?"

Imogen nearly choked. Young lass? The innkeeper had to be no more than thirty if he was a day, certainly only a few years her senior. Either he was in need of spectacles himself or was a consummate charmer.

Caleb drew her forward. "Imogen, this is Mr. Samson, proprietor of the Regal Swan, the finest inn in Northamptonshire. He and I grew up together, terrorizing the local populace, and so you must excuse his forward manner. Donald, may I present Miss Duncan? She is visiting from London for a short time."

Mr. Samson took up her hand in his, pressing it warmly. "I'm pleased more than you know to be meeting you, Miss Duncan. Let us hope you're here to reform this hardened rake."

Imogen blushed for what felt like the hundredth time that day. It seemed everyone in town saw her presence at Willowhaven as good as an announcement in the papers declaring her engagement to Caleb. And he, blast him, did nothing to dissuade his tenants from speculating to their hearts' content.

Like now. He chuckled, holding out his arm to her. She took it reluctantly. "Excuse us, Donald, but the ladies must be famished after an afternoon shopping. I shall see you later, my friend."

He guided them out past the busy commotion that filled the front courtyard and around to the back of the inn. There a gently sloping grass-covered hill ended in a small pond. It was a quiet spot, neatly shielded from the large building by the several mature trees that framed it. He laid out a spacious blanket under the obliging shade of an immense oak, and all four women sank gratefully onto it, adjusting their skirts. They dug into the basket with relish, and before long every crumb of meat pie, cheese, bread, and bright red berries was gone.

"Our thanks, Lord Willbridge," Miss Sanders remarked,

sighing happily. "This was a wonderful afternoon. I declare, Mrs. Samson is a fabulous cook."

"And now," Daphne announced, standing up and shaking out her skirts, "we must be off. I cannot wait to see Miss Russell—er, Mrs. Fuller. It has been an age. Rebecca, Hannah, shall we? Caleb, Imogen, we shall be back within the hour."

Without waiting for a response, Daphne ushered her two friends away.

Imogen watched them go, the glow she had begun to feel in such an idyllic setting fading away. She nervously smoothed her skirts. Beside her, Caleb leaned back on his elbows, and she could feel his eyes on her.

They had had such an easy friendship before, and now she could not be in his presence without feeling self-conscious and tongue-tied. She felt a small spurt of anger. His friendship had been one of the most important things in her life. But after what had happened between them, and given her feelings for him, it felt as if it were ruined beyond repair.

And if he could not find it in him to love her in return, she would be forced to break with him for good.

She sniffled, trying to control the sudden burning behind her eyes.

"Imogen, what is it?" Caleb reached out and took up one of her hands.

She shook her head. "Nothing at all."

"Are you certain?"

"Of course." She gave a feeble tug on her hand, but he held it fast. He stared at it, suddenly intent. Before she knew what he was about, he reached out with his free hand and undid the small buttons at her wrist.

And then his lips were there, hot on her sensitive skin. And she, quite simply, forgot everything. All that filled her mind was him, and the feel of his lips on her wrist. And it was the most glorious thing she had ever felt in her life.

• • •

Caleb could not think beyond the delicate skin under his mouth. Had she always tasted so sweet? Had she always smelled so mouth-wateringly amazing? He felt he could go on kissing her like this for the rest of his life and never tire of it. He could feel her rapid pulse against his lips, the unbearable smoothness of her skin, and thought he would burst for wanting her.

Her breathing grew fast and uneven, and still he kept his lips at her wrist. He knew somewhere deep inside of him that they were in a public place where anyone might come across them. But he was far from caring. He wanted her, and it only seemed to grow worse every day he was so close to her and yet unable to touch her. He could no more stop himself from kissing her right now than he could stop the stars from coming out at night.

She seemed to have finally regained her senses a bit, for she began to speak, her voice warbling slightly in her effort.

"I admit I am surprised at the ease with which you interact with your tenants." By her sharply indrawn breath he guessed she had not meant to say such a thing. He must have flustered her more than he had realized.

He smiled against her skin. "Surely you did not think I was an ogre to them. I think you know me better than that, Imogen." He brushed his lips again along her skin. He could see the blue-tinged vein just beneath the surface, her pulse making it flutter madly. He darted his tongue out to moisten the flesh there before blowing softly. He heard her breath shudder in an exhale.

"N-no," she stuttered, and then cleared her throat. "No," she repeated more forcefully. But then she paused again, as if baffled by what she had meant to say. He was pleased to note that, though she was attempting to converse normally, she didn't try to free her hand from his grip.

"I did not expect you to be anything but charming with them," she finally continued. "But I received the impression that you do not come to Willowhaven often. It surprised me at how well received and comfortable you are here."

He gave a short bark of laughter. My, but that was a lot of properly strung words considering her frame of mind. But when he raised his head to gaze up at her, he saw her cheeks were suffused with color and her eyes were heavy-lidded with passion. Her lips, however, were pressed into a tight line and her brow was furrowed.

"You really do not mince words, do you?" he murmured, returning his attention to her hand. It seemed he must renew his efforts. He obviously was not doing as good a job of befuddling her as he had thought. He began to tug at the fingers of her glove, slowly peeling the soft kidskin off. Her breathing sped up as the material slipped free.

"To answer your concerns, I do return here three or so times a year." He kissed her wrist. "I always make time to visit the village when I do." He let his lips linger at the fleshy mound under her thumb. "And when I am not here, I write weekly to my estate manager to make certain all the tenants' needs are seen to."

Not the most romantic speech he had ever made. But Imogen didn't seem to hear him a bit. He uncurled her fingers and kept his lips a fraction of an inch from her palm, his breath hot on her skin. Her limbs began to tremble. And then he pressed his mouth there, and a soft, incoherent cry escaped her lips.

Desire raged through his body at her response. Sweet heaven, he wanted nothing so much as to drag her beneath him and take her right there on the bank of the pond. His mind worked feverishly, calculating how much longer Daphne would be gone, if the branches of the oak tree hid them completely from view, whether any of the villagers could be expected to come this way.

But just as he was about to rise up over her and claim her mouth with his own, he paused. No. No, he could not do that to her, could not disrespect her like that. She would never forgive him, and he would lose her for good.

Placing one last kiss to her palm, he released her and raised his head.

It was as if she had been under a spell and suddenly freed. Her spine straightened and she hastened to move to the very edge of the blanket. She averted her eyes, digging her restless fingers into the grass beside her and tugging up clumps.

He was about to reach out to comfort her when her voice, high and tightly controlled, stopped him.

"You have seemed very distracted the last two days."

He felt his mood begin to plummet. Imogen's comment brought to mind his reason for being so withdrawn. Imogen and Emily's new and unexpected friendship had preyed on his mind all the day before. After a pounding ride over the land, he had travelled to visit with some local farmers. He had exhausted himself in his work with the tenants, joining with the men to help rebuild a wall that had been damaged by a wagon. By the time the day was about to come to a close, he was wearied in body. Unfortunately, however, it did not extend to his mind. All through dinner he had fought the fears that haunted him, half believing when he asked Imogen if she still intended to join him in a visit to the village that she would refuse. When she had confirmed their plans, her lovely turquoise eyes clear of any disgust for him, he had been relieved beyond measure. He could not help the kiss he had given her, had shocked himself at the tenderness he had felt for her, the nearly worshipping way he had claimed her mouth with his own.

He attempted a smile now. "Yes, and I'm sorry for it. I promise to be a better host from this moment on."

She blushed. "You are a perfectly wonderful host, and you know it."

He grinned, felt his mood begin to lighten at her grudging compliment. "Am I now? I admit, I was having my doubts."

She shot him a sly look. "I wonder, is my propensity for not accepting compliments better or worse than your propensity for fishing for more?"

He laughed. "Oh, certainly yours is much worse. For mine merely makes me all the more charming."

Her lips quirked. "Well, I am certainly glad you have not lost your modesty."

It was so like the way they used to banter that he was struck with a sudden joy. He reached down into the grass, plucking a few small violets and forget-me-nots from the mass of wildflowers that littered the hill. Reaching across the space she had put between them, he gently tucked the flowers into the braided coronet that crowned her head. She stilled, a blush stealing across her face.

"Do you know, you look every inch the magical wood sprite to me just now," he murmured. And indeed she did, with the soft white of her muslin gown embroidered with small yellow flowers and twining green vines, a pale green shawl around her shoulders, and the crown of pale blue and purple flowers surrounding her head like a tiara.

"Well, you'd best watch out, or I may just cast a spell on you and turn you into a frog."

"And here I thought only witches did that sort of thing."

"Witches are not the only vindictive creatures, you know."

"And will you kiss me after to turn me into a prince?"

She seemed to consider him for a moment, and her eyes took on that devilish gleam that was so rare to her and that he had missed so much in the last week and a half.

"No," she said, "I think I shall leave you as a frog. The birds can have you after that."

He chuckled and watched the answering mirth in her own face. "Blood-thirsty wench."

She shrugged. "We wood sprites must look out for ourselves, you know."

They shared a light laugh, and it was so pleasantly reminiscent that he unthinkingly reached out and covered her hand with his own. Immediately her smile faded as she stared down at his long fingers embracing hers. She pulled her hand from his.

He wanted to curse, to throw something. Why did she insist on pulling away from him? What was so bad about marrying him? Why could she not see that they would be wonderful together?

And then he felt it, what he tried so fiercely to bury deep down in the desperation of his pursuit of her.

He was angry.

Her unexplained refusal to marry him angered him. He knew she liked him, knew she desired him. So why did she continue to turn him away?

"Back to this again, are we?" he commented, and he knew from her startled glance that the lightness of his tone did nothing to hide his frustration.

Instead of answering him, she looked about their surroundings. "It truly is lovely here. Thank you for bringing me." Her voice was carefully measured, back to being painfully civil.

"I knew you would like it," he replied easily. Too easily. It was frightening, the ease with which they dropped back into politeness with each other.

She faced him, her hands folded primly in her lap, one still glaringly bare and hidden beneath the other. "It is a beautiful land. Why don't you return home more often?"

"I'm a busy man," he replied, attempting to sound casual even as his insides roiled. "And anyway, does it matter why?"

"It just seems strange, is all, seeing how you love it here," she replied carefully. "There must be a more essential reason for you to stay away."

His eyes narrowed at her choice of words and he peered closely at her. Was that little tick at the corner of her mouth a sign of distress? And her rapid blinking, what did that signify? But with a sudden bolt of insight, he knew exactly why she had chosen such specific words with such precision, why she watched him so carefully: Emily had said something to her after all.

His heart cracked.

"Why does it matter? You are not planning on becoming my bride and living here with me. Why do my comings and goings concern you so much?"

He saw her flinch, knew the words had been much harsher than they should have been. It was not anger at Emily that had prompted them. It was his fear of losing Imogen. His sister had gotten to her, had poisoned her mind against him, and Imogen was as good as lost to him now.

He wondered if his sister had done it purposely. But surely not. Emily was distant and aloof, and she surely still held some animosity for him for what he had done. But she was not cruel.

Imogen looked on him with uncertainty. He felt a sharp stab of guilt. He should have told her the truth himself instead of leaving her in the dark, praying she never learned of his past.

He was about to reach for her, to bare all. He obviously had nothing to lose now. But at that moment Daphne strode into view, the Misses Sanders following behind her like ducklings.

"What a lovely time we had. Oh, Caleb, I wish you could have been there. I have never seen Miss Russell—er, Mrs. Fuller, looking so well. I declare, marriage suits her splendidly."

She paused when she spotted Caleb and Imogen on the blanket. He imagined the tension was so thick she could taste it. He forced a smile and began packing up the rest of their luncheon, drawing Daphne's attention to him in order to give Imogen a moment to compose herself.

"Does it now? Well, I must say that after putting up with you for all those years, the poor woman deserves it."

The three young ladies laughed gaily, talking animatedly as Caleb continued to pack up. Imogen rose in silence and took up the blanket, quietly folding it. He watched her for a time, at how pale she had become and the tense line of her shoulders. He reached down to where she had discarded her bonnet and handed it to her. She looked at it uncomprehendingly for a time before reaching out and silently taking it. And then they were walking back toward the inn and home.

And Caleb did not know whether he wanted to sigh in relief or howl in pain that the moment was forever lost.

Chapter 26

Upon their return from the village, Daphne retired to her room and Caleb abruptly left Imogen in the front hall, mumbling something about needing to meet with his steward. She stared out the windows into the inner courtyard. The sky was beginning to darken with clouds, and she thought that her mood could not be reflected any better.

He had become so belligerent, so defensive. She had never seen him like that, had never been the recipient of his anger. She wasn't even aware he could be so cruel. But then a change had come over him. He had been about to say something of import to her. She knew he had. She wished they had not been interrupted.

She looked about, not sure where to go. But then her eyes lit on the entrance to the hall that led to the library.

Her father was there, seated at the large mahogany desk in the corner. Several piles of books littered the surface. His nose was buried in one unwieldy tome, and he was busy scribbling notes onto a sheet of foolscap.

Imogen approached and stood before the massive desk. She had a sudden flashback of more episodes than she cared to remember where she had waited for her father to acknowledge her. It had never bothered her overmuch, if truth be told. She had even made a bit of a game of it in her youth, counting the time as it passed on the mantel clock, making silent bets with herself to see when he would finally look up with a start, his eyes glazed over, his mind wrapped in the pages of his book, a sheepish smile on his lips.

As he did just now. "Imogen, my dear. I do hope you haven't been standing there long. You know how I get sidetracked while reading."

Imogen smiled and took a seat close by. "Have you been enjoying Lord Willbridge's library, Papa? I believe I have hardly seen you at all this past sennight," she teased.

"Oh, I am so sorry. The collection of books here is unlike any I have found elsewhere. I vow, I could spend the next ten years here and still not have unearthed all its treasures."

There was a spark in his eyes, so much like a small child with a crate full of puppies, that she couldn't help but laugh. "It's quite all right. I have not been lonely a minute, so do not worry on my account."

"Yes, I see you are getting along wonderfully with Lord Willbridge's sisters. Lady Daphne is a lively young girl. Reminds me a bit of Mariah."

"Yes, I was under the same impression. She is sweet. I think she will do wonderfully in town next year."

He sat back. "Now, Lady Emily, she is much more subdued. Though, if I am correct, it seems the two of you have struck up a bit of a friendship."

Imogen had learned over the years not to be surprised with the extent of things her father actually noticed, even while in the throes of a new intellectual pursuit. Most of what went on passed him by, but occasionally he was so in tune that it was almost shocking.

"Yes," she replied. "She is actually a lovely girl. We sang several duets together just yesterday. She has a beautiful voice." She hesitated.

Lord Tarryton's normally placid eyes sharpened on her. "What is it?"

"I worry about the relationship Lord Willbridge has with his family," she admitted, a frown marring her forehead.

Her father nodded. "He is unaccountably distant with them. I admit it surprises me, seeing as how easy his manner is with everyone else." He peered at her closely. "This bothers you a great deal."

"Yes," she murmured.

"But why?"

Her head drew back in shock. "I'm sorry?"

He sat forward, resting his elbows on the desk. "Why does it bother you, Imogen?

She cast about for an answer, but her mind came up blank.

"You have declared," he went on gently, "that you will not have Lord Willbridge. You have told me in no uncertain terms that at the end of our stay you will still refuse him."

Her mouth worked for a time in silence. Finally she managed, "Yes, Papa, that is correct."

"So why does it bother you so very much that he does not have a close relationship with his family?"

She shook her head, unable to tear her eyes from the kindness in his own.

"Can it be, Imogen, that you care for Lord Willbridge?"

She looked down at her lap, trying valiantly to fight back the tears that had suddenly sprung up behind her eyes. "It does not signify," she whispered.

He was at her side in an instant, offering her a handkerchief. She took it and wrung it between her fingers.

"On the contrary, I believe it signifies very much."

"No. It will never work." When he made to speak, she held up her hand. "Please, Papa. I have my reasons. Can we not leave it at that?"

He sighed and took the seat beside her. His hand was warm and comforting on her arm. "I have a feeling that this is due in some part to your sister's unfortunate situation. I know it has affected you greatly, seeing how unhappy she is. But I also know you have always been hard on yourself, Imogen. And so I can only assume that you believe yourself somehow not worthy of Lord Willbridge." He placed a finger under her chin and forced her gaze to his. "And let me just tell you, though I may be biased, that you are worth it, my darling girl."

Imogen could not suppress the sob that choked her. She buried her face in her father's handkerchief and let the tears flow, tears she had held in check almost from the moment she had been forced to refuse Caleb. She cried as she had not since she was a small child. And like a small child, she went to her father when he tugged on her hand, curling up on his lap and pressing her wet face into his shoulder.

His large hand stroked her back. And then he whispered into her hair, "And I am willing to bet my fortune that Lord Willbridge thinks you are worth it, too."

• • •

He was a coward. He personified the very essence of the word.

Caleb stalked through the house after he had left Imogen so abruptly in the hall after their return. In his mind he saw Imogen's face, hurt and bewildered at his harsh words. He'd had the chance to tell her everything, to clear his conscience and lay it all at her feet. The words had been on his tongue, burning his insides with the effort to get free.

When Daphne had returned, he had felt frustration that he had been forced to swallow the words back down. But overwhelming that had been a wave of relief. No matter how much Emily had told Imogen, hearing the whole of it from his own lips would have caused her distress, he reasoned. It was not something a finely bred young lady like Imogen could hear with any ease. The interruption had been a godsend; she would have suffered from the truth, as he had for these last ten years.

But he knew deep down that the relief had little to do with such lauded feelings of worrying about her well-being. No, it was all due to his fear. He feared telling her, seeing the look of horror on her face, having her turn from him.

He frowned as he exited the house. Heading for the stables, he hoped a good, hard ride would help to clear his head.

But as he passed the knot garden, he stopped. Slowly he entered the quiet, well-ordered space, and as if in a trance he walked to the spot where he had kissed Imogen. He looked down at the bed of hedges and herbs. His boot prints no longer marred the dark, soft soil, and the much-maligned lavender bush was trimmed back into proper shape.

He reached down and plucked a sprig from the plant. Crushing the soft purple blossoms and leaves in his fingers, he breathed in deeply, letting the fragrance fill him. In a flash he recalled the feel of her in his arms and the taste of her on his lips, and the raw triumph he had felt when she had begun to respond to him.

Yes, Imogen was his. There was no question as to that. And now that his body knew her, he found that he wanted her all the more. It mattered not why she was so important to him. The fact of the matter was he burned for her as he never had for any other woman.

He could not lose her.

His eyes narrowed as he considered the crushed sprig. There was one way he could secure her, one way that would guarantee her acceptance of his proposal.

He could ruin her publicly.

It would be a simple matter, really. All he need do was kiss her, have someone discover them, and her father would have no choice but to force his stubborn daughter to accept him.

He knew she desired him, that he could make her wild with passion for him. He could use that to his advantage. Why, if he put his mind to it, he could be engaged to her this very night.

But though his body hardened, he recoiled at the thought of manipulating her to such a degree. The realization of what he had been willing to do in order to secure her crashed down on him.

He stumbled back into the topiary, disgusted over the sick turn his mind had taken. How could he ever contemplate such a thing? After all, wasn't that what he had been trying to encourage at the start of their friendship, to fight back against what others prescribed for her and to live her life as she wanted to? If he forced her into marriage, she would never forgive him. And indeed, he would not deserve her forgiveness.

And even were he to manage to secure her hand without

admitting all to her, he would have to tell her eventually. He had deceived her for far too long. And with Emily's unintended interference, he had no more time left.

He set his jaw. Gripping the crushed blossom in his hand, he walked from the knot garden. Imogen was all that was sweet and good in life. No matter the consequences, she deserved to know the entire truth from him, to take the evidence and make a judgment herself. Only then would it be fair to marry her.

He would tell her tomorrow, he decided, ignoring the whisper of anguish his heart gave. He would tell her and see if afterward she deemed him worthy of heaven or of hell.

• • •

Imogen spent the rest of the afternoon in her room. She had pulled the drapes closed and lay on the bed fully clothed, staring at the ceiling. Her eyes were dry now, though her mind was fuller than ever, with her father's questions swirling about her brain as well.

She would be leaving in less than a week. She had no place worrying about the relationships between the people in this family. But no matter how she tried to rid herself of her concern, no matter how she tried to distance herself from the drama, she just couldn't. She cared for these people too much.

She turned on her side, but the wire frame of her spectacles pressed uncomfortably into her temple. Giving a huff of frustration, she sat up. She needed to think, and tucking herself away in her room was not benefitting her a bit.

Craving movement, she glanced at the small clock on the mantle. She didn't have much time before she would need to dress for dinner. She would stick to the house, then.

Stepping into her slippers, she walked from the room, striding down the hall and turning right into the Long Gallery. She remembered travelling this same path two nights before when she had met with Emily. She walked the length of the room, her steps slowing as she scanned the many faces of Masters ancestors that stared down at her from their lofty perches. So much history here. What joys and sorrows had these people seen? What had occurred within these walls to shape this generation? And how, she wondered, would the current turmoil affect future family members?

Imogen hugged her middle. What did it matter to her? She was not going to marry Caleb, after all. Who was she to worry about this broken family, to get involved? These long-dead people would never become her own ancestors, this home would never be her home. She would never call Caleb husband, would never call Emily and Daphne sister. She was a passing stranger who had been welcomed into their midst for a short time. That was all.

Except that you love Caleb and his family as if they were your own, her heart whispered.

Her breath caught in her chest, a sob that she would not allow to find purchase. Her steps grew more agitated, her shoes clicking sharply on the polished wood floor. But then she slowed, and stopped, and found herself looking into the forever-youthful face of Lord Jonathan Masters.

This boy's death was the key to all of the turmoil in this house. If only there was some way to learn why, to help this family find peace and to finally heal.

She shook her head against the thought. She had no right to meddle. But images of Caleb's tense, shuttered face, the pain in Emily's eyes, the longing in Lady Willbridge's, flashed through Imogen's mind in that instant. She expelled a breath, and with it all her doubt fled. Despite her refusal to marry into this family, the fact was that each of them had become important to her in a different way. Lady Willbridge was a caring, motherly presence as she had never known. Daphne was like another young sister, sweet and open and mischievous. Emily was a friend, plain and simple, and so much like her it sometimes pained her. And Caleb...

Ah yes, Caleb was her best friend in the world. No matter how much she had come to love him, no matter her desire for him, he was first and foremost her friend, the one who had helped her find her inner strength and enjoy life. She would always hold him in her heart, and would always be grateful to him for what he had given her. Because of him she had found the will to break away and free herself from the structure of her life.

The dressing bell rang then. Finding a new purpose, Imogen squared her shoulders and returned to her room. If there was nothing else she could do, nothing else she could leave him with, she could at least help Caleb regain his family.

Chapter 27

"I cannot believe you'll be gone in a matter of days. We have had so little time to become acquainted," Emily said.

Imogen smiled at her friend and gave her arm a squeeze as they continued on their slow promenade of the perimeter of the drawing room. From across the way, where he was playing a quiet card game with the other members of the household, she could feel Caleb's eyes on her. He had been watching her strangely all night, with a sad, almost fatalistic despair. She had been unable to interpret it.

"The time has passed so much more quickly than I expected it to," she responded. "I hope that, whatever we may be doing tomorrow, you will deign to join us. I hate the thought of missing even a moment to cultivate our friendship."

Emily paled and stopped, glancing around before leaning in close. "I'm sure you have seen, my brother and I do not exactly get on well."

"Perhaps spending some time together will do the two of you good," Imogen attempted.

But the other girl shook her head. "No. But it is kind of you to offer."

"Do you want to talk about what has come between you? I am a fine listener, I assure you."

Emily attempted a smile, but it did not reach her eyes. "It is good of you, Imogen. But truly, it is so long ago that I cannot recall what even started it." Her hand, however, reached up seemingly of its own volition to touch her scarred cheek. She quickly tried to hide the tell by moving her fingers to her hair, as if to pat a stray tendril in place.

"Very well. But should you ever need to bend an ear, I do hope you will take me up on my offer. And you must promise to write once I leave, and often."

"Of course." Emily looked at her oddly then. "But won't you be back?"

Imogen's lips trembled under the effort of keeping her smile in place. "No, I don't believe so."

Emily frowned and looked about to question her, but a noise across the room distracted her. Breathing a sigh of relief, Imogen followed Emily's gaze to the group that had a moment ago been playing cards. Lord Tarryton was packing the deck away and Lady Willbridge and Daphne were conversing quietly. Caleb had risen from his seat and was striding their way.

"Excuse me," Emily said, and before Imogen could react she was scurrying to join the rest of her family.

Caleb was at Imogen's elbow in seconds. "My mother was talking about having some music. I suggested you sing for us."

She glanced up sharply into his pale eyes. The sadness that had been present since before dinner was still there. She longed to reach up, to smooth the small line that had appeared between his brows. Instead she clenched her hands before her tightly.

"You know I cannot," she said. "I've told you that before. I hate to sing in front of others."

"And yet you sing with my sister."

Was that a hint of hurt she detected in his tone? But his features were calm, impassive.

"I have only ever sung for my family."

"Please, sing for me," he murmured. "I feel if I do not hear you now, I may never get the chance."

His words startled her. It was almost as if he were aware of something about to occur, something life-changing. Was he finally going to accept her refusal of him and let her move on? And why did that thought bring her not one bit of relief?

She laid her hand on his arm. "Caleb, is something wrong?"

He looked at her oddly for a moment but only shook his head.

She took a step closer, heedless of the eyes that must be watching them with curiosity. "Please, perhaps I can be of help."

For a moment she thought he would confide in her. But then he took up her hand, placing a delicate kiss on her knuckles. "Tomorrow," he decreed. "Tomorrow I shall tell you everything. For now let us enjoy the night. I have waited an age to hear your voice. Please sing for me."

If the words had not been enough to do her in, the vulnerable look in his eyes would have. He appeared fragile, as if he were about to shatter. She had never seen him thus. He had always appeared so strong, so capable. She never dreamed his naturally high spirits could be brought so low as they had been the last few days.

But the proof was before her. He was hurting, dreadfully. And if she could help alleviate that pain for even a small while, then she would do it. No matter how her stomach roiled at the thought of singing for him.

"Very well," she replied.

Relief seemed to explode from him in a sigh, and his lips turned up in a very real smile. He led her over to the pianoforte. Imogen sat at the bench and began to rifle through the music sheets laying there. Her hands trembled, the papers shaking in her grip. She forced her trepidation down as brutally as she could. This could be another gift she could give to Caleb, she decided. And perhaps, even more than that, it could be a gift to herself. She could not verbalize her feelings for him, or even allow him to guess at them. But she could put her very heart into this performance, to let him know in her own secret, private way just how deeply she felt for him.

She decided on "Sweeter Than Roses," a seventeenth-century aria. She spread the music before her and then, taking a deep, steadying breath, she positioned her fingers over the keys.

She started the song off low and languid, letting her voice dip into the notes, rising and falling with graceful melody. It was not an easy piece by far. But she put all herself into the song of passion. Every bit of love, every bit of desire, was poured into the words.

> "'Sweeter than roses, or cool evening breeze,
> On a warm flowery shore, was the dear kiss,
> First trembling made me freeze,
> Then shot like fire all o'er.
> What magic has victorious love!
> For all I touch or see since that dear kiss,
> I hourly prove, all is love to me.'"

She was achingly aware of Caleb at her elbow, his gaze hot on her face, his body but a short distance from her own. Her chest swelled with emotion, tears burning behind her eyes, and still she kept on, letting the words pour from her.

As the song picked up momentum she recalled the way he had loved her, how his body had fused with and moved within her own. She allowed the joy of that magical moment to enter her heart, to come through in her voice.

The song swept her along, until, finally, it came to a finish. Imogen closed her eyes as the last of the notes on the pianoforte faded, unable to bear being back here in the drawing room with their families. She positively ached for him. How would she live through this?

There was a long moment of silence. Suddenly the room broke out in applause. She hastily wiped at her damp eyes before facing her audience.

Her father, beaming, came to her and took up her hands. "My dear, never have you sounded better. What a waste that you hide that voice away from all of us."

She rose and allowed him to lead her to Lady Willbridge and her daughters. As she accepted their praise with silent smiles, she glanced at Caleb.

He was still standing by the pianoforte, watching her. His face was impassive as stone, but his eyes burned.

If only he loved her, she thought, turning back to the others, she would never have to leave him.

• • •

The night dragged on. There was a peculiar tension in the air like there had been the night of the thunderstorm, an electricity of anticipation. Strangely enough, it only touched Caleb and herself. Everyone else seemed blithely unaware.

When it was time to retire, Imogen was surprised to find Caleb at her side.

He held out his arm to her. "Will you allow me to escort you upstairs?"

She looked at him a long moment and then directed her gaze to the others. They were chatting amiably and already heading out the door.

Gingerly she placed her fingers on his arm. "Of course."

As he led her from the room, his steps slowed. She could feel an unexplained strain rolling off him in waves. More than once she thought he was about to say something as he tilted his head in her direction, but to her frustration he remained steadfastly silent.

By the time they reached her room, the hallway was quiet. The wall sconces glowed golden at intervals, not emitting enough light for her to see his expression clearly. His eyes in particular were deep in shadow.

"Caleb, what is it?" she whispered.

He shook his head with quick, jerky movements. "Nothing. It can wait."

But lines of tension bracketed his mouth and radiated from his eyes. She reached up and laid her palm on his cheek, unable to keep from touching him.

"Please tell me," she said. "Maybe it can help to talk about it."

He gave a tortured shudder and reached up, gripping her wrist and imprisoning her hand against his face. Turning his head, he pressed his lips hotly into her palm. Her breath felt trapped in her chest, and every nerve ending in her body seemed to have settled on that sensitive flesh.

"Imogen," he whispered against her skin. "Please let me kiss you." When she made no answer, he raised his head. His eyes glittered in the faint light, his breath coming in short spurts. "I swear, that's all I want, just a kiss. I won't ask you for more. Just let me hold you, feel you."

Her mind screamed that she should send him away and retreat to her room. But her body, her heart, cried out for his embrace. She gazed into his shadowed face, knowing what she should say. And yet the words would not form on her tongue. He held himself still, waiting for her answer.

Suddenly she caught the slight movement at his jaw. He was grinding his teeth together, forcing himself to be patient.

Her heart twisted. She knew the pain he felt was merely superficial, that he did not love her, only desired her. But even so she could no more deny him than turn back time.

Wordlessly she reached out for him. His eyes widened a moment before he grabbed her and hauled her against him. His mouth found hers, and she gripped his shoulders to keep her knees from buckling.

How badly she had wanted this. When last they had kissed, the night before their trip into Ketterby, Caleb had been infinitely tender with her, the kiss fleeting and yet heart-wrenching. Before that, in the knot garden, he had been wild, pulling a response from her that she had not wanted to give. Now he seemed to consume her with a focused intensity. His hands roamed over her back and hips, his movements slow, as if he were trying to memorize every detail of her. His lips devoured her own, eliciting a responding moan from her. One hand fumbled for the doorknob behind her, the other pressing her flush against him as he opened her bedroom door and pulled her through.

Once inside he closed the door and pushed her against the wall. Her body yielded to his, and she whimpered as she felt his arousal press into her belly. Heat and moisture flared in the center of her, and she writhed against him, desperately trying to get closer. His mouth moved to her throat, sucking at the tender flesh where it met her shoulder. Imogen gasped and arched her head to the side, silently pleading for more.

In reply he growled low, the vibrations on her skin leaving her shivering with need. One of his hands hiked up her skirts. He found the sensitive skin behind her knee, gripped it tight, hauled her leg up. And then he was between her legs, his hardness pressing through the barriers of their clothing.

"Caleb," she moaned. Her hands were in his thick, silky hair, pulling his mouth back to hers. She felt him shudder in response, was dimly aware as his hands reached between their bodies and fumbled for the fastening at his breeches.

But he stilled. His chest heaving, he gave her one final, achingly sweet kiss before he lowered her feet back to the ground, disentangling her arms from him and righting her clothing.

She stared up at him blankly, wanting to cry from the need that still filled her. "Caleb?"

"I will not break my promises to you, Imogen," he replied quietly. "You are far too important."

He released her. Before she had time to react he was through the door, closing it quietly behind him, leaving Imogen to stare mutely at the space he had been.

Chapter 28

Early the next morning Imogen opened the door to the gardens and peered out, securing her shawl about her shoulders. The air was chilly, the sun not yet over the horizon. A faint mist lay over the land, and along with the pale gray light the landscape was cast in a ghostly pall.

A perfect morning for visiting a graveyard, Imogen thought wryly as she stepped into the dewy air and closed the door behind her.

She took a moment to get her bearings before setting out in the direction the housekeeper had indicated. Small, cold droplets of moisture pelted her face, misting her spectacles. She wiped impatiently at them and pulled her shawl closer about her as she strode through the sunken garden, past the small pond to the far end. At the break in the hedge, instead of heading straight to the avenue of oaks and the stone bridge as she had with Caleb that first morning, she turned right. She had a sudden vision of Emily running into them during that very same walk, nearly toppling her in her haste to get back to the house.

Emily had been coming from the cemetery, she realized now.

She walked on, the trees appearing from the fog, their branches like upraised arms embracing their early morning shrouds. Shivering, she hurried her steps. She wanted to get this over with, to return to the house before anyone else awoke.

Imogen had not been able to sleep the night before. She had been appalled with how quickly and completely she had surrendered to Caleb. She would have given herself to him without a second's thought.

It had occurred to her, with a decided lack of surprise, that she was quickly running out of time. Not in the sense that she was leaving in a few days, but that her heart was once again winning the battle.

She knew she would refuse his offer of marriage when next he offered. Frances's pain was too fresh in her mind for her to do anything less. But that did not stop her from loving him, from wanting him, from nearly giving herself to him again. And that she could not do.

There was still the matter of helping Caleb regain his closeness with his family. But how could she possibly accomplish that in the short time she had left...and without succumbing to Caleb in the meantime?

It had been in that moment, as she had lain in her bed, exhausted but unable to find rest, that she'd thought of visiting the boy at the center of the turmoil. She would go to Jonathan's grave, she'd decided, and see if she could garner any inspiration from it. It was a mad idea at best. But she was willing to try anything at this point.

She had risen before dawn had lit the sky and dressed hastily by the light of a candle. And then she had sought out the house-keeper, who gave her directions to the family plot, and raced from the house before she could think better of it.

And now here she was, rounding the small parsonage. The sun began an earnest burn through the fading fog. As the ancient stone church came into view, the golden morning light hit it, giving a warm, honeyed glow to its hallowed walls. Imogen paused to soak the beauty of it in, taking strength from it, before she moved off toward the Masters family plot.

She let herself through the small wrought iron gate, breathing a sigh of relief as it swung on silent hinges. Immediately she saw a still figure at the far end in a dark gray cloak covering a pale blue dress. The lady had her head bowed, her bonnet obscuring her face. But Imogen knew who it was; there could be but one person here.

Imogen walked slowly through smaller graves and into the family plot, the large rectangular edifices and beautiful, elegant lines of the carved stone standing testimony to the status of the departed. Several of the older tombs were worn by the elements, pockmarked from wind and rain, moss dotting their surfaces. But as she moved further on she saw the graves here were newer, their stone smooth and cleared of growth. The tomb that rose up before the silent figure was particularly well cared for, its pale face soaking in the fresh light of dawn.

The woman at the grave showed no signs of hearing her approach. Imogen drew up quietly beside her. "Emily," she said softly.

Emily gasped, spinning to face her. "Imogen, what in heaven's name are you doing here?"

She motioned toward the stone edifice before them. "The same as you, I suppose. I came to pay my respects."

Emily looked at her oddly. "You never knew him."

"But you did. You loved him, and still do."

A tremulous smile touched Emily's mouth, pulling at her scar. She reached out a gloved hand, and Imogen took hold of it. Together they turned to face Jonathan's resting place. Imogen studied it, noted the meticulous way the grass and bramble had been cleared from it and the fresh bundle of flowers that adorned it.

"How often do you come here?" she asked.

Emily sighed, her breath carrying on the morning air. "Not very often. Perhaps once a month. Maybe less." She paused. "Well, more than that since Caleb has returned home, I suppose." She turned to face Imogen. "He has never been home for such a length of time. When he is here, it's typically only for a matter of days. It's because of you, you know."

Imogen blushed and kept her gaze on the stone, tracing over the engraved letters. "It was kind of him to invite my father and me."

"It was not kindness on his part," Emily replied. "I know he wishes to marry you. We all do. Surely you must realize as well."

Imogen was surprised to feel tears sting her eyes. "I know."

"And you won't have him?"

Imogen swallowed hard. "No."

Emily pulled on her hand, forcing Imogen to face her. "But you love him. I see it in your face when he's not looking."

It was not a question, and didn't need an answer. How appalling, Imogen thought with a sad humor, that her feelings were so glaringly obvious.

"If you love him, why won't you marry him?" Emily asked.

Imogen struggled for an answer. Finally she could only say, "It's...complicated."

Emily frowned. "I don't pretend to understand. Things must be much deeper than I'm aware, much more convoluted. But I do know," she said quietly, shyly, "that I would very much like to have you for my sister." When Imogen made to speak, she held up her hand. "I know things have been bewildering here. It's not natural for families to be as estranged as we are. I promise you, however, that my mother, sister, and I will move to the dower house once you marry Caleb. You can live here in peace. Just do please consider it."

Imogen felt her heart constrict. "How I wish I could. You have no idea how much. But," she said, her voice rising in strength, as if to convince herself, "I cannot marry Caleb. Not now. I don't think ever."

• • •

Caleb had not slept well. Actually, he had not slept at all. Imogen's response to him, her acceptance of his kiss, the feel of her in his arms, had left him aching for half of the night. The other half was spent in worry. He would tell her directly after breakfast. And after that, his future, their future together, would be in her hands. Anxiety filled him at the thought, and he tossed and turned in his bed, his sheets twisting about him.

As the horizon began to glow with the slow, gray creep toward dawn, he gave a harsh exhale and sat up. There was no use lying abed. He would dress, get out of doors, work off some of his excess energy with a brisk walk.

But as he set out, he knew no amount of activity could exorcise his demons.

He stopped at the sunken gardens, looked up at the sky, where the sun burned through the last of the fog. The warmth of it, so comforting after the coolness of the damp morning air, seeped into his very bones. In that moment he knew what he needed to do. For before he told Imogen of his past sins and asked her to marry him regardless, he first had to ask forgiveness from the one he had harmed the most.

The walk to the cemetery seemed to take an inordinately long time. He had only been once since his brother had been laid to rest, and that was for their father's funeral a few short years after. He could still recall the pain of seeing that fresh stone, the name carved into it sharp and new.

There were times when he was feeling vulnerable that he let the mantel of self-preservation go and he remembered his younger brother. It was then he could recall every heartbreaking detail, from the cocky, robust joy on his face, to the boundless energy that had him leaping from one forbidden adventure to another. He could see the shock of copper hair that never stayed put no matter how much it was brushed, the lanky frame that no seat could contain, even hear his infectious laughter that started from his belly and shook his whole body.

Caleb thought of that during his walk to the boy's resting place. The guilt rose up as it always did, bowing his shoulders, making it hard to breathe. But it was time he stopped trying to forget. If he was to have any future with Imogen, he had to come to terms with Jonathan's death and his own part in it.

Finally he was at the churchyard gate. He let himself in, walked unseeing past the graves of known and unknown people of the town, headed for the more stately tombs of his ancestors.

He was nearly upon the two figures at the far end before he even realized they were there.

The shock of seeing Imogen and Emily before Jonathan's grave froze him. In the next instant he had the horrified thought that he should move away. He could come back to make his peace another time.

But as he made to leave, Imogen's words reached him, sending a jolt of despair through him.

"I cannot marry Caleb. Not now. I don't think ever."

Chapter 29

Unable to help himself, Caleb turned back to the two women. Imogen's words swirled through his head. Had Emily been working at hurting his suit? Had she purposely sabotaged his chances with Imogen?

The answer was glaringly obvious. Of course she had. He was guilty, deserved every bit of pain he had received for it. But when would it end? Was he forced to pay for one mistake—as heinous as it had been—for the rest of his life?

Hurt, followed quickly by fury, lanced through Caleb, consuming the confusion that had overwhelmed him but moments before. He ignored the desperate reasoning in his head that told him Imogen had always been opposed to marriage to him, that her words could well be nothing more than a reflection of those earlier thoughts. Instead his heart took over, silencing all else.

He marched toward them, each step sending a jolt up through his limbs, feeding the rage that hummed through his body. He was hurting; he wanted to make someone else hurt as well.

He could tell by the stiffening of her shoulders that Imogen sensed him first. She released Emily's hand and turned to face him, starting violently. Her eyes widened behind her spectacles.

"Caleb, what in heaven's name are you doing here?" she exclaimed, attempting a smile. But she had always been an abysmal actress. The remembrance made his chest ache, and he pushed it aside.

Her voice, normally so quiet, was overloud in the hush of

the early morning air. Emily faced him with a sharp pivot, her surprise evident.

Caleb remained silent. He watched with narrowed eyes as Imogen's false smile wavered on her lips—lips he had kissed just the night before—and she peered sideways at Emily. His sister, for her part, had gone uncommonly pale. Her scar stood out, angry and red on her cheek. Pain overwhelmed him, as it always did when he looked on his sister's injuries. It was a visible reminder of the sins of his past.

"I could ask the same of you," he finally stated with barely controlled fury in his voice. "It is not a common place for two young ladies to walk at the break of dawn." He took a step closer.

Imogen watched him closely, guilt evident on her sweet face. "It is not *uncommon* to pay one's respects to the departed," she said, her voice full of false bravado.

"Am I to understand that you typically walk out of doors before breakfast to visit the grave of someone you never knew? My goodness, I seem to learn something new about you every day, my dear."

At his tone Imogen's eyes narrowed. "It is not unheard of, if one's friend was close to the departed."

The words shot like a barb. His guilt made him harsh as he turned to Emily. "Ah yes. Your friend. How could I forget that you two have grown so close in the past days?"

"We have," Imogen answered, a new caution coating her words.

"I wonder just how much my dear sister has told you of that long-ago day when Jonathan died," he mused, his voice cruel. Emily made a strangled sound in her throat and backed up a step.

He clenched his teeth. Her reaction was answer enough.

"Yes, I see you have been filling Imogen's ear with every detail," he choked.

Imogen stepped into his path, her eyes turquoise flames. Her action was blatant; she was protecting Emily from him. The thought was almost laughable. It had been Emily who had done the damage this day.

"She has told me nothing of how your brother died," Imogen said, her voice tight. "And, indeed, I do not know why you are attacking your sister, my lord. She has been nothing but your champion."

This he did laugh at, the sound harsh and raw even to his own ears. "My champion? Is that what you call ruining one's chances for marriage?" He turned back to Emily, his anger mounting. "You must have seen how I've been suffering all this time. Why did you do it? Why have you punished me even more?"

Suddenly Imogen's hand was on his arm, tugging him back. "Caleb, what in heaven's name are you talking about? What is wrong with you?"

He spun on her, his anger spiraling out of control. "And you," he said through gritted teeth, "I thought you were unlike everyone else. I thought you would not hold it over my head, would at least attempt to hear the story from my own lips before you rushed to judgment. But you could not give me even that, could you?"

A sudden movement drew his attention. He caught sight of Emily just as she crumpled against the smooth stone of their brother's tomb, her head bowed. Before he could move toward her, however, Imogen was there. She pulled Emily's arm up and over her shoulder, supporting her around the waist with the other. Emily's head lolled on her shoulder.

When Caleb made an instinctual move to help, Imogen looked at him. Her beautiful gaze was full of disappointment, confusion, and condemnation.

Suddenly an overwhelming weariness pressed down on him. All was lost. *Imogen* was lost.

He stumbled back, his hip ramming against the elegant, cold grave of an unknown ancestor before he turned and moved through the tombs to the gate. His feet felt as if they were encased in lead, his shoulders weighted with the burden of his sins.

As he left the two girls behind, he reminded himself he should have known, should not have allowed himself to hope. His past would never let him go.

• • •

Imogen watched in disbelief as Caleb lurched away from them, through the iron gate and into the trees, her heart aching. There was something that teased her just out of sight, something she knew was not quite right, a detail that would explain everything. She longed to go after him, to force him to explain. But Emily moaned in her arms, and she knew it would have to wait.

"Emily," she said urgently as the girl's weight settled more heavily in her arms. "You must get a hold of yourself."

But she made no indication of having heard her. "All my fault," she mumbled, her eyes closed, as if in pain. "I should have known, should have stopped him."

"Emily," Imogen barked, knowing she could not manage to get the girl home without some help from her. When Emily still made no sign of coming to her senses, Imogen released the arm that she had secured around her shoulder and slapped her. Hard.

Emily gasped, her eyes flying open, hurt and bewildered but cognizant of the world again.

"I need you to gain control of yourself until we reach home. Can you do that?"

Emily nodded, scrubbing at her wet cheeks. Soon they were heading out of the churchyard, past the parsonage and toward home.

By the time they arrived back at Willowhaven, Imogen was sweating from the exertion of half guiding, half supporting Emily as they stumbled along.

"Just a small while longer, dearest," Imogen panted. "Let me get you to bed, and then you may become insensible to your heart's content."

Emily merely nodded, but she seemed to rally. They managed to get through the house and to Emily's chamber, though not unseen. After Imogen tucked the girl under some blankets and left, closing the door softly behind her, the butler approached.

"Miss Duncan, I have heard reports that Lady Emily is unwell. Is anything amiss?"

"Lady Emily has had a fright and is overcome," she replied. "Please have a maid come and sit with her while I fetch her ladyship."

"Of course, miss," the butler responded, the slight widening of his eyes the only indication of his alarm. He turned to go, but Imogen stopped him.

"Has Lord Willbridge returned?"

He looked puzzled. "I'm sorry, I don't believe Lord Willbridge has risen for the day yet, miss," he said before hurrying off.

Imogen stood in the now empty hall, at a loss. Caleb had obviously not yet returned, or the staff would have been aware that he was awake.

Shaking her head, she hurried off to find Lady Willbridge. She had Emily to care for first. Only then would she search for Caleb. He could not be far.

• • •

Later that evening, however, Imogen still had no idea where Caleb was. He had not returned to the house, though she had been made aware sometime in the late morning that he'd stopped off in the stables and had a horse saddled before riding off at great speed for parts unknown.

Imogen took another look out the window of the drawing room before resuming her pacing. Dinner was over an hour past, the sky dark and starless. She was frustrated and worried. And angry. How inconsiderate he was being. The least he could do was be present so she could rail at him.

"Imogen," her father called to her from across the room, "you'll worry yourself sick if you keep that up. Please, sit down and relax dear."

"Your father is correct," Lady Willbridge said, lowering her embroidery. Her face was pale, new lines of strain radiating from the corners of her eyes. "My son is a headstrong young man. He will return when he's ready."

Instead of doing as they bid, she asked in a distracted voice,

"Do you suppose we should send grooms out to search for him? It is quite dark; if he went riding in this, his horse may have stepped in a hole and taken lame."

At that Daphne rose and went to her. She linked her arm through Imogen's, giving it a small squeeze. "Come and sit. Your worrying certainly isn't going to bring him home any faster."

"Lady Daphne has the right of it," her father said. "Lady Emily is resting soundly, and Lord Willbridge is a grown man who has taken care of himself for years. He is certainly too smart to take dangerous chances on the road on such a moonless night. He's likely staying with a friend and will return after daybreak."

"Very well," Imogen replied, reluctantly allowing Daphne to lead her back to the couch. She took up the glass of ratafia she had left there earlier, before her vigil at the window. The cloying taste washed over her tongue, but she welcomed it. A horrible dryness had settled in her mouth since her return with Emily that morning and she couldn't seem to rid herself of it.

Caleb's strong reaction to their presence at the cemetery only reinforced Imogen's suspicions. Jonathan's death was, indeed, the cause of the unrest here. It seemed, however, she had more questions than ever. What had happened when Jonathan had died? Why had Caleb attacked his sister because of it? She had tried to talk to Emily, but the girl had been given laudanum to help her rest and was beyond conversation at the moment.

Her fingers tightened on the delicate stem of her glass. If only Caleb would return. There were answers he owed her, answers he owed his family. She looked into the dark burnt orange liquid, swirling it in her glass, her jaw tensing as she watched the light struggle through it.

Once she saw him, she would get those answers or die trying.

Chapter 30

Dawn was just beginning to break when Imogen heard it: a pounding at the heavy front door, not loud enough to wake the entire household but with enough sound to capture the attention of someone who had lain awake all night long, listening for something just like it. Her eyes flew open and she threw off her covers, bounding from bed. She quickly donned her spectacles, night robe, and slippers before hurrying from her room.

Billsby was just opening the door when Imogen raced into the front hall. The sight that greeted her eyes, however, had her skidding to a shocked stop.

Large, jolly Donald Samson, proprietor of the Regal Swan Inn, was propping up a very disheveled, very inebriated Caleb.

"Dear me," Imogen breathed. She stepped forward. "Mr. Samson, is Lord Willbridge injured?"

"Miss Duncan, lovely to see you, though perhaps not under the circumstances." He grinned at her. "No, he's not injured, though it's not from lack of trying."

"Perhaps we'd best get him to bed and you can tell me what has become of the good marquess." She turned, Donald trudging along behind her, half guiding and half carrying Caleb.

Suddenly the butler intervened, his hands flapping frantically. "Miss Duncan, you cannot accompany Lord Willbridge to his bedchamber. It isn't proper."

"Nonsense," Imogen said, stopping to face Billsby. Donald halted behind her, heaving a bit at Caleb's weight. "Lord Willbridge is in need of care, and I would rather it not be common knowledge below stairs what has become of him. I also would not want to upset his mother any further with his behavior."

Luckily the butler reacted to the note of command in her voice and dropped back. Unluckily, Caleb chose that moment to realize she was there.

He raised his head, gazing at her blearily. His eyes were red-rimmed and heavy-lidded, a day's growth of coppery beard shadowing his face. "'S that you, Imogen? Donald," he said in a loud whisper, "it's my Imogen. I want t' marry the girl but she wo—won't have me. Can't figure 't out, m'self."

Donald turned his head away from his friend and wrinkled his nose, presumably from the strong odor of liquor on Caleb's breath. "I don't know, I can think of a few reasons right now."

He grunted as Caleb suddenly made to step toward her. The loss of balance almost sent them both tumbling to the tiled floor, but the larger man kept his hold on the marquess, widening his stance to provide support. Even so, Caleb was a tall man, and Donald was breathing hard from the exertion of holding him upright.

Imogen stepped toward Caleb, her face burning. "Now you listen here," she said firmly. "You are going to help poor Mr. Samson as he brings you to your room, and you will remain quiet to keep from waking the rest of the household. Am I understood?"

To her surprise Caleb nodded meekly. Just catching Donald's approving look, she turned and marched away, the two men lurching along behind her, slowly but blessedly quiet.

Several stumbles and near topples later and they finally reached the master bedchamber. As Imogen opened the door and made to enter the room, Donald stopped and made a distressed sound in his throat. She raised one brow in question.

"You shouldn't be going in there I think, Miss Duncan." His face was red, and not just from his exertions.

"I assure you, Mr. Samson, I am no milk and water miss. Lord Willbridge requires my help at the moment, and I have no qualms helping him into bed."

She entered the room and Donald reluctantly followed. He

reached the bed, heaving Caleb onto it. Caleb fell into the soft mattress with a grunt.

"M' heads spinning, Donald. What the devil?" he said before his head fell to the side. At first Imogen thought he was unconscious, until a healthy snore reverberated from his chest.

Imogen sighed and took hold of Caleb's foot, pointing to the other. "If you would be so kind, Mr. Samson? And while we're at it, perhaps you can fill me in on Lord Willbridge's whereabouts over the past day."

"Well," he began, grabbing Caleb's leg and working at removing his boot, "as you probably know this one's as stubborn as they come. He came to the inn early last evening, his horse in a lather, calling for drink. We sat about for some time talking, and before I knew it he'd gone through a good portion of a bottle of my best scotch. By then he was more than a bit drunk. Even though the hour was late and it was darker than the inside of a witch's cauldron, he insisted on returning home. I tried to get him into a bed at the inn, but he would have nothing to do with it, said he wanted to return home."

He'd finished with the boot and together they moved to his jacket. While Donald rolled Caleb onto his side, Imogen worked the material from his arm. "And so, though I hate to admit it, I kept him at the inn drinking, hoping he'd just pass out and that would be an end to it. It was either that or risk him toppling from that beast of his and breaking his damn foolish neck. Oh, my pardon, Miss Duncan."

Imogen waved one hand in the air. "Please, think nothing of it. I am just grateful you were there for him." She looked up at him. "You are a very good friend to his lordship."

Donald blushed, dipping his head in acknowledgement before turning Caleb on his other side so she could reach his other sleeve.

They worked in silence for a time, the only sound their labored breathing as they worked to divest Caleb of a portion of his clothes, and Caleb's own soft snores. Finally they had him down to his breeches and shirt. Propping him on his side with a pillow behind his back in case he vomited while sleeping, Imogen and Donald stood back, looking down at the blissfully slumbering marquess.

As one they turned for the door. Imogen closed it quietly behind them and they started down the hall to the main staircase.

"What I cannot figure," Donald said in a hushed voice, "is what got him so riled up to begin with. I've never seen him in such a state."

Imogen's eyes narrowed. "You can be assured, Mr. Samson, that I will find that out."

• • •

The first thing Caleb was aware of was a bright, burning light. It shined through his eyelids in a haze of red, tearing into his head with a searing, hot pain.

"Close those damn drapes," he growled. But even that sound made him gasp as it ricocheted about his skull. He winced, and at the indrawn breath felt the dryness in his mouth. He smacked his lips together ineffectively. His throat felt raw, his mouth like cotton.

He sensed movement at the side of his bed—it *was* his bed, wasn't it? Must be his valet. Several violent thoughts coalesced in his head. He'd be sure to dock the man's wages after this. What kind of a human being woke a man up in so brutal a manner after he'd spent the better part of the night drinking himself into a stupor?

He received an answer to that a moment later.

He sputtered and gasped as what felt like the entire contents of the River Spratt was poured over his face. The utter unexpectedness—as well as the chill—of it shocked him to complete wakefulness. His eyes flew open in outrage, his hand coming up to slough the water off of his face.

Who he saw standing over him, however, was not anticipated.

Of course, he'd really had no idea who would be nearly drowning him in his own bed. But he certainly hadn't expected Imogen. Holding an empty water pitcher. With a glare like an enraged Fury.

"What the devil are you doing?" he bellowed.

To her credit, she didn't even so much as flinch. "I want some answers from you, and I feel I've waited long enough," she said with impressive hauteur. He had never seen her thus, and felt he would have been aroused if he wasn't so damn mad. And wet.

He glanced in disbelief down at the bed, the sheets dripping, the pillow sodden, his shirt and breeches clinging to him in an uncomfortable, clammy way. "And you had to drown me to get them?"

She cocked one eyebrow, her lips twisting. "As it is already late afternoon, I thought it prudent to wake you."

His head swung in disbelief to the window—he winced again at the sudden movement—and sure enough, only indirect light filtered in. His window faced east, which meant the sun was well on its daily journey at the other side of the house. He had slept all day? What in hell had been in that whiskey last night?

He turned with careful movements to Imogen. "And what answers would you be wanting, madam?"

She placed the pitcher on the bedside table, a muscle in her jaw ticking. "I would like to know why you reacted so harshly to your sister yesterday morning when you found us at the cemetery."

With a sudden flash of insight he remembered everything, why he had stayed away all day yesterday and why he had drunk himself insensible. Emily and Imogen at Jonathan's grave; Imogen proclaiming to Emily that she could not marry him; their fight after; the pain he had felt at Imogen's betrayal.

Rage began to pound within him, pushing aside the thick-headed befuddlement that had been present since he had been woken in such an abrupt manner. He swung his legs over the side of the bed and stood slowly, breathing deeply, trying to rein in his temper. Rivulets of water dripped from his clothes, pooling on the polished wood floor, but he paid it no mind. He towered over Imogen, expecting to see her shrink back, but she only stuck her chin out and narrowed her eyes.

"Perhaps you are the one who should be providing answers," he said in biting tones.

"I get the distinct feeling," Imogen said, not in the least cowed by his demeanor, "that you believe yourself to be wronged somehow."

"No, just unfairly judged."

"I assure you, the only thing I am judging you on is your asinine behavior to your sister yesterday."

"Is that true?" He curled his lip. "Then why did I hear you declare that you cannot marry me? Do you mean to tell me that comment was not brought on by something Emily told you?"

Imogen blushed, but her eyes narrowed. "You know I have always been opposed to marriage," she said, her voice low and saturated with pain.

A twinge of doubt crept in.

"You seem to be under the impression that somehow your sister sabotaged your chances," she continued. "That could not be further from the truth."

"What do you mean?"

"I did not lie yesterday when I said Emily has been your champion. She had just gotten through with trying to convince me to accept you before I declared I could not marry you."

He stared at her a long moment. "That cannot be."

"Why, because you cannot conceive that I made my decision on my own? You think my mind would be altered by anything she could have told me?"

Pain washed through him. "Yes."

Her eyes tensed at the corners like they used to when she went without her spectacles. "Perhaps you had best explain."

Bitterness mingled with the pain. "What is the point? You have already declared you will not have me."

He suddenly turned from her, unable to bear being so close to her now that he knew she was lost to him. He strode for the door to his dressing room.

"Where are you going?" Imogen cried. He could hear her scuttling after him but didn't turn around.

"I'm going to change out of these clothes," he said, the weary defeat in his voice apparent even to him, "and then we can see about getting you ready for your journey back to London."

Chapter 31

Imogen's steps faltered. He was sending her home before she could get the answers she needed to help this damaged family. But a second later she resolutely put her head down and marched forward. She grabbed Caleb's arm just as he was about to go through the door and spun him to face her.

"Now you listen to me," she ground out. "I will not stand by and watch you completely destroy whatever tenuous peace this blasted family is living under. You will give me answers, and you will give them to me now."

His eyes had dulled, and he regarded her with a weary defeat. "Why? You'll be leaving soon. Telling you will change nothing."

Her heart ached at the lost look in his eyes. But she could not have put that there. He did not love her, after all. He would forget her soon enough.

That did not mean, however, that she had to leave him with nothing.

"That may be. But then again, telling me may help everything," she said. "Let me in, Caleb."

He regarded her uncertainly for a moment. It was now or never.

"I have already figured that it has to do with Jonathan's death."

Such pain flared in his eyes that her chest constricted. She reached for his hand and squeezed it reassuringly.

"If Emily did not tell you, how did you find out?" he asked, his voice hollow and resigned.

She smiled sadly. "All part of being a wallflower, I'm afraid. I'm unbelievably observant."

Still, he looked uncertain. She pursed her lips, and then gave him a little push toward the dressing room door. "Why don't you change into something dry? When you return, I expect answers."

He nodded distractedly and disappeared inside. Imogen went to a set of heavy mahogany chairs before one of the windows, sinking onto the slate blue damask cushions.

It wasn't long before Caleb appeared, dressed in a dry linen shirt open at the chest and soft buckskin breeches. His hair was still damp but now brushed back from his forehead. He regarded her with hooded eyes for a moment before joining her. Imogen clasped her hands primly in her lap, turning her eyes to the landscape out the window, patiently waiting for him to start.

"I loved my brother," he said haltingly. "Before I begin, you must know that."

She shifted her gaze to his and nodded. For some reason her heart was thumping like mad in her chest. She clasped her hands tighter to keep herself from reaching for him.

"I always allowed him to follow after me. We were ridiculously close, he and I. I am not being conceited when I say I know he looked up to me. And he was such a jolly fellow, a veritable ray of sunshine, that I admit I admired him as well.

"That last morning, however—" Here he stopped. He cleared his throat and stared unseeing out the window. "I was twenty. I had my two closest friends visiting, Tristan and Morley. Perhaps you remember them?" At her nod he continued. "We were young men and wanted to discuss women and gambling and all things inappropriate for younger ears. We had made plans to spend the following morning together by the fishing pond, reveling in this new level of adulthood we had reached. I did not want my younger siblings tagging along. And I told Jonathan so."

His mouth twisted, but not in humor. There was a deep self-loathing in that expression. "He did not take it well, I'm afraid. We fought. I told him I didn't want children with us, that he would ruin it for us. I told him he was a burden, an infant, a loadstone I didn't need around my neck."

Imogen's heart ached as she watched Caleb's profile. The muscles in his jaw worked painfully and he swallowed hard.

"We set out early the next morning. I had no idea that Jonathan and Emily had snuck from the house to follow us. They had taken a circuitous route, you see, not wanting to be spied, and had tried to make their way over an embankment of rocks. But I saw them. I was so angry…" For a moment he sat silently, seemingly lost in his memories. Suddenly, he cleared his throat, looking at Imogen quickly before resuming.

"I climbed up to them. We fought." He pressed his lips together, seemed to struggle for words. "So many words I said, that I wish I could recall. I finally turned to leave. But Jonathan grabbed at my arm. I threw it up, trying to ward him off. He flailed. The look on his face was full of such surprise. And then the rocks gave way…"

His voice trailed off. Imogen could stand it no longer. She reached out and gripped his fingers. To her relief he gripped hers back fiercely, as if she were his lifeline.

"There was such a sound. As long as I live I shall never forget it. The deep rumbling that fairly split my ears, the screams. I thought it would never end. As if in slow motion I saw him scramble, try to get purchase on the tumbling rocks. I reached for him, but it was too late. When the dust cleared there he was, at the bottom of it all. He was so still."

His voice was guttural, infused with pain. The words seemed to speed up as they poured from him. "There was so much blood. And Emily was trying to get to him, stumbling over the rocks. She fell, tore her cheek open. She was like a wild animal, trying to reach him. I remember her clawing desperately at the rock still lodged on Jonathan's chest. She would not stop screaming. Her face was pouring blood from the gash, her nails torn and bleeding from pulling at the rock. We tried to drag her away, but it was as if she didn't know we were there. We finally managed to subdue her, to remove the rock from Jonathan. When she saw he was gone, truly saw he was dead, she fainted. We carried them home. I can still remember the blood on my hands, that horrible smell."

Imogen's heart drummed painfully and her eyes burned. What they must have endured. And yet—

Still things did not add up. Why had there been ten years of estrangement following that?

"Caleb," she said gently, "I don't understand. Why this breach with your family?"

He looked at her, the raw agony in his eyes overlaid with disbelief. "But don't you see?" he said, his voice hoarse. "It was my fault."

Imogen looked at him in shock. "Oh, no, Caleb."

But he was shaking his head. "If I had only let him join us, he would still be here today. But I was so full of pride. I hurt and disparaged him. And when he made to hold me back, I practically pushed him to his death."

Imogen could see from the hard glint in his eyes that he was not about to let this go easily. Like Donald Samson had said early that morning, he was so damned stubborn.

She sat forward. "Caleb, did you mean to throw your brother off balance?"

A look of horror and anger suffused his face. "Of course not."

"Then how could you possibly be at fault?"

"How could I not be? It was because of my actions that he fell."

"Do you mean to tell me," she pushed, "that had it been Emily who had accidentally thrown Jonathan off balance, you would expect her to take the full guilt onto her shoulders?"

"Of course not," he scoffed. "What mad idea is this?"

"Then tell me how it is any more sane for you to do so."

Caleb went to the window, looking down into the gardens. "You don't understand. You were not there."

Imogen watched him, noting the stiff cast to his shoulders under the fine lawn shirt. That was true. She hadn't been there. She could never fully know the details of what had occurred, and so she knew her words would forever fall on deaf ears.

Her eyes narrowed as she considered what to do. There had been others there. Sir Tristan and Lord Morley, of course, who were back in London. But also Emily. If she could just get the two to talk, for Emily to make him see that she did not blame him, perhaps he could let go of some of the guilt.

She thought long and hard on this as Caleb stood silently at the window. His reaction to Emily yesterday morning told her all she needed to know. He believed Emily blamed him, that she was punishing him. They had to make him see that this was not the case.

But would Emily go for such a plan? Especially now that she was so fragile? She recalled the girl's advocacy on her brother's behalf, trying to get Imogen to accept his suit, and she knew in her heart that Caleb's sister would help.

Imogen straightened. "You believe Emily blames you for Jonathan's death."

He glanced at her over his shoulder, the indirect light of the fading day throwing his features into harsh lines. "Of course. Why wouldn't she? I took away the person she loved best in this world. She is scarred for life because of it."

"And have the two of you ever talked of it?"

As he turned back to the window he gave a harsh laugh. "Of course not. Her feelings are plain on her face. We have no need to bring it up and court more misery."

"It is why you believed so easily that she would try and turn me against you."

He gave her no response but a shifting of his weight, a further tensing of his shoulders. It was answer enough.

"And yet," she mused, "that conjecture, which you were so certain of, was wrong."

A peculiar stillness settled over him. He faced her. "Yes," he admitted gruffly. "I did her a disservice by thinking such a thing."

The pain in his eyes nearly made her falter. But she could

not back down now. No matter the grief he was feeling at this moment, it would be well worth it if she could reconcile these two damaged souls.

"Couldn't it be possible, then," she said, "that your other ideas regarding her could be wrong as well?"

But he was already shaking his head. "No——"

Imogen held up a hand. "Do me the honor of hearing me out before you discount what I have to say. You cannot possibly know what is in Emily's heart until you make an attempt to understand it. I have gotten to know her a bit in the past few days, and I can say that she is one of the sweetest girls of my acquaintance. She has never, not once, said anything to make me believe she holds you in any contempt. Indeed, I get the distinct impression that your distance grieves her."

He stared at her in disbelief. "That cannot possibly be true."

"I assure you, it is."

Several emotions flashed across his face. "Then why did she not come to me?"

"Why did you not go to her?" Imogen shot back. "And besides, your sister is shy, even more shy than me in some ways. Do you honestly believe she would have put herself forward with you, who has become in so many ways a stranger to her?"

Caleb flinched. "What would you have me do?"

Imogen stood and moved toward him. "Go to her. Talk to her. Truly, you have nothing to lose and everything to gain. If she verifies your feelings, you will be in the same position you have been for the past decade. But, if she does as I think she will and tells you that you were not to blame, you both can begin to heal this wound that has been festering. You can regain your sister. And, I hope, you will also begin to forgive yourself."

At his dubious look, she took hold of his hand, giving it a tug. "You won't know until you try. Do you truly want this doubt hanging over your head for the rest of your life?"

It was with a burst of relief that she saw his shoulders slouch in defeat. She gave another tug on his hand and he followed, to what she hoped would be a healing for them all.

• • •

The distance between Caleb's room and his sister's was not long, and before he was at all ready they were there. Imogen knocked sharply at the door. There was no answer. Caleb glanced down at Imogen uncertainly. To his surprise she pressed her lips together and took hold of the handle, pushing in, pulling him in after her.

He stood frozen for a moment, allowing his eyes to adjust to the sudden lack of light. Despite the hour of the day, Emily's room was plunged into gloom, the curtains drawn tight. Only a few candles had been placed about, barely penetrating the darkness. He finally spotted his sister, seated before the empty hearth, a guttering candle at her elbow, an unopened book beside her.

"I told you before, Mother," she said, her voice painfully brittle, "I'm not hungry."

"It is not your mother," Imogen murmured. Her voice was gentle and soft. Even so, Emily looked in their direction sharply.

Her face immediately paled when she saw Caleb. Pain flared in her eyes. Pain, Caleb noticed, not blame or hate. Was it possible that Imogen was right? Had he only seen what he expected to see?

"What is going on here?" she rasped. Betrayal saturated her features. "Why is he here, Imogen?"

Imogen pulled Caleb further into the room. "He is here to talk."

"Talk?" Emily asked in disbelief. "What is there to talk about? I cannot think of anything more he might wish to say to me."

As his sister presented them with her stiff profile, Imogen gave a small growl of frustration. "Both of you are more alike than you know, stubborn as the day is long. You will have this out, now. Do you know, Emily, that your brother has been blaming himself for Jonathan's death all these years?"

Pain flooded Emily's face and she gave a shuddering breath. "Yes," she whispered.

"Did you not think it wise to disabuse him of that notion?"

Emily swung her eyes to them. "Our mother and father tried for years to tell him he wasn't to blame. If he would not believe them, what would make me think he would listen to the likes of me?"

"Because," Imogen said, her voice gentling, "it was your opinion that mattered most."

His sister's pale eyes, so like his own and Jonathan's, settled on him. His breath caught at the incredulity there. "But why?" Emily whispered.

Imogen, at Caleb's side, nudged him forward. He gave her one last doubtful look before he moved closer to his sister and sank into the chair beside her. It went against everything he had been taught to sit in Imogen's presence. But he could not tower over Emily for this.

"I know you must blame me, Emily," he said. His voice came out rough and broken, and he cleared his throat. "You saw what happened. I practically pushed him. He is dead because of my selfishness and pride."

But his sister sat forward, her formerly dull eyes suddenly blazing. "No, it was an accident. I know you never meant to throw him off balance. You did nothing wrong. If anyone is to blame, it is I."

Caleb was certain he must not have heard her right. "What did you say?"

Emily's eyes filled with tears. When she spoke, her words poured from her in a rush. "It was my fault. I should have told you long ago. I knew you blamed yourself. But I was so young, and the years passed, and it just seemed easier and easier not to say anything. It was horribly selfish of me. I am so sorry." Her voice broke on a sob. She covered her mouth with her hand.

Caleb could only look at her in shock. Of anything she could have said, he had certainly not expected this. He glanced up at

Imogen, who was looking at them both with wide eyes. When she caught Caleb's gaze, she gave a quick shake of her head. So she had not known of this either.

He turned back to his sister. "How could you possibly be at fault? You were a twelve-year-old girl. You loved him so much, more than any of us could understand."

"But that is just it, don't you see? I was jealous of you."

He stared at her. "Jealous of me?"

She looked down at her hands. They were gripped tightly together in her lap. "We laughed at what you had said to him the night before. You had acted so important in front of your friends, were becoming a man of your own. Jonathan admired you so very much, and I could see that, even though he made light of it, he was hurt by what you had said. But he was so ready to forgive you, to let it pass. I, however, was not." She swallowed hard. "I provoked him, used his small hurt, enflamed it. Jonathan was my best friend, but he looked up to you so very much, at times he hardly saw me."

Her breath hitched in her chest. "I didn't know my taunting would compel him to follow you. I caught him that morning, sneaking from the house. And instead of stopping him, I went with him. I should have stopped him—"

Her voice broke off on a sob.

Tears burned in Caleb's throat. What she had suffered all these years. All this time he had been blaming himself, she had been thinking herself guilty. And with the reminder of the scar on her face, reflected to her from every mirror, was it any wonder it had dragged her into the shell of a creature she was now?

He left his seat and went to his knees in front of her, reaching out and gently pulling her to him. He folded his arms about her thin form, and for a moment she sat frigid in his embrace.

"It is not your fault, you know," he whispered into the top of her head. "It is not your fault."

She gave a violent shudder before, with a soft cry, she crumpled in his arms. He held her up, gently rocking her, as her fingers dug into his shirt, her tears soaking the fabric. He caught sight of Imogen's face as she made her way to the door and quietly let herself out. There were tears in her eyes, but she was smiling.

Caleb knew in that moment a lifting of the burden that had propelled him on for so many years. The ever-present crack that throbbed so painfully in his heart began to heal. For the first time in too long, he felt peace.

Chapter 32

Imogen had just packed the last of her things away for the trip back to London when a knock sounded at her door.

She hurriedly wiped at her eyes, which had been continually moist since she had left Caleb and Emily an hour or better before, and called out, "Come in."

It did not surprise her to see Caleb stride into the room. Nor did the painful twist her heart gave. What did surprise her was the lightness in his eyes. She could not remember ever seeing such a free expression on his face.

She smiled. "You are reconciled."

"Yes." He looked amazed, as if he could not quite believe it was possible.

"I am glad," she whispered. "So glad. It was my fondest hope."

He stayed silent for a long time, gazing at her. Without warning, he strode to her, taking her face in his hands. She gasped as he bent and brushed his lips against hers.

"Thank you," he whispered. "Thank you for giving my family back to me."

She could only stand there mutely as his lips traveled butterfly soft over her mouth, her cheeks, her eyes. She reached up, gripping his shoulders. She thought of returning to London the next day, of never seeing him again, and just barely stopped the sob that threatened to burst from her lips.

She would miss him, so much that even the thought of it nearly broke her. Just one more memory, she thought greedily. Just one more kiss, one more embrace to sustain her.

Imogen pushed herself onto her toes, her lips pressing to Caleb's. Her hands found their way into his hair, dragging him to her, deepening the embrace. She had never been so bold, had never taken charge in such a way before. She could feel the shock of it freeze up every muscle in his body. But he didn't remain that way for long. With a groan his arms went around her back, crushing her body to his. His mouth opened over hers and Imogen felt as if her very breath were being stolen from her lungs. She would not think of tomorrow, would not even let a whisper of the future intrude right now. She was in the arms of the man she loved—that was all that mattered.

She arched into him, pressing into the lean strength of his body. His hands splayed over her back, kneading through the layers of material and into her muscles, moving down until he cupped her bottom. Heat pooled between her legs as she felt him, hard and insistent, pressing into her belly. Desire snaked across her limbs, down her thighs, leaving her knees too weak to hold her. His arms tightened, pulling her even more completely into his body. She wanted nothing more than to sink to the floor, to pull him atop her, to feel him fill her.

But even with these thoughts, when he made to move deeper into the room toward her bed she froze. *No*, her mind screamed, even as her body ached, begging for him, begging for release. Her mind desperately fought for dominance. She knew once they reached the bed that there was no turning back. Finally, with a strength she didn't know she possessed, she wrenched herself free.

She scrambled across the room, trying to distance herself from him, knowing if he came near her that she would fall back into his arms. He watched her intently, his face a blank mask, the only sound in the room their labored breathing, but he made no move to go after her.

"I'm sorry," she gasped. "That was a mistake. That should not have happened." With trembling fingers she straightened her spectacles.

He considered her for a long moment. Without warning he

began walking toward her. She scuttled along the wall, away from him. He paused.

"It was no mistake, Imogen," he said carefully, his voice low and measured, as if he were talking down a frightened horse. "Don't you see what we have together?"

"Yes," she said shakily as she rounded a chair. Her fingers dug into the cushioned back. "We have friendship, and passion. But that is not enough, Caleb."

Her throat closed up before she declared herself. For heaven's sake, she was practically begging him to admit to stronger feelings. But even as she knew those words would not come, she found herself holding her breath. All it would take, she knew, to keep her here, was some hope that he could love her. Just the smallest kernel.

Instead he said, with a hint of impatience, "Of course it is enough. Imogen, we have had this discussion before."

"Yes, we have," she agreed hollowly.

"I believed you could be made to come around." He ran a hand through his hair, his agitation apparent. "I do not know why you have proven so stubborn in this. It is ideal on both sides. You get a husband, will get out from under your mother's thumb. I get an ideal marchioness, one who understands me and whom I feel a great deal of passion for."

Imogen shrugged off the mounting despair, instead drawing herself up before him. "It may be ideal for you, my lord. But it is not for me."

Caleb threw his hands up, his voice rising. "No? And what is ideal, living the life of a spinster, falling back into a shadow under your mother's tyranny?"

She flinched. He saw it, a look of contrition falling over his face. "Forgive me. That was not well done of me."

"I'm sorry, my lord," she managed through a throat tight with tears, "after those glowing words, but my decision stands. I will not marry you."

With as much dignity as Imogen could muster, she went to the door, pulling it wide. It was an unmistakable dismissal.

He was silent for so long that she felt her forced calm begin to crumble. When he spoke, his voice was saturated with disbelief. "Imogen, you cannot mean that."

She straightened her back until it ached, keeping her gaze straight ahead. "I assure you, I do," she replied, putting as much cold certainty into her voice that she could muster. "You have known all along that I won't marry you. It should come as no surprise."

"Is this your final answer? Because I promise you, I will not repeat my offer again."

His voice was so filled with confusion and hurt that she nearly relented. Instead she gripped the doorknob tighter and swallowed past the lump in her throat. "Yes," she whispered, "it is." She took a deep breath. "My father and I will be leaving at first light tomorrow morning. Please don't see us off. And please don't seek me out in London."

There was a heavy silence. Out of the corner of her eye she saw his head swivel to her trunks, packed and stacked against one wall, and then return to her.

"As you wish."

He brushed past her, his steps faltering for only a second. Then he was out the door and down the hallway. She closed the door before, with a violent sob, she sank to the floor and let loose her tears.

• • •

Caleb stood at one of the tall windows in the Long Gallery the following morning, his hands clasped behind his back. Below him, in the front courtyard, the carriages waited in the early morning sunlight, the first rays of dawn having just broken through the tree line. Footmen were putting the last of the trunks into place, Imogen's maid and Lord Tarryton's valet disappearing into the smaller carriage.

A minute later Lord Tarryton himself appeared. He looked

briefly back at the house, shaking his head mournfully before climbing into the larger carriage.

Caleb's eyes eagled in on the space directly beneath him. Suddenly she was there, Emily's arm tight about her shoulders. Imogen's back was straight, her hair back in that infernal bun. She received Emily's hug stiffly before climbing into the carriage. He could just make out her dim profile through the window, could see her pale cheek and the tight line of her mouth.

His eyes locked onto her, devouring her, taking in what he could. He willed her to look up, to acknowledge him, to show even a small bit of the loss he felt at their parting. But she did not, and with a jolt, the carriages lurched forward, and he could see her no more. Within moments they were rounding the circular drive, slipping through the tall stone columns and down the long avenue.

He didn't know how long he stood there. He only knew the carriages had disappeared from view long ago and the sun was climbing to its zenith when he felt a gentle hand on his shoulder.

He pulled his tired eyes away from the horizon reluctantly to look down into Emily's upturned face.

"Caleb," she said softly. Her own eyes were red-rimmed as she looked at him, but she gave him a small smile.

"Do you know what I could use right now?" she asked him. "A good pounding ride. What do you say to joining me?"

He wanted to return her smile, but his mouth would not respond. He was about to tell her he wanted to be alone right now, but he looked at her and saw a near reflection of his own grief mirrored. Emily had come to care for Imogen as well and had to realize what this sudden leave-taking meant.

He felt humbled. That she was opening herself to trust him, to need him, after what had occurred between them, was brave indeed. And if she could be brave enough to show her need for him, then he could as well. He held out his arm to her, his heart lightening a bit when he saw relief pass over her face.

They made their way to the stables, and before long they were mounted up and galloping over the vast back lawn. Caleb let his gelding have his head, concentrating on the feel of the horse beneath him, the rhythmic sound of the hooves pounding into the ground, the way the wind whipped past him and burned into his eyes. Emily kept pace beside him, leaning low over her mare's neck. He had not known she could ride so well, and found himself wondering what else she could do, what else she liked and disliked. He truly didn't know a thing about his sister. He felt a biting regret of the years lost, but pushed it away as he thought of the time they had ahead of them to know each other again. He had his sister back, his entire family back.

And it was all due to Imogen.

He frowned and pulled his mind back from where it had wandered. He could not think about her. It would drive him mad.

They stopped for a short time to rest their horses before heading back to the stables. As one they turned their mounts over to the grooms and began the short walk back to the house, but as they approached it he remembered that *she* was no longer there, with her calming presence and quiet smile. He thought of the long night ahead of him and clenched his jaw painfully, walking on.

Back in the house he turned to Emily. She had been a silent support throughout the day. Now she reached out with only the smallest hesitation and took his hand, giving it a small, reassuring squeeze.

"Thank you for today," he said to her, returning the pressure of her hand, hoping she could see the deep gratitude that his paltry words could not convey.

She smiled and nodded before turning away, heading for the music room. He watched her go, and after a short while he could hear the delicate strains of the pianoforte through the closed door. He started for his study, not wanting to remember how Imogen had played for him that one night, her voice sweet and swelling with emotion, as if she were trying to convey something important to him.

He suddenly stopped, his hand on the study door. She *had* been trying to tell him something that night. He thought of the expression in her turquoise eyes as she had sung, the same emotion he had glimpsed more than once when she believed he wasn't looking.

In an instant he knew, deep in his heart, just what she had been so desperately trying to say.

"She loves me?" he murmured in disbelief. His voice echoed about the hall, as if mocking him for his stupidity.

He sagged against the door. But no, how could that possibly be? She had refused him. Why would she do so if she loved him? Now that the thought had been brought into being, however, he could not let it go. He shook his head, unable to wrap his mind about this new information. With that disbelief came an energy that filled his tired body and had his feet taking him unseeing through the house. When he stopped and looked up, only to find himself outside Imogen's bedroom door, it did not surprise him one bit.

He opened the door, letting it swing wide before he stepped over the threshold. As it felt with the rest of the house, the space was cold and empty without her in it. He let his eyes take in the room, looking on the dressing table she had used, the mirror she had gazed into. The bed she had slept in.

It was there he went, letting his fingers trail over the neat coverlet. Everything was in its place, the maids having erased all sign of her. Tension worked into his shoulders, making his body stiffen and his fingers curl in on themselves. It was several seconds before he realized what it was that was saturating his body with such fearsome force. Panic.

She was gone. Truly gone. She had loved him, and yet had left him. Why? He leaned over and pressed his fisted hands into the bed. His panic ripened, turning to anger. Why had she left him? They loved each other. Wasn't that the very best reason for two people to marry?

In the next second he realized just what he had admitted to himself.

That could not possibly mean what he thought it did. Surely

he loved her just as a friend. Not in the romantic sense. Not in that ridiculous way that sent young girls' hearts fluttering and turned men into imbeciles. In that moment, however, he felt it, the realigning of the pieces of himself, and the pattern was suddenly clear. He *did* love her.

Dear God in heaven, he loved Imogen.

How had he not seen it? How had he been so blind to something so very important? But before the questions had even formed in his mind, he knew the answer. She had so quickly become a dear friend to him, though he didn't deserve it. Over the last weeks he had been so afraid of losing that friendship that he had been oblivious to the true nature of his deepening feelings for her.

Would he have ever seen it if Imogen had not healed his family, if she had not released him from his guilt? If he had not felt worthy of having her for a friend, there was no way he would have ever accepted that what he felt for her was love. But he could see it now, in all its beauty and brilliance.

"I love Imogen," he murmured in wonder.

But in the next moment he realized the futility of the realization. She had left him. She was gone and never wanted to see him again.

Exhaustion overwhelmed him. With a great sigh he turned about and sat on the bed. He'd had his chance at happiness and had lost it. He propped his elbows on his knees, resting his head in his hands. But no matter how he squeezed his eyes shut, no matter how he pressed his fingers into his scalp, he could not erase her from his mind. The recollections came and he gave in to them, like a floodgate collapsing under raging waters.

It was random at first, a jumble of memories, her sweet face at the center of them all. Soon, however, they began to rearrange themselves. Imogen the evening before, telling him that she needed more in marriage, the look of pleading in her eyes, his callous words that their union of friendship and passion was so ideal. The achingly sad look she had given him after her love song to him three nights ago. And then a flash of her first night at Willowhaven, when they had met in the library and he had told her he wasn't the type to fall in love.

All that time, had she been begging him for even the possibility that he could love her? Had she been telling him in her own way that she felt more, and needed more from him? Caleb felt his agitation grow. He had been such a dunce. And now he had lost her forever.

He straightened, frowning. No, he could not believe that. There had to be a chance for them still. He would go to London, would make her see that he loved her, that they could make a go of it. A tentative hope bloomed in his chest. Yes, he would make her see, they belonged together.

In the next moment he was up and bounding from the room. "Billsby!" he called as he sprinted down the hall and through the Long Gallery. "Damn it man, where are you when I need you? I need to leave for London at once."

He had just reached the main staircase when his mother emerged from the room adjacent. "And so you are finally leaving, my darling boy," she said. "Granted, I do wish I had you to myself for a small while longer now that I have you back. But I can only be glad it is Imogen who captured your heart."

Caleb stopped and stared at her. She was smiling broadly, none of the strain of the past years evident on her still lovely face. Their reconciliation had been quiet, natural, as if no time at all had passed, no heartache had come between them. As he stood there looking at her, he could not now imagine what could have made him think that she could ever lose her love for him.

His throat tightened with emotion. "How long have you known?"

She came closer, taking up his hand. "That you are in love with Imogen? From the first moment she set foot in that drawing room."

He looked at her in bewilderment. "But even *I* didn't know."

"Some things are obvious to a parent." His mother gave him a satisfied smile and squeezed his hand before releasing it. "Now, as much as I'd love for you to stay, I think you'd better leave with all due haste. And when you finally secure that wonderful girl, you come straight back here. I've a mind to know both my son and new daughter better."

The hope that had begun to bloom in him blossomed then to vibrant life. Grinning, he took his mother in his arms and planted a kiss on her cheek. Spinning about, he sped down the stairs, leaving the marchioness smiling after him.

Chapter 33

Imogen was glad she had given herself free rein to cry her heart out the night before their departure from Willowhaven. During the long carriage ride to London, when she'd had nothing to do but sit and think, she had been blessedly drained.

Her father only once attempted to ask what had happened. "Dearest," he said once they were under way, "did you and Lord Willbridge fight? This leave-taking of ours seems too sudden. I feel something is not right here."

"No, Papa," she answered in a dull monotone, "we did not fight."

He sighed and settled back in his seat. "I don't understand it. I can see you care for him, my girl. Why won't you have him? Did he change his mind? Has he done something despicable?"

She felt weary to her very bones. She trained her eyes on the passing scenery, the long avenue of trees they had entered through on that first day. It seemed so long ago now. Another lifetime entirely.

"No, nothing like that. I refused him, is all."

"But you love him!" her father finally exploded.

She turned to him, too numb to feel surprise, though it was the most agitated she had ever seen him. Having lived with her mother for nearly thirty years, he had perfected the art of outward calm, and rarely lost his composure.

"Papa," she said slowly, "you promised you would abide by my decision at the end of our trip. Please keep that promise to me, I beg you."

He must have heard the slight catch in her voice at the end.

"As you wish, my dear," he replied gently. After giving her one last solemn look, he took up his book and buried himself in the pages.

The rest of their journey was spent in near total silence. Now it was late afternoon of the following day and they were just pulling up to their London townhouse. Her father took up her hand before the door to the carriage opened.

"I just want you to know, dearest, that I shall support you. Always. Don't take your mother's words to heart. She may be harsh, but she does love you."

Imogen looked deep into her father's gentle eyes and felt the first stirrings of tears since their departure. There was nothing in his expression but utter love.

"Thank you, Papa," she whispered just as the door was flung open. They were handed down to the pavement and made their way up the townhouse steps.

The butler stood there to greet them and divest them of their outer garments. "My lord, Miss Duncan, I trust you had a pleasant trip."

"Thank you, Gillian. Are Lady Tarryton and Miss Mariah at home?" Lord Tarryton murmured, his eyes sweeping about the hall. Imogen could sense his worry for her as a palpable thing and felt what was left of her heart give a twist.

"Yes, my lord," the butler answered. "They have just returned and said to inform you they will be down momentarily."

Before the words were out of Gillian's mouth a vision in sage green came tearing down the stairs. She launched herself at Imogen, nearly knocking her from her feet. As Mariah's slender arms came about her, Imogen felt a terrible crumbling of the barricades she had erected. A small sob escaped her before she could stop it, and she hugged her sister back fiercely.

"Oh, Imogen," Mariah murmured mournfully, stroking her back, having gained every bit of knowledge she needed at Imogen's reaction.

Suddenly a strident voice carried across the hall. "Well, you're back, and a day earlier than I had figured. I trust you bring me joyful news?"

Imogen squeezed her eyes shut and buried her face in her sister's shoulder. Mariah hugged her tighter.

"Not now, Harriett," she heard her father mutter quietly.

"But what is this?" Lady Tarryton continued. "You can't mean to tell me she refused him again?" Her voice rose as she spoke, until it was nearly a shriek.

"Give her some time," her father said, his voice growing tense. "Can't you see Imogen is overwrought?"

"Overwrought?" her mother screeched. "She should be overwrought! Refusing a marquess, and twice? The girl is mad. I am ashamed to call her my daughter. I want nothing more to do with her. I disown her."

At that pronouncement, a shocked hush fell over those assembled in the hall. Imogen let the words clang about in her head for a time, soaking them in. Her tears subsided, a calm settling about her, a strange surge of steel travelling down her spine. She straightened, pulling away from Mariah, and turned to face her mother.

Lady Tarryton's mouth hung open like a trout's. She looked at her eldest with wide eyes. Apparently she had shocked herself as much as everyone else. Even at her worst she had never made such a horrible proclamation. But a moment later she pulled herself up to her full height and regarded the room with her typical haughty stare.

"I don't know what I've done to deserve your censure and disapproval all these years," Imogen said with quiet dignity. "I have done everything I could to please you. But it was never enough. I understand that you were upset when you spoke those words just now, and therefore I will not hold them against you.

"However, please know that though I was happy to come to London for my sister, I will be returning to Hillview Manor tomorrow. I'm sure you all realize I have not been content here in town, and I know you only want what is best for me, which is to return to the country with all due speed. If when you return home it pains you to have me in the house, I will set up my own household with Papa's help."

With that she turned and walked toward the stairs. Her hand on the railing, she said over her shoulder, "Now, if you'll excuse me, I have to make plans for my trip tomorrow."

She walked up the stairs without a backward glance.

• • •

Mariah stole into Imogen's room late that night, her face drawn from worry. But there was a certain unconcealed awe in her eyes. She stood with her back pressed to the door, studying Imogen.

"What is it?" Imogen said, pushing aside the covers on her bed and rushing to her sister.

"You have changed so much," Mariah breathed. "I never thought you would stand up to Mama as you did."

Imogen winced. Though she felt empowered, though it had been the right thing to do, she felt a twinge of guilt. Having been brought up to obey, she doubted it would ever be comfortable for her to go against her parents' wishes. "Was she very upset?" she asked, pulling Mariah over to the bed and settling onto it with her.

A twinkle entered Mariah's cerulean blue eyes. "Very. She slumped right to the floor. Papa had to revive her with smelling salts. And when she came to and began thrashing about, moaning and carrying on, he just left her there." She giggled. "When Mama saw she had no audience she got right up, gave a sniff, and called for the carriage to take her shopping."

Imogen clapped a hand over her mouth to keep from laughing. "You are jesting, surely."

"On my honor, it's the truth." She chuckled. "Oh, Imogen, you were fantastic. If nothing else, Lord Willbridge has done wonders for your self-worth." Mariah suddenly gasped, her eyes filling with regret. "Oh, I am so sorry, dearest."

The shock of hearing Caleb's title hit Imogen like a kick to the stomach. She patted Mariah's hand, hating the misery on her sister's face, though her heart felt as if it were breaking anew. "Why should you be sorry?" she whispered. "It's true. He did give me a strength I never knew I had. Or, at least, he helped me to realize the strength that was already in me."

"But why did you refuse him, Imogen? I can tell you love him."

Imogen laughed without humor. "Dear me, everyone seems to have been able to guess at my feelings for him. It's amazing that the man himself never realized. Though I should be grateful, considering his decided lack of that particular sentiment." Her voice had turned bitter, and she took a deep breath to calm the ugly emotions clamoring inside her.

Mariah looked at her in confusion. "But I don't understand. Lord Willbridge cares for you very much."

"Yes," Imogen replied, suddenly beyond weary, "as a friend and no more."

"But even if that were true—which I do not believe it is—shouldn't you give it a chance, to see if something stronger could develop?"

"Mariah, you have seen what has happened to Frances."

At the mention of their sister, Mariah's face fell. "But that is a different matter entirely."

"Is it? She loves her husband, desperately. And he does not love her. You have seen what that has done to her. She used to be so very jolly, always happy, always laughing. But I cannot remember the last time I saw her smile. I cannot live that life, Mariah. It would kill me. You know it would."

Even Mariah could not fight such logic, she saw. The younger girl's shoulders slumped in defeat. Imogen buried her grief and forced an apologetic smile. "I'm sorry, dearest, but I really do need to get some sleep if I'm to leave on the morrow."

Mariah roused a bit at that and looked as if she were about to argue the matter, but at the last moment she pressed her lips together and nodded. As she leaned in to embrace her sister, however, she whispered, "You are wrong about his feelings for you, you know. I only hope you see it before it's too late."

Chapter 34

A soft tapping sound woke Imogen some hours later. She jolted awake, staring with wide eyes at the darkness around her, listening intently but hearing nothing further. Just as she began to relax back into sleep, thinking perhaps she had imagined the entire thing, she heard it again.

Tap, tap, tap. Something was hitting her window softly, with rhythmic regularity. Could it be the branches of the tree that loomed nearby?

But a second later she heard a soft curse. Fear coursed through her. Trees certainly did not curse.

And then someone began to push her window open...*from the outside.*

She bolted upright, fumbling for her spectacles, her hands shaking as she reached for the book on her bedside table, the only heavy object within reach.

She slipped from the bed, eyes wide and anchored to the dark figure slithering into the room. Keeping to the shadows, she held the book tightly to her chest. The intruder moved toward the bed on silent feet, pausing when he saw it was empty. A chill stole through her.

She watched as he began feeling about the bedside table. Moving behind him, she raised the book high above her. Her muscles tensed, ready to bring the tome down on his head. She gave a fervent thanks for the heavy volume of Shakespearian plays she had decided to bring to bed with her when a candle flared to life. The intruder turned, his face illuminated.

Imogen gasped and dropped the book. It landed on her bare toes and she winced, dropping to the floor to rub away the pain.

"Imogen," Caleb whispered, bending down beside her. "Are you hurt?"

Foot throbbing, eyes stinging, she looked up at him incredulously. "Caleb, what are you *doing* here?"

Instead of answering, he gripped her hands, helping her up. As soon as she was standing, she pulled away from him. Her mind was whirling, her heart beating hard in her chest.

He stepped toward her, but she held up a shaking hand. He stopped, his face tight with frustration.

"Why are you here in London?" she repeated. "Why aren't you back at Willowhaven with your family?"

"I had to see you." There was something new in his voice that she was vaguely aware of, even in the midst of the turmoil she was feeling.

"You saw me just two days ago," Imogen said harshly. "I think we said everything there was to say to each other then."

"No, there's more."

He looked as if he were about to draw close to her again. Desperate to put more distance between them, she moved to the open window, looking down at the three-story drop to the ground. She imagined him scaling the spindly tree, using the narrow stone ledge of the building to access her window, and shuddered.

Her back to him, the chill night air cooling her flushed skin, she rasped, "So you raced halfway across the country? You climb in through my bedroom window in the middle of the night? Why couldn't you wait to use the front door?"

"I knew you wouldn't see me."

"No. No, I wouldn't. And you know why, Caleb." She concentrated on slowing her agitated breathing, on steadying her heartbeat. But her voice still came out strained. "Why can't you leave me alone? Please, respect my decision. I said I will not marry you."

She could hear him moving closer. She tensed, but he didn't reach out to touch her.

"How can I respect your decision when I don't understand it?" He paused, and the air was rife with tension. "I know you love me, Imogen."

Imogen's knees nearly buckled. She reached out a hand to catch herself, but he was already there, his hands warm on her arms.

"What did you say?" She swung about, her eyes flying to his face.

His gaze softened, and he brushed a strand of hair from her cheek. "Why didn't you tell me you loved me, Imogen?"

His expression nearly undid her. More than anything, she wanted to melt into his embrace. She had used too much of her strength to leave him; she felt completely vulnerable now. She wasn't supposed to have seen him again. How was she to build her defenses up against him now, when she had been torn raw from the pain of leaving him?

"It makes no difference," she said through stiff lips.

His arms came about her and he pulled her against his body. She was acutely aware of how thin her nightgown was, of how completely unclothed she felt.

"It makes all the difference in the world," he said, brushing her lips with his own. She closed her eyes and shuddered at the sensations bombarding her. But somehow, when her hands made to move up and grip his shoulders, she was able to reach deep down in herself and find one small shred of strength left. She placed her hands flat on his chest and pushed herself away from him.

"No, Caleb," she choked, stumbling free from his grasp and turning from him. "Please, I cannot bear it."

She rushed for the door, desperate to escape him, to escape the pain that seared her very heart. She didn't care why he had chased her back to London. She could not do this anymore. This time she was certain it would destroy her.

"But I love you," he whispered.

She gasped and reached out for the wall to steady herself.

"What?" she breathed.

He was suddenly at her back, his arms about her waist, his breath hot in her ear. "I love you," he repeated, his voice tender. He pulled her back against his chest, his hands strong as they splayed across her middle.

But she was shaking her head, her hair rasping against his coat. "I know you love me. As a friend."

"No, I *love* you, Imogen. As the other half of my heart." He spun her to face him. His pale gray eyes held new worlds of emotion in their depths. "Yes, we're friends. Yes, we have passion. And you were right, for a marriage to work, we would need more. Imogen, we *have* more."

It wasn't until he reached up and wiped at her wet cheek with his thumb that she realized she was crying. "You were crying the first night we met," he murmured. "Do you remember?"

She nodded, unable to speak, too overcome with the emotions welling up in her. For so long she had forced them down. Now, however, they were breaking free.

Her eyes searched his face frantically, looking for any doubt there. This could not possibly be real. She had to be dreaming; that was the only excuse. But no, his body was solid and warm, pressed to hers. And his eyes were open, and honest, and true.

Hope uncurled like a sleeping bird in her heart, woken after too long a slumber. And it began to sing.

"I will forever be grateful that you stumbled upon me that night," he said. "You have brought a calm and happiness to my life that I never thought to have again—indeed, never thought I even deserved."

"You love me?" she whispered.

He smiled and pulled her closer. "How could I not? You are beautiful and kind and generous. I'm only amazed it took me so long to realize."

Still Imogen could find no words. She was dizzy with the whirl of emotions—first such utter despair, followed by such staggering joy she was afraid to grasp onto it. She reached up, gingerly touching his face, his lips. He clasped her hand, pulling it to his mouth, pressing a fervent kiss to her skin.

"I have been a fool," he said, his eyes roaming greedily over her face. "I was so blind to the truth that it nearly cost me you. If I had only realized before. It came on me so gradually, I couldn't see it for what it was. Though I think I have loved you since I saw you transformed at that masquerade ball."

Imogen felt a sudden dimming of her joy. He had loved her since she had changed into a completely different person? She began to pull away from him, but he held tight.

"Since," he continued, reaching a finger under her chin to tilt her face up, "I realized that I'd rather have you as you are, and not as a copy of every other debutante out for the Season. Since I realized that I could not deny the pull you had on me. You ground me, make me a better man. My life was a shell before you stumbled into it. And thank God you did."

He pulled her flush against him and she opened her arms to him. His breath stirred the tendrils of her hair that had escaped her braid as he embraced her.

"Marry me, Imogen," he pleaded, his lips moving at her temple, his hands cradling her like the most precious of treasures. "Marry me, and make me the happiest of men."

She smiled into his shoulder as all the doubt and sorrow in her heart melted away. "Yes," she whispered.

He stilled, and then pulled away just enough to look into her face. His eyes, dim in the candlelight, flared with a fierce joy. "Say it again."

She laughed. "Yes, I will marry you, Caleb."

Before the words had completely left her mouth, his lips covered hers. His fingers splayed over her hips, digging into their roundness, pulling her against him. Her thin nightgown was barely a barrier to the hard press of his body. Her skin felt as if it were bursting into flame. She reached up, her fingers diving through the thick softness of his hair, her heart singing as he bent over her, forming his body to hers. She felt wrapped up in him, safe and cherished.

His lips moved from her mouth, trailing over her cheek, to the sensitive skin near her ear. "I love you," he growled against her flesh, his voice sending waves of pleasure through her body, his words sending pure joy to her heart. "I love you so very much, Imogen."

She gasped as his lips worked a path down her neck to her collarbone. She strained against him, needing more, needing to be closer to him. "Please, Caleb," she moaned, her fingers tugging at his clothing.

His hands released her and she nearly collapsed, her legs were so weak from wanting him. But the world suddenly tilted, and she was cradled against his chest for a short moment before being lowered gently to her bed.

"I will get a special license," he promised, his lips trailing down to her breast. He took possession of the straining tip, and Imogen nearly choked at the feel of his hot mouth through the thin material.

"Yes, you will," she panted, unable to bear the thought of even one night without him in her bed.

"We can marry as soon as tomorrow," he went on, sitting up and rapidly divesting himself of his clothing, his eyes hot on her, raking her body with fierce possessiveness.

Imogen chuckled low in her throat. "You may have a battle ahead of you. Do you think my mother will allow her daughter to marry a marquess and not gloat to all of society about it?"

"I don't give a damn about your mother, or for society either."

She smiled, getting up on her knees, the better to watch as he stripped off his clothing. "We can give her two weeks," she suggested. The heat between her legs only grew hotter as his muscled chest was revealed. She cleared her throat and adjusted her spectacles.

"One week," he growled, looking at her, devouring her. His face was pure need. Need for her.

Imogen felt a power she never had before shoot through her at the realization that this incredible man hungered for her. And not just her body. He hungered for her love as well, so much so that he had raced across counties to get to her, had scaled a three-story building to proclaim his love for her.

She smiled and placed her spectacles on the bedside table before, reaching down, she located the hem of her nightgown and pulled it slowly over her head, letting it fall from her fingers to the carpet. Caleb watched her with an intent, raw yearning. She reached for her braid and brought it over her shoulder, working the plait apart. His eyes fastened on the movement, on how the strands came free and curled over her breast. Her nipples hardened under his stare.

"Sweet heaven, Imogen," he rasped, shoving his breeches and drawers over his lean hips, discarding them on the floor. And then he kneeled on the bed before her, pulling her into his arms, his body pressed tight to hers.

Imogen gave a long sigh of pleasure at the sensation of his naked flesh against her own, at his arousal pressing into her stomach. She was overcome by the undeniable urge to touch him. Her lips pressed into the strained cords in his neck, lathing him with her tongue, pulling at his skin with her mouth. A ragged breath escaped him. He fell back into the softness of the bed, bringing her with him, pulling her over him.

Imogen gave a small squeak of surprise at the change in position. But then she smiled into his skin, reveling in the sense of control it gave her. She continued her attentions, pressing her lips to his chest, taking one of his small, flat nipples in her mouth. He groaned, straining against her.

Suddenly his hands were at her thighs. He gripped them tight, pulled them wide until she was straddling his stomach. Her mouth opened in surprise.

"Can it be done this way as well, then?" she whispered.

A wicked smile spread over his face. "This and so many more, love. And we have the whole of our lives to try them out."

Imogen's heart nearly burst from her chest, it felt so full.

Blinking back tears, she sat up and, taking hold of his hands, guided them to her hips. "Show me how."

His lids grew heavy as he regarded her above him. His eyes traveled leisurely over her breasts, her gently rounded stomach, the soft thatch of curls between her legs. Finally, when Imogen thought she could bear it no longer, he lifted her and brought her down on himself.

Imogen gasped, her eyes rolling back in her head at the sensation. He filled her so completely she felt there was no room for anything else but him inside of her.

"Like this," he said, his voice strained as he gripped her hips tight and moved her rhythmically, first up and nearly off of him, then back down the hard length of him. And then he removed his hands.

Imogen began with small gyrations, testing the position, trying to get a sense of motion. Pure fire shot through her as she rubbed against him. Her eyes focused on Caleb's face, watched as he threw back his head and the strong cords of his neck stood out in harsh relief. She tried another small circle with her hips, saw him gasp. At the sight of his pleasure, her uncertainty melted away.

She quickly found her rhythm, riding him, the pressure building in her own body to a dizzying height. His fingers dug into her thighs, his breath coming in short, harsh pants. Faster and faster she rode until, in a blinding burst of light, her body exploded around him, throbbing with its release. As she collapsed atop his sweat-slicked chest, she heard his own muffled shout of completion. Smiling, she slowly drifted off with his arms tight about her.

• • •

The room was just beginning to lighten with the faintest hint of dawn when Imogen was woken by a soft kiss. She opened her eyes, a smile of pure contentment spreading across her face at the sight of Caleb, adorably tousled, leaning over her. So it had not been a dream after all, she thought happily as he captured her lips once again. Imogen felt an immediate response in her body. She reached for him, deepening the kiss. He groaned softly, his naked body hard against hers under the covers, his arousal immediate. But a moment later he pulled back.

"I have to go," he said, regret thickening his voice.

"I know," she whispered, but then smiled. "You have an archbishop to see, after all."

His eyes softened as he gazed down at her. "I do."

Imogen gazed up at Caleb, happiness coursing through her. And for once she didn't care that her heart was in her eyes. For his heart shone through now as well. She certainly didn't need her spectacles to see that, she thought with a smile as he lowered his head to hers.

Acknowledgments

The path to publication has been a long and winding one for me. I have been incredibly blessed to have so many people in my corner through it all.

Thank you to my incredible agent, Kim Lionetti, for working tirelessly to find the perfect home for my book.

Thank you to Eliza Kirby, Mallory Soto, and everyone at Diversion Books for your incredible support and for making my lifelong dream become a reality.

Thank you to the Romance Writers of America, to my Golden Heart 2017 Rebelle sisters, and to Silicon Valley RWA for being a safe haven for me through the storms.

Thank you to my beta readers for this book: Maria, Katie, and Heather. Your advice was invaluable.

Thank you to the Le Bou Crew: Julie, Hannah, Joni, Debbie, Rich, and Silvi, for being there for me week after week and making sure I never gave up.

Thank you to Gerry O'Hara for mentoring a wide-eyed fourteen-year-old girl all those years ago and fanning the small spark of a dream into a flame.

Thank you to my late grandfather, Robert Jette' Sr., for being the best Papa a girl could ever be blessed with and who, with a letter found again years after his passing, set me on the path I'm on today.

And thank you to the friends and family who have been by my side through every up and down, most especially my husband and children. Whether I needed a shoulder to cry on or a cheerleader, you never gave up on me. I love you.

CHRISTINA BRITTON developed a passion for writing romance novels shortly after buying her first at the tender age of thirteen. Though for several years she turned to art and put brush instead of pen to paper, she has returned to her first love and is now writing full time. She spends her days dreaming of corsets and cravats and noblemen with tortured souls.

She lives with her husband and two children in the San Francisco Bay Area. A member of Romance Writers of America, she also belongs to her local chapter, Silicon Valley RWA, and is a 2017 RWA® Golden Heart® Winner. You can find her on the web at **www.christinabritton.com**, Twitter as **@cbrittonauthor**, or **facebook.com/ChristinaBrittonAuthor**.